THE VOYAGE OF THE DOLPHIN

Kevin Smith

SANDSTONEPRESS
HIGHLAND | SCOTLAND

First published in Great Britain
Sandstone Press Ltd
Dochcarty Road
Dingwall
Ross-shire
IV15 9UG
Scotland.

www.sandstonepress.com

The publisher acknowledges support from
Creative Scotland towards publication of this volume.

ISBN: 978-1-910124-82-6
ISBNe: 978-1-910124-83-3

Cover design by Mark Ecob
Typeset by Iolaire Typesetting, Newtonmore.
Printed and bound by CPI Group (UK) Ltd, Croydon CR0 4YY..

In memory of my grandfather

Walter Edwin Crozier

(1893 – 1982)

A man that is born falls into a dream like a man who falls into the sea

– Joseph Conrad, *Lord Jim*

Contents

1

Mr Fitzmaurice Has Exciting News

Dublin, February 1916

The gunpowder had been packed into a yellow tin with red lettering on it that said FRY'S PURE BREAKFAST COCOA. A copious amount of adhesive tape sealed the lid and a hole had been punched in the base of the container, into which a length of fuse wire had been inserted. This dangled now as the young man, working with stealth, attached the bomb with more tape to the door, halfway down between the hinges. Playing out the wire, he shuffled backwards along the corridor the ten or so paces to where his comrades were crouched in readiness, scarves pulled up to hide their faces. A match was struck and the fuse lit. It sparked and sputtered and went out, was ignited afresh, and again died. The third time it caught fully and the tenacious orange flare set off along its line.

Sunk deep in an armchair in his shared chambers at Trinity College, Walter Crozier, his face full of angles and shadows, looked up from the sports pages of the *Irish Times*. For twenty minutes or more he had been distracted by scurrying footsteps and hissed conversation in the passageway. Now there was shouting. He hauled himself to his feet and in a few swift strides crossed to the door...

Blinded, and a split second later deafened by the blast, he staggered backwards at speed across a furlong of threadbare Axminster and over a green leather steamer-trunk, where, stunned and winded, with his boots in the air and blood dribbling from his nose, he regarded the high ceiling (the tide marks, he noted, were getting worse). As the muffled pounding in his ears subsided, he fancied he could hear, receding along the corridor, the sound of hysterical laughter.

*

'It's absolute bloody anarchy.'

Hugh Fitzmaurice, resplendent in a peacock-blue smoking jacket, was perched on the arm of the sofa filling his new Meerschaum pipe with pinches of aromatic flake. Behind him, a man in overalls was running a measure over the splintered doorjamb.

'That's the third one this month. The bastards are going to kill someone sooner or later.'

Fitzmaurice had hair of a type – soft chestnut frills – almost exclusive to the minor aristocrat, sleepy grey eyes, and large, liverish lips that he seemed unable to prevent from forming into a pout; all this atop a long sturdy frame hardened by many hours of brutality on the playing fields of successive private schools.

'I mean, I know I'm no angel, but we can't have fresh-men going around blowing people's doors off, can we? I mean, we need doors. They keep draughts out, for one thing.'

He looked up, struck by a sudden thought.

2

'The Fabians! I bet it's the bloody Fabians. Everybody knows they're a bunch of bloody anarchists.'

He tamped the tobacco down with a pencil stub, his latest affectation so far lacking the relevant paraphernalia, and fumbled in his pocket for a match.

'Do you think we should inform the constabulary?'

'Probably.' Frank Rafferty, a first-year medic, was standing at the window peering down into the square at three young women attempting to attach a purple banner to a pole. 'But I'd say College will deal with it themselves. I doubt they'll want to risk the Press getting wind of it.'

A match sizzled into life, followed by the effortful *mwap-mwap* of pipe ignition, and a foul odour filled the room. Fitzmaurice stared into space for a moment and then succumbed to a coughing fit that lasted nearly a minute.

'This tobacco can't be right,' he croaked, wiping away a tear. 'I knew I should have gone to Petersons.'

Rafferty, who had been eyeing his room-mate with mild scientific curiosity during the closing paroxysms, turned back to the window, and clutching the frame for leverage, stood on tiptoe to get a better view. The banner bore the legend, UNITED IRISHWOMEN.

'To be honest, I don't really understand it.'

'Understand what?'

'This craze for blowing things up. I mean, what's the point? Where's the fun?'

'Well, to be fair, it probably *is* rather good fun.' Fitzmaurice slid onto the sofa proper. 'What I'd like to know is where they're getting the bloody gunpowder... Ah, here he is. Any ideas comrade?'

The unfortunate Crozier had returned from sickbay

3

and was making room on the rack for his overcoat, a heavy tweed ulster purchased for him by his father before his departure from Belfast's Great Victoria Street station the previous year. ('That'll stand to you, so it will, keep the damp Dublin air at bay, eh?' The awkward half-embrace, the fumbled handshake, his father's face pale above the clerical collar, the eyes a fragile blue.) He resumed his previous seat in front of the fire and gazed into the flames.

'Crozier?'

'Sorry, what?' He pulled a wad of cottonwool from his ear.

'I was just saying, Crozier old man, where are these anarchists getting the gunpowder?'

'Oh, that's easy enough.' Crozier rolled up the wadding and lobbed it into the hearth. 'The Gunpowder Office on Sackville Street would probably be your first port of call.'

'Yes, I dare say. By the way, how are you? Will you live?'

Crozier sniffed. 'Just about. My ears will be ringing for a while.'

'Mild tinnitus due to acoustic trauma – nothing to worry about.' Rafferty turned from the window. 'Which nurse was it?'

'Didn't catch her name.'

'Nurse Buckley probably. She looked after me when I fell off the campanile during Freshers' Week. Very pretty. Sweet smell off her... like cloves.'

He stood, fingering his sand-coloured moustache, his eyes unfocused behind the thick lenses of his spectacles, then moved towards the door.

'Meeting Miss Maguire for tea. Arrivederci.'

After Rafferty had left, the other two sat in companionable silence, Fitzmaurice sunk in a tobacco trance, Crozier working half-heartedly through Salmon's *Infallibility of the Church*. Having never seriously considered any other line of study (it was fully expected that he would follow his father into the clergy) he was now wondering whether Divinity was really for him. Without faith, to adapt a Salmonism, he might win all the pieces on the chessboard, but what use if he were already in checkmate?

The afternoon light had begun to fade when three chimes from the Trinity clock rolled across the ancient cobbles.

'I'd better cut along too,' Fitzmaurice said. 'The Senior Dean wants to see me.'

'That's nice. Any particular reason?'

Fitzmaurice pondered the possibilities, his lips twitching.

'I suppose it might be something to do with my academic progress. Or rather, the lack of it.'

'I thought you'd squared all that last term?'

'Not really. Seeing as I didn't show up for the supplementals.'

'*What?*'

Fitzmaurice had risen and was at the grate, tapping the dottle out of his pipe.

'You knew that. I went climbing in the Highlands instead, remember? With Cousin Ninian and the Westmeath crowd.'

Crozier gave an incredulous snort. Fitzmaurice turned and stood pouting into the middle distance.

'Well, the dates really were very inconvenient. And the trip had been planned for a long time. I'd been looking forward to it.'

'Fitz, you'd better watch your step. They're going to have your head on a plaque in the Common Room if you're not careful.'

'Oh, I'll be fine. They're too in awe of Uncle Ernie to sack me.'

Fitzmaurice was related, on his mother's side, to Sir Ernest Henry Shackleton, veteran of the *Discovery* and *Nimrod* expeditions, planter of the Union Flag within spitting distance of the South Pole, and at that moment – although the public was not yet aware of it – marooned on an ice floe in the Weddell Sea, his ship, the mighty *Endurance*, crushed like a meringue beneath the leaden Antarctic water.

'You know,' he slipped out of his smoking jacket 'that's really part of the problem.'

'Mmm?' Crozier was picking flakes of plaster out of the turn-ups in his trouser-legs. He had heard this speech, or a version of it, before.

'Bloody Shackers. People are always expecting me to be more like him. Steel-chinned, full of grit, an example to my peers. It's a lot to live up to. In fact, I bet you the first thing the Dean says is,' (he adopted an effete nasal falsetto) '"Really, Fitzmaurice, it's just not good enough, why can't you be more like your Uncle Ernest?"…'

He pulled on a camphor-scented blazer with piped lapels, that was a little too tight across the back.

'Although, it's funny,' he continued, 'now that I think of it, Mother said when they were children he was a complete crybaby: blubbed if he so much as grazed his knee. Made it her business to bully him at every opportunity.' He checked his hair in the oval glass above the mantle. 'Oh well, wish me luck.'

After a couple more hours of reading, and a short nap, Crozier gave in to hunger and strolled over to the College dining hall for a bowl of soup. Then, deciding a turn around Stephen's Green would clear his head, he exited the side gate of Trinity and, having narrowly avoided being hit by a tram, crossed to Dawson Street.

The gaslamps were lit and there was more than the usual activity, with a large group of people, mostly men, gathered outside the headquarters of the Irish Volunteers. The pavement was blocked by the throng, forcing him to the other side of the road. The crowd was being addressed from an upper-storey window by a darkly-bearded man with brilliantined hair. A banner draped across the brickwork below him read, NO CONSCRIPTION, STAY UNITED, and in smaller letters beneath, OGLAIGH NA HEIREANN – GOD BLESS IRELAND.

'To extend the Military Service Act across the Irish Sea would be no less than a declaration of war,' the man was telling them. 'We cannot be forced to aid the British Empire in an unjust campaign and, if they try to compel us,' he scanned the crowd, then held up a warning forefinger 'if they try to compel us, we will resist and we *will not slacken.*'

A round of enthusiastic cheering and clapping broke out.

'Why,' the man continued, '*why* should we fight for a power that denies us the right to govern our own country?'

More cheering.

'Sure, your lot couldn't govern a graveyard,' someone shouted.

A ripple of laughter ran through the group closest to the heckler but didn't catch. He tried again.

7

'Yis couldn't organise a two-ticket raffle!'

The orator continued undaunted.

'Ireland is *not* the Empire,' he roared, leaning forward onto the window sill, veins popping on his forehead. 'The Empire is *not* Ireland!'

The audience was very excited now, adding foot-stamping and hat-waving to the general hubbub. Some youths detached themselves from the periphery and took off at speed. Crozier, who was uncomfortable in crowds, was unnerved by the growing sense of menace and resumed his walk in the direction of the park.

At the top of Dawson Street he paused to look in the window of the recruitment office: 'A Call To Arms', 'An Appeal To Gallant Irishmen', 'Remember The Women Of Belgium.' His eye was drawn to the latest image, soldiers marching between velvety hills and fields of gilded wheat, encouraging the farmers of Ireland to 'Join Up And Defend Your Possessions'. He pictured the tender greenery of his home county, its plush Ulster pastures and meadows rolling out from the edges of the city, and suddenly the face of Jenny Gilmour loomed up from behind a drumlin, poster-style, and his mind flashed back to the letter he had so recently held in shaking hands: '... *Please don't think badly of me, Walter, I never set out to make you fall in love.*'

Crozier waited for a carriage, with its sharp stink of horse, to pass, and made his way towards the park. As he stepped onto the opposite pavement there was a loud crash and he turned to see the window of the recruitment office smashed, shards of glass hanging round a gaping hole. The youths – from earlier, he was almost certain – were sprinting towards Grafton Street. Passers-by were shouting and jumping out of their way. A whistle sounded and two policemen hurtled into view from the west side of the Green, drawing their truncheons as they ran. The Dublin Metropolitans were tall, Crozier noted. He was nearly six feet himself but he hadn't the bulk to be a policeman in this city, whose motto, *Obedientia Civium Urbis Felicitas* — 'Happy the city where citizens obey' – was surely becoming a bit of a joke.

The quarry and their pursuers disappeared down King Street, a handful of inquisitive citizens trotting in their wake. Crozier completed his circuit of the Green without further incident and headed to McDaid's public house nearby, where he met a couple of fellow Divinity students earnestly discussing points of doctrine. He found he wasn't in the mood for debate, and excused himself after one drink.

Outside, a yellowish fog had descended, and as he peered into the murk a *gurrier* materialised in front of him, hand out in supplication. The child's face was streaked with grime and its feet were bare. The boy (he was guessing it was male, though the hair was long) was saying something urgent in a low, wheedling mumble. From a prosperous quarter of a city awash with the proceeds of linen and shipbuilding, Crozier had been shocked at the scale of Dublin's slums and the degradation of the inhabitants who strayed across the river to beg. He had long since stopped trying to give money to every needy case, but such was the anguish in this creature's gaze he couldn't help but root in his pocket for a coin. The urchin dissolved.

Crozier stepped onto the downward slope of Grafton Street, where he fell in behind a throng of students —-- he recognised a couple of them from his short-lived membership of the rowing club – belting out a boisterous drinking song that boomed about the thoroughfare: '*I went down to Monto Town to see young Kill McArdle,*' they sang, '*but he wouldn't give me a half a crown to go to the Waxies' Dargle*' (And then, with extra gusto) '*What will you have? Will you have a pint? I'll have a pint with you, sir!*' The lads, thanks to a fresh victory on the River Liffey, were in high feather and oblivious to the disapproving stares of the citizenry. '*And if one of you don't order soon, we'll be thrown out of the boozer!*'

He diverted right, into Duke Street, and after a moment's deliberation in the doorway, entered the velvet-dark interior of the Bailey, with its gleaming wood and twinkle of starry lamps. Rafferty was in his usual berth at the far end of the bar, the remains of a meal in front of him.

'Crozier, excellent timing. A pint, while you're at it,' he called, holding up his empty glass.

The Northerner ordered the drinks, another stout for the Dubliner, a Bushmills and water for himself.

'Going to the devil, I see,' Rafferty said, noting the whiskey. 'What would the church fathers say?'

'They'd assume... Cheers.'

'*Slainte.*'

Crozier savoured a taste of home, the spirit's floral heat, imagined for a second he detected the salt tang of a North Atlantic breeze.

'They'd assume I'd been brought low by degenerate southern Papists like yourself, corrupted into your ways of strong liquor and fornication, and remind me in no

10

uncertain terms that drunkards shall not inherit the kingdom of God.'

'Romans?'

'Corinthians.'

'Interesting. And what would you say to them?'

'I'd probably say, drink thy wine with a merry heart for God now accepteth thy works.'

'Proverbs?'

'Ecclesiastes. Anyway,' he took another sip, 'all things in moderation, including moderation itself.'

'Leviticus?'

'Oscar Wilde.'

A skeletal woman in a black pinafore ascertained with her eyebrows that Rafferty was finished with his plate and whisked it away.

'How was the steak?' Crozier enquired.

'First class. Best in town.'

'It's well for you. I've barely enough left to pay my Commons fees.'

Rafferty grunted. Crozier looked around. The place was busy but not full, its clientele made up largely of newspaper-men and politicians, clerks, and a smattering of tormented writers mumbling into their pints. Seated further along the bar, among them the orator from earlier, was a group of drinkers. One of them glanced over. Catching Rafferty's eye, he nodded in recognition and approached.

'Friend of yours?'

'Acquaintance,' said Rafferty, sitting up.

The man was tall and fleshy with shiny jowls and a face too small for his head, and had on a heavy coat of navy-blue wool such as a bookmaker might wear. He was swaying slightly.

11

'Didn't see you down the road earlier, Frank. Were you busy studying?' he said, winking at Crozier.

'Haha, you got it in one, Joe,' Rafferty replied. 'Sure, there's no rest for the wicked.'

'You have that right. Will we see you on Tuesday at the hall?'

'I'll do my best.'

'Good man.' He was regarding Crozier with a smiling but calculating eye. 'Quick word, Frank, do you mind?'

As Rafferty climbed to his feet he set a coin on the table and gestured for another round. His drink was waiting for him when he returned a few minutes later.

'Sorry about that,'

Crozier grinned.

'Are you with the rebels now, Frank?'

Rafferty extracted a Wild Woodbine from his pack and lit it.

'Not exactly,' he said, exhaling.

'What does that mean?'

'They want me to be. They think I am...'

'But?'

'I'm not sure. I mean, I believe they have a point, or at least I think I do, thought I did.'

'How involved *are* you?'

'Oh, nothing serious. A couple of meetings, a bit of fundraising, that sort of thing. And I got caught up in some of the high-jinks in the Phoenix Park.'

'I heard there was mayhem.'

'There was drink involved, I can't deny it,' Rafferty conceded. 'Anyway, enough of my problems, what about you? Any word from Jenny?'

12

Crozier gazed into the remains of his whiskey and shook his head, his eyes brimming.

'Come on, ye black-hearted hallion,' Rafferty said. 'One for the road.'

The streets, as the pair rolled back to College, were still thick with fog, the gaslamps casting barely a glimmer on the ghostly human shapes that passed beneath. Aside from an occasional mumbled 'excuse me' at a near-collision, neither man spoke, immersed, as they both were, in their own troubles: preoccupations that, though neither could have known (or imagined), were about to be forgotten in an instant, dwarfed by a sudden and unusual development.

When they arrived back at chambers, Fitzmaurice surged from the sofa like a spaniel fresh from the reeds.

'Where the hell have you two been?' he cried. 'I was looking all over town.'

Taken aback, both began to speak at once but Fitzmaurice rushed between them and, putting his arms around their shoulders, propelled them towards the hearth.

'It doesn't matter now. Come in, come in. I have news.'

Crozier and Rafferty exchanged perplexed glances while Fitzmaurice threw the last of their scuttle allowance on the fire and jabbed at the embers.

'Fitz, what on earth's going on?' Rafferty slowly unwound his scarf. 'Why the drama?'

Fitzmaurice sat on the arm of the sofa. The fire cracked and fizzed.

'There has been an extraordinary turn of events,' he said at last. His tone was grave.

'Well?'

13

Fitzmaurice took his pipe from a side table, and holding a shaky match above the bowl, puffed it briskly to life, watching them both all the while.

'For Godsake, Fitz, that stinks to high heaven,' Rafferty snapped, fanning the air. 'Stop teasing us and tell us this news.'

'What would you say,' Fitzmaurice had moved into high theatrical mode, 'if I told you I could offer you the adventure of a lifetime?'

'I'd say, what the hell are you talking about?'

'Hmm. And if I said I could make you famous throughout these islands, and guarantee you a place in the annals of history?'

'Again, what the hell?'

'I see. And if I advised you to prepare for a momentous journey?'

'Fitz,' Crozier interjected, 'this is ridiculous, what are you..?'

'To a place beyond your wildest dreams?'

'Rafferty, pass me that cricket bat.'

Flame-shadows quivered across the ceiling and around the walls.

'Gentlemen,' Fitzmaurice's eyes gleamed and he revealed many teeth, 'lace up your stoutest boots and pack your warmest underwear. We're all off to the bloody Arctic!'

2

The Masters

Earlier that afternoon the College cellarer, a melancholic man with poor posture and a melted eyelid, had been dispatched to fetch a bottle for the Senior Dean, who was hosting a small luncheon in his office. Not given to belief in the supernatural, the cellarer found himself unnerved nonetheless by the strangely human sound that drifted from time to time through the tunnels beneath Trinity College. There it was again: a low mournful monotone rising and falling like ghostly plainsong before fading back into the rock. It was caused, no doubt, by the rush of air through a faulty duct or drainage well, but down in the gloom, alone in the empty passageways, it was easy to imagine...

He held up the lantern, letting his nostrils fill with the damp perfume of the vault. Bottles gleamed darkly in the shadows: Magnums and Jeroboams, Methuselahs, Salmanazars, Nebuchadnezzars, the mighty Melchiors. He was struck, as he always was, by the gravid nature of the hush, by a sense that delicate, dream-like activity was taking place within the containers around him, and he became careful in his movements.

Stacked along the wall facing him were the clarets, their indented bases like rows of artillery, and he edged along, squinting at the labels. Some of them were worth multiples of his yearly wages. When the time came, he mused, he would have his list at the ready. He eased a dust-slippery bottle from its cradle and made his way back along the corridor towards the steep stone steps that led to the light.

In his lofty-ceilinged room three floors above, the Senior Dean was deep in contemplation of a portrait of himself that had been hung, just that morning, on the wall opposite the big window. He cocked his head to one side, then the other. He took three steps back; a moment later, two forward. He hunkered down for a fresh angle. He stood up. The painting, in bold, lustrous oils, depicted him in full academic garb, crowned with a gold-tasselled mortarboard, holding a rolled-up scroll and surveying the viewer with majestic leniency. It was quite magnificent. Except for one detail, one flaw, one minor error in perspective that, now he had spotted it, ruined everything. He leant his head back and squinted, then opened his eyes very wide. He fiddled with his snow-white goatee. That *imbecile* of an artist. There was no way around it: the hand that clutched the scroll was *tiny*. Like a *withered* hand... Like a vestigial forepaw.

There was a knock at the door and an elderly servant arrived pushing a trolley tinkling with silver containers, which he set about transferring to the dining table. A minute or two elapsed, then he coughed. 'Did you hear, sir, there was another gunpowder incident this morning?'

The Senior Dean was sitting on the edge of his desk, still transfixed by the painting.

'Mmm, really? Another one? Where?'

'Botany Bay, sir. Another door off, I'm afraid.'

'Botany Bay, I might have known. That place is an absolute nest. Anyone hurt?'

'No, sir. Though I hear an undergraduate had a lucky escape.'

'That's good. Is Front Gate onto it?'

'I believe so.'

When the servant had finished, the Senior Dean called him over.

'What do you think of this portrait?' he demanded.

'To be honest, sir,' the old retainer said, having learned many Senior Deans ago to keep his own counsel, 'I wouldn't be the best person...'

'Nonsense, man, how does it seem to you?'

The servant peered up at the painting.

'It's very handsome, sir. It...'

'Look at the hand. *The hand*. Is it normal?'

'It looks...'

At that moment there was another tattoo at the door and into the room marched the All-Faculty Master of Discipline, long, thin and hawkish, and walking with the aid of a horn-handled cane, followed by the roly-poly figure of the Regius Professor of Zoology and Comparative Anatomy. The servant seized his opportunity. 'By the way, sir,' he called over his shoulder, 'the cellarer said to tell you the wine was decanted at midday.'

The academics admired the new likeness (the hand was not mentioned) and sat down to their lunch: Brown Windsor soup followed by venison casserole, all washed down with a perfectly aerated 1900 Chateau Margaux (declared 'excellent'). Afterwards they lit the lamps and withdrew to the armchairs, the Regius Professor taking

17

with him an apple which he began to carve into sections with his pocket knife.

'So,' the Senior Dean folded his hands across the tweed expanse of his belly. 'We're all agreed that this expedition must go ahead?'

The other two nodded. The Regius Professor cleared his throat.

'Absolutely,' he said in his fluting, feminine voice. 'I can tell you that the Royal Irish Geographical Society met this morning and it was the view of every last one of us on the board that we may never have this opportunity again. We believe this could very well be our last hurrah. Once Home Rule comes in, God only knows what will happen.'

The Master of Discipline tapped the brass tip of his walking stick against the toecap of his shoe. 'Are you suggesting it may not be all "nougat, velvet, and soft music"?'

'I'm saying, gentlemen, we'd better hold on to our bloody hats. As soon as this war is over we'll be totally at the mercy of the natives.' The Regius Professor examined, with an expression of great sorrow, the chunk of fruit on the end of his blade. 'Beauchamp says we should start hiding the good wine right away.'

There was silence as each man contemplated the potential wear-and-tear of the coming turmoil on his privileges.

'Well, Beauchamp is correct,' the Master of Discipline said at last. 'These are deeply uncertain times. We need to do all we can, as *soon* as we can, to bolster the standing of this College.'

'Good, we're agreed then.'

'There is one further matter we should perhaps consider.'

'Yes?'

'The war.'

'What about it?'

'Well, do we know if His Majesty's government will even permit such an enterprise?'

The Senior Dean shrugged.

'They let Shackleton go. I can't see it being a problem for us.'

'Is there also,' the Master of Discipline continued, 'a safety aspect to all this? I mean to say, the Boche are pretty lively at the moment, according to the papers. I'm just wondering, with the U-boat threat and so on, should we really be risking...?'

The Senior Dean flashed a business-like smile.

'The U-boat threat is much diminished since the Americans kicked up a stink over the *Lusitania*, and anyway, on the route they'll be taking, the odds are very slim. I'm told if they give the North Sea a wide berth they'll be fine. Now,' he held his hands apart, palms upraised, 'nothing further? Good. Then we'll proceed. I've asked Fitzmaurice to join us, he should be...,' he drew out his fob watch, 'yes, any moment now.'

In fact it was to be nearly another half-hour before Fitzmaurice joined them, having lingered in Library Square to watch a group of students attempting a human pyramid (two sprained ankles and a concussion). As he took his seat across the table from the three masters, each sporting a mortarboard, it dawned on him that he might be in more than the usual degree of trouble. The Senior Dean thanked him (a little icily, he thought) for attending,

19

introduced the other two (who regarded him in a manner reminiscent of a pair of elderly crocodiles basking on a riverbank), and flipped open a thick leather folder.

'I'm assuming, Fitzmaurice, you have an idea why we wanted to see you today?'

'Not really sir. Is it about the re-sits? You see my cousin Ninian...'

'The re-sits, the failed exams,' the Senior Dean flopped a hand around, 'the absences, the disciplinaries...'

'Sir, there's a perfectly...'

'The goat incident, that business with the vice-chancellor's wife. Everything really. It's all in here.' He tapped the dossier.

'I appreciate how it looks sir, but if I could just explain.'

'I'm afraid, Fitzmaurice, the time for explanations has passed. I've spoken to both the head of the Law Faculty and,' he gestured to his right 'to the Master of Discipline and it's my sorry duty to have to inform you that we have no choice but to send you down.'

Fitzmaurice stared from one to the other and then beyond them at the Senior Dean's new portrait.

'I...' he was momentarily distracted by the withered hand, 'you've *what?*'

'I'm afraid so. It gives us no great pleasure, but your record... well, even you must realise, it's... *bad*.'

'Yes but... How bad sir?'

'Very bad, Fitzmaurice. Atrocious.'

'I'm very sorry to hear that sir.'

'We did our best. We gave you a lot of leeway.'

'Yes but...'

'It's a long accumulation of things really, I mean, of course we appreciate your prowess on the rugby field and in the mountaineering club, but it's not enough to overcome the rest of the... Let's face it, you have no academic aptitude...'

'Yes but...'

'Whatsoever. There are a lot of avenues open to you Fitzmaurice, it just happens that the legal profession isn't one of them. Try not to take this badly.'

'Yes, but what's my mother going to say?'

'I'm sure she'll understand.'

'I think I can say with some certainty she won't.'

Fitzmaurice's lip quivered. He saw his mother's face snapping tight at the news, many tiny creatures scuttling for cover on boundless, wind-whipped sands.

'Please, sir, you have to give me another chance.'

'Our hands are tied.'

'Sir, I promise, I can fix everything.'

The Senior Dean petted his goatee for a moment, then whispered with his two colleagues in turn. Slowly he removed his mortarboard and set it on the table.

'There may be an alternative,' he said.

Fitzmaurice blinked back a tear.

'Yes?'

All eyes were on him.

'There is something we would like to have in our possession.'

'Sir?'

'Something valuable. Something that could help us add to the store of human knowledge and bring immeasurable prestige to the College,' he paused, 'something that would reflect well on all of us.'

'Yes sir, I... and what would that be?'

'A skeleton.'

Fitzmaurice turned the word over several times in his head but failed to extract meaning from it.

'A skeleton, sir?'

'Yes, but no ordinary one. We're talking about the skeleton of a giant.'

Fitzmaurice looked from one to the other. He considered the possibility that some sort of prank was being perpetrated.

'Sorry sir, did you say *giant*?'

The Senior Dean nodded gravely.

'Sir, by any chance would this giant be at the foot of a very tall beanstalk?'

The masters exchanged chuckles.

'Haha, no Fitzmaurice. The skeleton is that of Bernard McNeill, the last of the so-called Tyrone Giants, men who, for reasons not yet fully understood, grew to outlandish heights. It lies beneath a cairn of stones on the southern tip of a small island in the Arctic Archipelago.'

Fitzmaurice's brow performed a series of vigorous exercises.

'I see. And what's it doing there?'

'I take it you've heard of Sir Hamilton Coote?'

'No.'

'My God, your uncle would be ashamed of you. Coote was one of our finest explorers, County Tipperary man, passed away a few years back. In eighteen sixty-three he led a search for Sir John Franklin, who had disappeared two decades earlier while navigating the Northwest Passage. McNeill the Giant was one of Coote's crew. He died on the voyage.'

'I see. And may I ask, sir, why you're telling me all this?'

'Because, Fitzmaurice, we'd like *you* to lead another expedition to bring McNeill's bones back to Trinity.'

The room was silent except for the stiff to-and-fro of the mantel clock's pendulum and the faint sound of the Regius Professor's pug-like breathing. From the square below came the murmur of voices and the muffled tip-tap of rugby boots on cobbles; a tram on Nassau Street sounded its gong. Fitzmaurice leant back and glanced around him at the room's green-shaded lamps and polished surfaces. Time had become slurred, dream-like.

'Why me, sir?'

The Senior Dean appeared momentarily nonplussed, then recovered himself.

'A number of reasons. Setting aside your lack of academic commitment, you are hale and hearty, intrepid, ebullient and outgoing, and evidently have the ability to make people like you. You possess, in other words, leadership qualities. More importantly, for current purposes, you are closely associated with, and indeed tied by blood to one of the great heroes of the modern era, which lends you a degree of public credibility.'

Fitzmaurice hadn't understood all that had been said, but felt justified in puffing himself up a little, causing the seams of his blazer to creak.

'You were the first person we thought of for the job,' the Senior Dean added.

This was untrue. Their first choice, Captain Herbert 'Eagle-Eye' Eagleton, the man who had prepared their expedition with such efficiency and whom they had to thank for the ship that would shortly dock in Queenstown harbour, had drowned in his bath three weeks previously. Their second, Sir Robert 'Iceman' Clapperton-Fox, it had transpired, was in prison for stock market fraud, whilst a third, 'Biffo' Heffernan-Parry, a Trinity man, had been shot down over Dusseldorf during an air raid on a Zeppelin shed. Most of the remaining eligible candidates were dodging German shells and choking on chlorine gas along the Western Front.

'And if I were to undertake this expedition, what would happen afterwards?'

The Senior Dean again conferred, *sotto voce*, with his advisors.

'Then, I think it's fair to say, you would be in *very* good standing with the College.'

'And how long would I be away?'

'We estimate six months, maybe more.'

'That's a long time. I'm not sure I...'

'The other factor you may need to consider, Fitzmaurice, is that, unfortunately, this voyage would prevent you from going to the Front.'

'On the other hand, there's nothing really... Could I take anyone with me?'

'You could take Crozier with you, that's a good explorer name.'

'And Rafferty?'

The masters consulted.

'It would be useful to have a medic around, but... Fitzmaurice?'

'Yes?'

'For Godsake don't let him operate on anyone.'

Over the next hour Fitzmaurice took in more information than he had in the entire term. From the Regius Professor he learned how science might benefit from study of the giant, the potential advances in the fields of osteology and genetics, and how boffins would come scurrying from all four corners of the Earth just to behold him. From the Master of Discipline, who lectured in the School of Medicine, he heard about 'adenomas' and 'pituitary malfunctions' until his head swam. The Senior Dean talked of Atlas and Cyclops, Gog and Magog, Orion, Antaeus, Polyphemus – the sons of Uranus and Gaia who were brought to Earth by Hercules; regaled him with tales of the Giants of Crete, the twelve-foot prehistoric Castelnau Giant, the Prussian infantry regiment of 'Potsdam Giants', and the Irish giants 'Big Frank' Sheridan, Patrick Cotter, the Knipe Brothers, and finally, Charles Byrne, the toast of eighteenth century London.

'Byrne's skeleton is in the Royal College of Surgeons of England,' the Regius Professor squeaked. 'Seven foot seven inches, and a wonder of the age. Our man, McNeill, stood eight foot nine in his stockings – *eight foot nine*! Imagine that. We'd outclass them by more than a foot.' And his little eyes gleamed.

On the huge, ornate globe that stood beside the window, they traced the route the ship would take, sailing up through the Atlantic to Reykjavik, snaking around Greenland and across Baffin Bay to the mouth of the Northwest Passage, and thence into the slow-churning waters of the Arctic Archipelago.

By the time the masters had finished with him, Fitzmaurice could barely see for the visions of heroism that swirled in his head: silver-oxide portraits of courageous men (himself mostly) with rime-crusted beards and eternity-haunted eyes, straddling chasms and planting flags on cathedrals of ice; front-page ticker-tape blizzards and hysterical crowds. As he tottered down the stairs from the Senior Dean's office and out into Front Square he pictured the parade that would greet his homecoming, himself at the head of it, carried shoulder-high.

'This calls for a celebration,' the Senior Dean announced, ringing the bell for a servant. 'Another bottle of the Margaux, I think.'

As he trimmed the wick on his lantern, the cellarer glared up from the cobbles at the Senior Dean's window and softly cursed the shadows that cavorted on the ceiling. The temperature had dropped and a chill, eye-level fog was forming. He crossed the square and unlocked the door to the vertiginous stairwell, took a couple of deep breaths, and still swearing to himself, began his descent. Somewhere in the dark below, in the furthest passageway, the spirit of the labyrinth started up again its strange threnody.

3

Rigged and Ready

Standing on the edge of Queenstown harbour that late March morning, breathing plumes of sharp, briny air, Crozier was seized by a dizzying sense of imminence. The *Dolphin*, a three-masted barquentine of oak and Norwegian fir, had arrived from the re-fitting yard in Bristol during the night and now rocked gently on the early tide, gulls wafting and yelping above it. The prow was painted with gold curlicues on bands of pale blue, while a gleaming figurehead of a white, bottle-nosed dolphin chortled beneath the bowsprit. On the dockside, stacks of packing cases awaited loading. Voices could be heard from below deck. It was suddenly clear that, after all the talk and speculation and imaginings, the voyage was *actually* going to happen.

Since arriving at the southern Irish port the previous morning, the room-mates had passed the time wandering the streets like out-of-season tourists, or scouring the stores for stray provisions. Food and drink for the journey, and equipment for the expedition, had been arranged by Captain Eagleton before his untimely death, and would be stowed shortly. Last-minute purchases included dried fruit, tinned beans and a hot water bottle for Fitzmaurice's iguana Bridie (a souvenir from his father's South

American travels) that he was insisting on bringing along despite strong objections. 'There's no one to look after her. She'll die otherwise,' he protested. When reminded of the well-known reptilian aversion to low temperatures, he harumphed and said she would snooze out the voyage in some cosy nook near the ship's furnace.

Neither Crozier nor Rafferty approved of Bridie, a weighty conglomeration of clammy green frills and warty dewlaps measuring over three feet from nose to tail. They did not like her haughty demeanour and malevolent stare, nor the way she kept very still for hours on end, then *moved very quickly*. Nor did they care for how she would some-times hold up a tiny, chainmail-gloved hand before emit-ting a loud, propulsive sneeze, usually in their direction. Rafferty, in particular, refused to be in a room alone with the creature following a high-pitched late-night encounter that had every resident of Botany Bay bolt upright in their beds. Fitzmaurice loved her dearly, however, and much to the horror of his friends, would occasionally let her sit in his lap and take chunks of carrot from between his lips.

As a concession to the presence of Bridie, Rafferty had been allowed to bring along his banjolele, an instrument he had taken up in the first term after finding it in a pawn shop in the Liberties at a knockdown price. The reason for the discount was a warp in its frame – unadvertised and invisible to the naked eye – which meant it could never fully be brought into tune. That any prolonged solo induced a debilitating headache in everyone within ear-shot was unfortunate, as Rafferty had a mellifluous voice and a rich repertoire of songs gleaned from his maternal uncles who were in music hall. He was not entirely insen-sitive to the effect of the instrument on others, but was convinced that practice would make perfect, and he was nothing if not persistent.

'Ahoy there.'

A stocky man with a shaggy white moustache and black button eyes was making his way down the gangplank.

'Are you Fitzmaurice?' he asked, surveying Crozier with suspicion.

'No, but I'm one of his party,' Crozier said, and introduced himself.

'Right y'are. Ewan McGregor is my name. Skipper of yon tub,' he jerked his head sideways 'God preserve us and keep us.'

'And a handsome vessel she is too.'

McGregor shot him a quick look, coughed richly and spat something heavy into the water.

'She's Glasgae-built, like myself, but I'd say my mother did the better job,' he said. 'She floats, though, that's the main thing. Will your party be ready tae leave on the morning tide, first light?'

'We'll be ready whenever you say the word.'

A Navy Cut appeared between McGregor's fingers.

'I'm led tae believe, and correct me if I'm wrong,' he struck a match, 'that you boys have never been tae sea before. Is that the case?'

Crozier met the full force of the Glaswegian's obsidian stare.

'Well, technically speaking,' he replied. 'I mean, Fitzmaurice has done some sailing and Rafferty, I seem to remember, took a ferry to...'

'So that's a no then.'

'Yes.'

There followed a pungent silence in which Crozier gazed at the horizon with intense interest while the skipper reduced his cigarette to a red-hot spike.

'Right then, me and the boys are going to hae a wee bit of shore leave.' The dog-end hit the water followed by another oyster from the sea-bed of McGregor's lungs. 'So that puts you in charge. Keep your eye out for strangers sneakin' aboard, and try not tae sink her.'

With the help of two porters, the adventurers spent the morning lugging their belongings from the guesthouse to the *Dolphin*. The ship was more spacious below decks than it appeared from the outside and smelled of shaved wood and tar. It was planked throughout with oak, and the walls and ceilings webbed with rope netting in which was stored bales of sailcloth, lanterns, spools of twine. After some token argument, Fitzmaurice bagged himself a master's cabin, which was larger than all the others except for the skipper's, and featured, along with a single bed, a writing desk, bookshelves and a porthole. The other two took smaller lodgings under the fo'c'sle. Bridie, in her glass cage, was installed on top of some boxes of provisions in a corner of the galley next to the stove flue.

When they had arranged their baggage, they convened at the big table in the mess for a pot of tea and some hard, flavourless biscuits they found in a tin. Above them they could hear the shouts of the stevedores, who were winching aboard cases of canned food, medical supplies and trekking equipment. McGregor and his crew had long since disappeared up the pastel-terraced hillside of Queenstown in search of a sailor-friendly early house.

'Well gentlemen,' Fitzmaurice said, 'here we are. Almost at the point of no return.'

Neither of his companions responded. Rafferty, cradling his banjolele, plucked a chord, frowned, tweaked a peg.

'Who'd have thought?' Fitzmaurice continued. 'Just shows you, doesn't it? You never know what's round the corner. I mean, a month ago I was facing the sack, destined for some ghastly desk job in Dublin Castle or a commission to the Front, and now here I am with you two fine fellows on our own ship headed for the top of the world, and, providing all goes as planned, for fame and...'

He was halted by a sudden flurry of discordant strumming.

'Actually, let me stop you there,' Rafferty said. 'Here's a quick question. What exactly *are* our chances of finding this giant? I've been thinking about it and it doesn't seem to me that we've really got much to go on.'

Fitzmaurice's mouth formed an outraged pout.

'Of course we'll find him. It's imperative.'

'How though?' Rafferty set down his banjolele. 'We don't even have a proper map.'

'What are you talking about? We've *plenty* of perfectly decent maps.'

'Yes, but not an *accurate* map, a map that actually shows where the body's buried. As far as I can work out, the grave could be anywhere within a hundred-mile radius.'

'Rafferty's right,' said Crozier. 'It's all a bit vague.'

Fitzmaurice tapped a rhythm on the table with his fingertips.

31

'And has that only just occurred to you? Why didn't you mention all this before we left Dublin?'

No response.

'And what if it *did* turn out to be a wild goose chase, would you pass it up? The gangplank's right outside. Be my guest.'

Rafferty adjusted his spectacles.

'No, but I just wish we had a better idea of where we're going.'

Fitzmaurice thought for a moment, then rose and left the room. Rafferty embarked on an uncertain tune.

'Seriously Frank,' Crozier said. 'A skeleton? The Arctic? Do you think we're wise?'

Rafferty set his instrument down.

'Jaysus, definitely not,' he took another biscuit, 'but the way I look at it, we have the rest of our lives to...'

Fitzmaurice had returned, holding an object aloft.

'I was saving this as a surprise but I suppose now's as good a time as any.'

He set on the table a tattered, leather-bound notebook tied with a length of cord. The other two stared at it. And then at him.

'This, my friends, is the lost journal of Sir Hamilton Coote,' he tugged at the fastening, 'from the expedition in search of Franklin.'

The book was fragile, and its spine creaked. The pages – a number had come free of their binding – were crammed with notes written in a sloping, elegant hand, along with sketches of miscellaneous flora and fauna, and roughly drawn maps in pencil and ink.

'Where on earth did this come from?' Crozier demanded.

Fitzmaurice smiled.

'The masters. It turned up a year ago at the bottom of a trunk in the Old Library, along with a Gutenberg Bible that had gone missing from the Vatican. Look at this,' he leafed towards the end of the journal, then stopped, tapping the page, 'here's our man.'

They leaned in. It was a map showing a small island off a stretch of coastline, with the sea represented by squiggly waves, hills by upside-down 'V's, and various scribbled sets of bearings. A more detailed sketch on the facing page appeared to depict the lower tip of the island, and a cluster of mountains. At the top of one of them was an 'X', below which was written:

'The remains of B.F. McNeill, ship's cook, and last of the Tyrone Giants, died 9th of July, 1865, of the consumption, aged 27 years. May God have mercy on his soul.'

Fitzmaurice sat back with a pleased expression.

'There, that make you feel any better?'

His companions absorbed the new material.

'Seems a bit more specific, I suppose,' Rafferty conceded.

'Would appear to narrow it down,' Crozier agreed.

'Of course it does. Now buck up and stop worrying.'

Refreshed and reassured, they spent the next hour exploring the ship. Though showing signs of age on the interior, the *Dolphin* had been skilfully bolstered on the outside, every joint and fitting cross-braced, the bow thickly sheathed in greenheart wood to crash through ice. Of her three masts, the forward one was square-rigged, while the other two carried fore and aft sails, like a schooner. In the stern, below the galley, there was a coal-fired steam engine capable of driving the ship at around six knots, although as the coal bunkers were relatively small, this was a limited option. For warmth, the inside ribs had been tarred and panelled, and iron-clad hearths installed in both the captain's cabin and the mess, the exhaust fumes vented by pipes to the main funnel.

'I still don't understand,' Crozier peered in at the long, low galley, 'how a giant would manage on a ship like this. My head is nearly scraping the ceiling and I'm not much above average.'

'I believe,' Fitzmaurice said, 'that Sir Hamilton was so fond of McNeill's cooking that he wouldn't travel anywhere without him. The ship was designed with a vaulted galley and a specially extended cabin just to accommodate him.'

'That must have been some good grub.' Rafferty rubbed his hands together. 'Let's hope we're in for something similar.'

At dusk, McGregor and the rest of the crew, half a dozen in all, returned. Crozier, who was up on deck, heard them before he saw them, rolling along the pier, arms about each other's shoulders, singing a ragged shanty. The quality of the performance indicated that a local tavern had enjoyed a good day's takings.

'Yis're all settled in then?' said McGregor, barrelling off the gangway. Behind him two of his shipmates were having trouble assisting a third.

'Indeed we are, Skipper,' Crozier replied. 'And you and your men found refreshment, I see.'

'Ah, don't worry about the cabin boy, he's only young – cannae sniff the barmaid's apron without...'

The struggling trio fell onto the deck, gasping and

swearing. A gaunt man with red-blistered cheeks sloped into view.

'Are you hungry? Cookie here's going tae feed us all, aren't you, Victoor?'

The cook gazed morosely at Crozier, then, putting a hand to his mouth, lurched sideways and vomited over the side of the ship. Two of the fallen men, meanwhile, were upright again, both of them broad and blond with red beards and pinkish blue eyes.

'The twins,' said McGregor. 'Magnus and Mikkel, but for Christ's sake don't ask me which one's which.'

'Skål!' the pair shouted at Crozier, saluting and laughing as they headed for the hatchway.

Two more men followed, Doyle the bosun, a Sligo man with huge, dark eyebrows and a hard handshake, and Harris the first mate, a genial Londoner whose frizzy grey hair was tied back in a nautical ponytail. McGregor blocked their way.

'Get the cabin boy down tae his scratcher,' he ordered. 'But first, one of yis needs tae go back for Bunion.'

'Bunion?' said Crozier.

McGregor jerked his thumb. Crozier peered over the side. Down below, shivering next to a mooring bollard and staring up at him with watery eyes was a pale, squat dog with a wedge-shaped head and skin the texture of scuffed baize on an old billiards table.

'What's the matter with him?'

'He's a f---ing wee bastard is what's the matter wi'im,' McGregor growled. 'Disn'ae like the sea.' He paused, hawked, and launched an audible projectile onto the dockside. 'F---ing wee boaker.'

Crozier watched as Harris went back down and engaged

in a brief *pas de deux* with the beast before grappling it in his arms and attempting to lift it clear of the ground. There was a crack of compacting vertebrae and a sharp grunt of pain. Harris staggered sideways.

'He's doin' Stiff Dog,' he cried over his shoulder.

McGregor slammed a calloused hand on the gunwale. 'Pay no heed. Grab him by the ballocks if ye have tae!'

At that, man and hound disappeared abruptly from view, and there were sounds from below as of the thrashing of a large fish.

'F--- sake.' McGregor made for the gangway, rolling up his sleeves.

While the skipper and his mate wrestled with Bunion, the ship's cook was coming to terms with the lizard in his kitchen. He tapped at the glass, causing Bridie to tense and regard him with her customary primordial contempt.

'It's important that she stays in her little house,' Fitzmaurice warned. 'If she gets out and you upset her, she will, in all likelihood, hurt you.'

The cook was from Antwerp and had the look of a figure from the background of a Flemish painting depicting the unsavoury nature of peasant life. He stared uncomprehendingly at Fitzmaurice, then drew back and resumed his supper preparations. Around his malnourished midriff he wore, like an outsized charm bracelet, a leather belt hung with ladles, knife-sharpeners and corkscrews that chimed and clanked as he walked.

Later, the ship's company (with the exception of the cabin boy) sat down to a horrifying soup-like stew in whose khaki depths bobbed nubs and gobbets of blubber and cartilage, and dumplings the texture of wet sand. Fortunately there was also bread from a local baker and beer for those that could stomach it. (The new arrivals exchanged glances to the effect that next time, presumably, the cook would be sober.) McGregor, meanwhile, enhanced the eating experience by regaling them, in funereal tones, with tales of terror on the high seas and icy death in extreme latitudes. It was clear soon enough that he was sceptical about both their mission and its leader, whom he addressed with a curled lip as 'your Lordship'. Fitzmaurice, in the manner of his caste, was oblivious – 'Really, there's no need to stand on ceremony in this day and age' – and, if anything, appeared to find him charming.

Afterwards, the skipper, showing no sign of the effects of his earlier intake, invited them down to the officers' cabin, where a fire had been lit in the grate. He poured them each a measure of Wee Jimmy Finest Scotch Whisky, then spread some charts out on the table. He and Fitzmaurice studied the route while the other two warmed themselves and listened to the wind plucking at the rigging. At length, the older man straightened up with a sigh and stared at each of them in turn. On receiving a kick from Crozier, Rafferty, who had been attempting to pick out *The Lass That Loves A Sailor* on his banjolele, stopped.

'I'm going tae square with yis lads,' McGregor began. 'Ma gut tells me this expedition is a load of old bahookie.'

'Now hold on a minute.'

'If I might just finish, "your Lordship"?'

Fitzmaurice's lip inflated.

'Thank you. You've not a jot of experience between yis, no training tae speak of and, from what I kin see, very little chance of finding what it is you're supposed tae be seeking. There's also a risk – it's a *wee* risk but a risk nivertheless – that we could all be blown tae kingdom come by the Hun. I have tae ask... are yis sure yis want tae proceed?'

Fitzmaurice swept his hair back with emphatic hauteur.

'Let me assure you, Mr McGregor, that we are fully prepared for this expedition in every respect and that we fully intend to achieve our aims and return home safely to reap our just rewards. There is no doubt in our minds.' He paused for an elongated sniff. 'We are Trinity men after all. Perhaps it is *you* that wishes to reconsider?'

McGregor's moustache bristled to twice its original volume.

'Not at all, "your Lordship", I've no fears for my own part. I earned ma stripes long before any of yis so much as keeched in a nappy. I'm just making sure yis are aware of the dangers. The freezing...'

'McGregor, we're fully aware of the...'

'The freezing temperatures are only half the battle. There's an ocean of ice tae get through and...'

'McGregor, please...'

'And if the wild animals don't get yis, the natives'll...'

'McGregor! Please!' Fitzmaurice reached out and gripped the skipper's arm. 'Please. We'll be fine. Everything's going to be fine... Now I'd like, if I may, to propose a toast, to you, Skipper, to your handsome ship and your trusty crew, to my companions, who have risen, as I knew they would, to the occasion, and to the success of our expedition. Gentlemen,' he lifted his glass, 'to the voyage of the *Dolphin*.'

The adventurers hoisted their drinks high.

'THE VOYAGE OF THE *DOLPHIN*!'

McGregor reached for the whisky bottle.

'... skin yis like seals and f---ing eat yis.'

4

A Queasy Start

Crozier had never seen a chicken being sick before. Forgetting his own misery for a moment, he clutched the top of the coop and watched as the bird, red of eye and damp of feather, performed a solo *do-si-do* in time with the pitching of the ship, its wings raised in the manner of a baptist preacher at full tilt, and then, with convulsions of its sweaty neck and a series of strangulated burps, hunched over and relieved itself of several days' worth of corn. Its companions, including a poleaxed cockerel, were slumped in a corner of the run in a collective trance, their time having come and gone.

An image of eggs glistening in a frying pan flashed in Crozier's mind and his gorge rose. Further back in the darkness of the hold a joist groaned and something shaken loose by the swell skittered across the floor. Struggling to stay on top of a ballooning heave, he held tighter to the woodwork and splayed his legs for better balance. Another unknown object clattered in the shadows. He edged his way along the stack of cases until he located the box marked 'Spices' and, rummaging through it, withdrew a package of powdered ginger – the only half-effective remedy for seasickness, according to Harris, aside from an infusion of black horehound. Or death.

Above him, in their turbulent cabins, Fitzmaurice and Rafferty were both very much regretting having gone to sea, and in the case of the latter, curled on the floor hugging a wooden bucket, having been born. 'I swear, I have nothing left to give,' he sobbed into the maw of his pail. Fitzmaurice, though not yet quite at the depths reached by his friend, was nevertheless holding onto the sides of his cot and flailing from side to side with his eyes screwed shut, like a chimpanzee strapped to a nightmarish fairground ride. In the passageway, the ship's dog, which had been vomiting at regular intervals since leaving port, had long since collapsed, the only sign of life being an occasional shiver through its stubby legs.

It had been an unfortunate start to the voyage. Intending to avoid the Atlantic's prevailing southwesterlies and the danger of seasonal gales, McGregor had elected to sail east out of Queenstown and head north through St George's Channel. Almost immediately, however, they had hit a powerful swell that persisted for nearly six hours. Even the crew, veterans most of them and therefore more confident the horror would eventually pass, would later concede that it had been a particularly testing stretch. The only one unaffected was McGregor himself, braced at the wheel with his captain's hat on. 'Ye'll feel better if ye sit under a tree' was his helpful advice to anyone who happened to lurch by.

In the early afternoon the chop began to abate and, his stomach restored to semi-equilibrium by Harris' hot-water-and-ginger trick, Crozier ventured up on deck. The sea was a muscular grey-green, with scurrying white-caps disappearing in the direction of the Waterford coast. A scattering of gulls busied themselves above the ship's wake. The bearded twins, tending to the tautness of various ropes, looked up and bade him a stereophonic 'Skål!', but it lacked the cheer of the previous evening.

After the torrid morning below, the stiff breeze was immensely refreshing and Crozier found himself gulping down ravenous lungfuls, until eventually he felt much better and even began to countenance the possibility, at some distant point in the future, of food. The *Dolphin*, still pitching, was a solid craft, he thought, listening to the thump of the hull against the waves, the crack of the breeze through the rigging. He felt relatively safe on her. He gazed up at a complex geometry of buntlines and ratlines, the crossbeams dark against the creamy blankness of the sails. She smelled good too: ancient wood, long seasoned; forest and ocean; turpentine and spice; a thousand cargoes loaded under hot suns.

As he stood there being filled by these pleasant sensations, some of his misgivings began to fall away: perhaps he *had* been right to put his studies to one side (it was only a year after all and it would be an opportunity to think things over); maybe the trip *would* be a success (and the making of him, as his father would say, *test him as a man*); and, who knew, perhaps there was a small chance that Fitzmaurice wasn't, in fact, stark raving mad... At that moment, the ginger wore off without warning, and leaning over the rail with a groan of resignation, he gave the seagulls something to fight about.

'That really is a most unwholesome creature,' Fitzmaurice said. 'It's rather putting me off my eggs.'

The other two turned to look at the ship's dog, which was perched on its hindquarters on the floor nearby attending noisily to its testicles. Alerted by a flicker of jungle-sense it paused, glared at each of them in turn, suppressed a belch, and returned to its work.

'What sort of a breed is it anyway?' Rafferty asked.

'Not sure,' Crozier said. 'Could be a bit of bulldog in there. Or Staffordshire terrier. It's definitely got those funny little ears. What's that thing on its chin though? Is that the bunion?'

'No, that's not a bunion. A bunion – or a *hallux abducto-valgus* to give it its scientific name – is a deformity of the big toe. That's just some kind of horrible wart.'

A becalmed sea and a good night's sleep had revived everyone onboard and some had even managed to hold down the Antwerpian's version of porridge, which appeared, mysteriously, to have had prolonged contact with the frying pan. The crew had disappeared about their duties, leaving the late-rising non-sailors to linger over their breakfast.

'My grandmother had a bunion,' Fitzmaurice said. 'Frightful thing it was. Size of an apple. Very hard to look at.'

'Was it painful?'

'Extremely – pass the teapot would you – my grandfather accidentally hit it with a croquet mallet once and I'd say they probably heard the scream three counties away.'

'Anyone want the last bit of sausage?'

'All yours, old man. Anyway, she didn't speak to him again for years. I think it put her in a bad mood for the rest of her life.'

'Is it just me, or does that dog look a bit like Mc—'

Just then Bunion jumped up and stared at the door, and a moment later McGregor entered with the bosun

42

and the cabin boy, who had been absent earlier. They sat. McGregor ignited a Navy Cut and leaned back in his chair.

'Right, having been on the bridge the whole night I think I've earned the right tae a bit o' kip so I'm going tae retire to ma cabin. Which brings me tae the wee matter of you young gentlemen and how yis're going tae earn your salt.'

Three sets of eyes flashed in his direction.

'Obviously, yis cannae be doing anything that would endanger the lives of the rest of us, so for the time being yis'll busy yourselves with the cleaning and maintenance of the ship.'

'Just a minute,' Fitzmaurice broke in. 'May I remind you...'

'I'm afraid, "your Lordship", every man has tae pull his weight at sea, regardless of his position on land. You're in my jurisdiction now.'

Fitzmaurice noted the Scotsman's tone, hesitated, and settled for a semi-inflated lip.

'The deck will need scrubbing and the bilge pumped, and there's a whole length of ship could do with sanding and varnishing. Yis'll also need tae take it in turns helping out in the galley. Doyle there will assign your duties from day tae day.'

The bosun said nothing, but moved his fearsome eyebrows up and down, twice.

'Now look here, McGregor,' Fitzmaurice said, 'I'm really not sure about this bilge business. Isn't that the cabin boy's job?'

The boy in question, an intensely self-conscious sixteen-year-old with a bubonic neck, stared down at the heavily-bandaged hand that was not engaged in foraging for leftovers. McGregor doused his cigarette-end in a teacup.

'Cabin boy's lucky he's not danglin' from the f---ing yardarm.'

During the morning the wind strengthened in their favour and they began to make up lost time, fairly scudding along the coast of Wexford, the shore gleaming white in the distance. Crozier and Rafferty, side by side like a couple of old plough horses, set to scrubbing the planks, while Fitzmaurice made an ill-tempered start on the first six inches of several miles of brightwork. Around them people came and went, attending to mysterious nautical tasks. The hen coop had been hauled up from the hold and its inhabitants, revived by the fresh air, were finding their sea legs, the cockerel even venturing a tentative strut. Crozier and Rafferty conversed for a while but the noise of the wind in the sails, and the heat of the spring sun on their backs, made it an effort.

'Be passing Dublin port soon,' Rafferty observed at length. 'Last chance to do the sensible thing.'

Crozier grunted. In his peripheral vision he could see that Rafferty had stopped scrubbing and was resting upright on his hunkers, gazing towards the horizon. He wondered what it felt like to be a Dubliner, what it must mean to be an unwilling subject in the second city of the Empire. In his mind's eye he tracked upriver along the quays towards the centre, picturing the sunshine on O'Connell Bridge, hearing the clatter and clack of carriages and trams, the cries of the gurriers and the flower sellers. He thought of Daniel O'Connell, the great emancipator of Irish Catholics, further up the street on his plinth, impervious in his stolidity to pigeon droppings, weather, the passage of time. '*...The alternative to live as slaves or die as free men.*' Rousing words. And yet, '*The altar of liberty totters when cemented only with blood...*'

It occurred to him that they had made no provision for religion on the voyage and that Rafferty, a modest attender of Mass, was in a tight minority. Though the Antwerpian was more than likely a Catholic. A recruitment poster flashed in his mind. 'Remember The Women Of Belgium!' Another small Catholic country, already overrun, its womenfolk defiled by the drooling Hun in his jackboots and *pickelhaube*.

He recalled dinner at the Rafferty home before they left for Queenstown: a handsome terrace in Phibsborough, on the city's north side; crucifixes, the Child of Prague in the entrance hall, a framed copy of Batoni's 'Sacred Heart' on the wall of the dining room where they sat down to boiled ham and parsley sauce, conversation that was itself like two sets of best crockery laid out for mutual inspection. Rafferty's mother, a wiry, confident woman, did most of the talking and that was the way his father, a large, slow-moving man with a country complexion, seemed to like it.

It was Rafferty's mother who had gone to the bishop to secure dispensation for her son to attend the Protestant university ('You'll have as good an education as *they* have or I'll die trying'); his mother who had straightened his tie and spat on a handkerchief to rub dried soap off his cheek as he waited to be interviewed by the Fellows; his mother who wept with pride when he was accepted into the School of Medicine.

Crozier knew all this because Rafferty had told him after a particularly maudlin session in the Bailey during his first term. He had also confessed to fear verging on panic when confronted with his first cadaver in the high-vaulted anatomy room that smelled of formaldehyde and disinfectant: a man freshly dead of heart failure, shades of pink and blue, the puckered skin peeled back 'like a joint of pork'; how he realised, as his vision fizzled and the room became distant — the professor repeating his name, demanding an answer — that he could not bear the sight of blood.

'Goodbye Walter, we hope you'll come again when you're back from your trip.'

'I'd like that very much, Mrs Rafferty.'

He remembered her turning to her son, her reproachful 'Frank, are you mad altogether?' tinged with fear and admiration, the flush of withheld emotion below her cheekbones, and 'I'll light a candle for you'; his father's brisk, formal handshake and 'Sure, it'll keep you out of trouble here' delivered with a look that warned, *break your mother's heart and I'll break your...*

There was a sudden stink, like burning guano, and the two deckhands turned to find Fitzmaurice sitting astride the capstan puffing at his pipe. He gave them a cheery salute.

'Ahoy me hearties.'

They joined him. Rafferty, struggling against the wind, lit a cigarette.

'Life on the ocean wave, eh lads?' Fitzmaurice said. 'Lets you see the world afresh, don't you think? Look at that sky, smell that air.'

'All I can smell is that filthy pipe,' Crozier grumbled. 'What on earth are you putting in it?'

'Now, now, there's no need to be dour. The sun is shining, the wind is in our sails and we're heading for adventure. That, my friend, beats sweating over books in a boring old library any day.'

His companions concurred and all three took their ease for a while, enjoying the breeze. A voice called from the quarter-deck.

'Mr Fitzmaurice?'

It was Doyle, his eyebrows at full mast. He held up the bilge bucket.

5

The Western Isles and a Surprise

Three days later they had skirted the northeastern edge of Ireland, Crozier's homesickness not helped by Rafferty playing *Mountains of Mourne* on his banjolele, accompanied by a howling Bunion. They threaded their way among the Inner Hebrides, through the Sound of Mull and the Sound of Skye, and into the Minch, heading for the Western Isles. The light, as they made their way north, thinned and became more delicate, the distant hills on the islands they passed shimmering behind a silvery haze. At night, under starscapes of breath-taking clarity, lamps in the windows of crofters' cottages flickered yellow in the deep darkness.

Though sheltered from the turbulent Atlantic, the going in some of the channels was surprisingly choppy, but in the calmer stretches they fished for mackerel, which were plentiful. Cooked simply, fresh from the sea, they were a welcome relief from the standard rations. (Victoor, it had transpired, was actually marginally worse at cooking sober than he was drunk.)

Excitement had been provided for Crozier, who was a keen amateur naturalist, by a sighting of a golden eagle (*Aquila chrysaetos,* according to his reference book) riding a thermal above one of the islands off

Skye. He watched through field glasses as the bird, with a wingspan, he estimated, of some seven feet, spiralled downwards, intrigued by a pair of goats and their kid that were traversing the cliffside. Legs splayed, it made several speculative swoops towards the youngster but eventually climbed back to the clifftop and disappeared. Later that same day they were joined by a pod of seals that kept pace with the ship for half a mile, stealing curious sideways glances with their oddly affectionate eyes before vanishing beneath the waves.

Working life on board the *Dolphin* had quickly settled into a routine, with the three greenhorns following, more or less, the instructions of the bosun and starting to take on a little nautical training, largely ropework, but also some rudiments of navigation using charts and quadrants. Having spent a couple of summers sailing in his youth, Fitzmaurice was making most progress and even won some grudging approval from McGregor for his knotting prowess. Overall, though, the ship's captain, who had by dint of hard labour and sheer desperation hauled himself from the echoing squalor of a Glasgow tenement, remained suspicious, scornful even, of the half-millennium of unearned privilege he perceived in the sheen of the younger man's curls. He was none too pleased either to discover Fitzmaurice's pet. According to Harris, who had been in the galley at the time of the encounter, both parties had performed a double-take, a disk of dried banana halting sharply on the way to Bridie's mouth, a teacup en route to the skipper's. They had then stared at each other for a full minute before McGregor turned on his heel, muttering something about 'Noah's f---ing Ark'.

The ship's dog, meanwhile, long shunned by the crew, had attempted to ingratiate itself among the new recruits and, after much rejection (and many unkind words), eventually found Crozier's resistance to be the weakest. It took to following him around and sat watching him from a distance while he worked. It scraped at his cabin door at bedtime, and each evening having been denied entry, snored loudly in the passageway. One night, the latch having failed to engage, Crozier awoke to find the beast's gnarly snout opposite him on the pillow, its tongue lolling, its swamp-gas breath condensing on his cheek.

The port of Stornoway, with its dark stone buildings and looming church steeples, was their last land contact before the open sea. They dropped anchor in the deserted harbour – the fishing boats, according to McGregor, having pursued the shoals of silver herring north to Shetland – and the first mate and the cook rowed ashore. After several hours they reappeared, accompanied by two youths pushing barrows full of vegetables, and a man on a horse pulling a cartload of coal. Harris and Victoor between them also lugged rum, tobacco, milk, cured meats, strings of kippers, and another half-dozen chickens, tied by their feet, to replace those abducted for the pot.

Later that afternoon the *Dolphin* cleared the Isle of Lewis, and with a fresh magnitude of wind in her sails, bore northwest into the marble-green sweep of the Atlantic. The new hens were acquainting themselves with the resident fowl (and a somewhat reassured cockerel); the Antwerpian was picking over his supplies and making plans; Doyle and the twins were fine-tuning the rigging. Having finished their scrubbing duties for the day, Crozier and Rafferty were lolling on deck and Fitzmaurice, tired of the endless sandpapering, was idly scanning the horizon off the port side.

'A whale!'

The others rushed over.

'I don't see anything,' Rafferty said. 'Are you sure?'

'Yes, yes, it was just there.' Fitzmaurice indicated the middle distance. 'It was half out of the water. I saw its fin and everything.'

'What size was it?' Crozier said.

'Not giant, but big enough. And grey and shiny.'

'Probably a minke. Though it could have been a right whale.'

'As opposed to a…'

'Yes, indeed. Although, I suppose there's also a chance it was a small sperm whale. Though I doubt it.'

'I'm not sure it *was* a whale. Probably the seals again.'

'It was definitely a whale,' Fitzmaurice snapped.

'Or a sea cow.'

'Too cold for sea cows,' Crozier said. 'They prefer warm, shallow waters.'

'I wonder if sea cows' milk is salty,' Fitzmaurice mused. The other two looked at him and Crozier opened his mouth to say something, then didn't.

'Imagine falling overboard and being swallowed by the brute,' Rafferty said. 'How dark it would be in there.'

They pondered this and Fitzmaurice shivered.

'Makes you wonder how old Jonah survived.'

'Well, he couldn't have,' Rafferty said.

'Couldn't have what?'

'He couldn't have survived.'

'How do you mean?'

51

'I mean he would have been dissolved by the whale's gastric juices. He would have been digested. It's just a parable.'

'I'm sure you're mistaken old man. Jonah and the Whale's a true story, isn't it Crozier?'

'All stories are true,' Crozier replied. 'And some of them actually happened.'

'See, I told you.'

'I read a real-life account of a man being swallowed by a whale once,' Rafferty recalled. 'Fell off a harpoon boat. When they cut the whale open he'd been bleached white and gone completely blind. And he'd only been in there for half a day.'

'Crikey.'

They watched for a while longer but the sea was keeping its secrets.

'Right,' Fitzmaurice said at length, 'I suppose we'd better make a start on the photographs.'

The others groaned. Along with Jacob's Cream Crackers, and O'Shea's Tinctures, Salves & Balsams, one of the main sponsors of the expedition was a gentlemen's outfitters, Savage Newell of Kildare Street, a firm that had gained a foothold selling cheap, tight uniforms to British regiments during the Boer War. They required, in part-return for their donation of one hundred pounds, a set of publicity photographs of the intrepid lads sporting their outdoor clothing in a variety of rugged scenarios. To this end they had provided a handsome square-bellows camera (the latest model) and several boxes of trousers, pullovers, vests, mitts, balaclavas, reindeer-hide boots, stiff gabardine coats and prickly woollen longjohns.

'I'll fetch the equipment, you fellows go and put on the garments.'

The camera, a Magiflex Rectograph Imperial, was a large and unwieldy device made of brass-bound mahogany, and it was with some difficulty that Fitzmaurice secured it to its tripod. He stared at the instructions.

Once fitted to the tripod and with glass plate inserted on the rear standard (fig.1), open the shutter on the lens (fig.2) to focus and compose the image. Straightforward enough. *The taking lens may be stopped down (fig.3) to help gauge depth of field and vignetting, and a focusing cloth may be used in conjunction with a Fresnel lens (fig.4) or a loupe (fig.5)...* He frowned. *To make a photograph pull back the ground glass (fig.6) and slide the film holder into place within the plane of the lens (fig.7) taking care not to damage the springback mechanism (fig 8)...* Breathing heavily through his nose he skipped twenty or thirty pages ahead. *Close and cock the shutter (fig. 193) and set speed and aperture before removing the darkslide...*

'Christ.' He looked up. Crozier and Rafferty were loitering bulkily around the companionway in their Savage Newell coats, knickerbockers and gaiters. Rafferty was additionally wearing a thick balaclava, that combined with his milk-bottle glasses to give the impression of a diving helmet, or an insect head on a human body.

'Right-o, stand over there by the rigging and act as though you know what you're doing. As if you're expert sailors.'

Crozier seized a brush and made sweeping motions; Rafferty attempted to reach up and grasp the rigging but the seams beneath his armpits refused to yield and he had to settle for resting his hands on his hips in an approximation of a jolly tar about to dance the hornpipe.

'Good. Now hold it like that.'

Fitzmaurice squinted again at the manual then reached into the box and drew out a pane. It slipped from his fingers and shattered. He extracted another and after several attempts from a number of angles managed to insert it into the rear standard *(fig.1)*. He opened the shutter on the lens *(fig.2)*.

'How long do we have to stand here?' Rafferty wanted to know.

'I'm not sure.' Fitzmaurice peered at *fig.3* and wondered whether he should use a focusing cloth. 'Just bear with me.'

Not having any idea what either a Fresnel lens or a loupe was, he moved on to *fig.6* and pulled back the ground glass to slide the film holder into place within the plane of the lens *(fig.7)*. There was a crunching sound. He adjusted the film holder but this caused a sharp snap, as of an over-stretched spring returning to an unextended position, and a fragment of glass shot out of the side of the bellows.

'Come on Fitz, what's taking so long?'

'Just another minute. We're almost there.'

He opened the lens wide and peered through the viewfinder at the ghostly forms in front of him. It was no good. He removed his jacket, draped it around his head and leant over the apparatus, pulling the fabric close to block out the light. He began to ease it all into focus, and slowly, slowly, the picture began to form. Slowly... And then, the dinner gong sounded, a low rumbling came from the bow and the cabin boy and the twins thundered into and through the camera's range of vision plucking Rafferty, without a word or backward glance, into their slipstream.

'Bloody hell,' shouted Fitzmaurice.

Crozier wasn't hungry (it was salt-beef and boiled cabbage and he could abide neither) so he stayed on deck and settled himself on a perch below the bridge to watch some gannets *(Morus bassanus)* diving for fish. The *Dolphin* was managing a good six knots and it wasn't long before they were gone from view. He lay back and listened to the myriad sounds of the ship: the creaking and ticking of her timbers, the seethe and plash of the ocean against the hull, the whip-crack of the sails; all the various inexplicable tinklings and clankings sought out by the wind. Above him a gull was dreaming at the masthead, floating with barely a wingbeat, and he marvelled at its effortless detachment. What would it be like to be as free as a bird?

Just as the question formed he was distracted by a sound on the starboard side of the deck. It was coming from the lifeboat. Shielding his eyes against the sun, which had just pierced the clouds, he watched as the canvas tarpaulin that was stretched over the mouth of the craft went slack and dropped away, and to his utter amazement a face appeared. It was deathly pale. A pair of wild eyes peered from beneath a tangle of dark hair. He squinted. The creature looked around, listening intently, then rose further into the light and after one more scan (Crozier was largely hidden by the mainmast) vaulted nimbly onto the deck and loped with silent footsteps over to the water butt that stood beside the hatchway.

He could see now that the figure was a young woman in a grimy white blouse and ragged grey skirt. She took the tin scoop from its hook and drank, droplets spilling down her chin. And again. She replaced it, then froze, head on one side. She had sensed him. He shrank back into the shadow of the mast, holding his breath, his heart pounding. When he ventured another peek, she had vanished.

He sat thinking about what he'd just seen, wondering if he had, in fact, seen it. Could he have hallucinated? There was no doubt that he'd been feeling unusual of late, what with the seasickness and the hit-and-miss nutritional value of Victoor's *basse cuisine*. Or had he witnessed an apparition? It wouldn't have been the first time. As a child he'd described to his nervously-smiling family a number of other-worldly encounters, later referred to, *sotto voce*, as 'Walter's visions'. These included a conversation with a neighbour's wife dead some fifteen years, and a premonition, relayed with great excitement to an uncle who worked for Harland & Wolff Heavy Industries, of the sinking of a mighty ship between 'white mountains'.

'Are you sure it was a woman?'

'I told you, she was wearing a skirt.'

'And how did she look?'

'Thirsty. Fierce.'

Crozier and Fitzmaurice were standing a little way back from the lifeboat. Invitations to the apparition to make itself known, along with tentative tappings on the hull, had yielded nothing.

'Mmm, very interesting. And you say this kind of thing has happened to you before?'

'A few times. When I was seven I talked to the ghost of Mr Gillespie-next-door's wife and she told me where she'd hidden the key to their summer house.'

'And?'

'There it was, where she'd said.'

'Fascinating, and...'

There was a clatter at the opening of the companion-way and Rafferty, his chest heaving, hauled Bunion onto the deck.

'What kept you?'

'Little brute,' Rafferty panted, 'was doing Stiff Dog. Jaysus, he's heavy.'

The hound stared about him indignantly, his demeanour softening when he spotted Crozier.

'Animals are sensitive to the supernatural,' Fitzmaurice explained. 'It's a known fact. If there's something in there, this little fellow will tell us.' He pointed at the lifeboat. 'Off you go, good dog.'

Bunion sniffed the breeze.

'Go on boy, fetch.'

Bunion sat down.

'Sic, Bunion. Sic!'

Bunion yawned.

'Squirrel, Bunion! Rabbit! Squirrel!'

Bunion shifted onto one haunch, extended his other back leg at an upward angle and with a look of defiance plunged his snout into the shadows.

'Great,' Rafferty said. 'I've given myself a hernia for nothing.'

'Don't worry,' Fitzmaurice started for the hatch, 'I'll get my lizard. She'll flush it out.' He stopped dead. 'What the hell was that?'

All three turned towards the source of the muffled but unmistakable sound of a female scream. The canvas cover pinged, and the head and shoulders of the screamer burst into view. An astonished silence fell. Crozier had been correct on all but one count: this was no phantom.

'Do *not*,' she warned, pointing a vital finger at each of them in turn, 'bring a f—ing lizard anywhere near me.'

6

Interrogation

The stowaway finished her second portion of suet and sultana pudding (it had been preceded by three helpings of salt-beef and cabbage) and laid down her spoon. 'Compliments to the chef,' she pronounced, apparently without irony. Quivering with unaccustomed pride, Victoor moved forward, his belt clanking, and began gathering up the dishes. Ranged around the mess table, the Trinity men, Harris, and McGregor remained mute, the latter having added nothing further to the single hoarse profanity he had uttered on the bridge earlier.

'So,' she said, when the cook had gone. 'You probably have a few questions.'

She gazed at them levelly. Her pale face was oval-shaped, her expression defiant. A smear of fat shone on her chin. The others turned to McGregor, who made a noise in his throat like a bull mastiff approaching a burglar. He coughed, then spoke.

'Well, how about ye start by telling us why ye picked the *Dolphin*? And how exactly ye managed tae get on board.'

There were some scattered breadcrumbs on the table in front of her and she began rounding them up with a fingertip.

'Oh, it was easy. Your ship was the only one that wasn't guarded,' (McGregor glared at Crozier), 'and I came aboard while these three were arguing about a ukulele.'

'It's a *banjo*lele, actually,' Rafferty said. 'There's a difference.'

'Well, it sounds like a ukulele, and, by the way, your A-string is flat.'

'No, it's not.'

'It is, it sounds terrible.' (Rafferty blinked at her, taken aback.) 'Then, when they went below, I hid in the lifeboat and made myself a little nest among the ropes, using my bag as a pillow. It was cosy at first but during the night the temperature dropped and I was freezing, so between watches I crept down to the hold, found some food and blankets and slept behind some packing cases with the chickens who, I have to tell you, are surprisingly good company, if a bit smelly. And then before dawn I'd sneak back to the boat and sleep some more. I did a lot of sleeping.'

'I can't believe you managed to stay hidden for so long,' Crozier said.

She shrugged.

'I only moved around when absolutely necessary and then only at night. I did nearly get caught a couple of times, once coming back from the… well, the you-know-what … by that man there.' She pointed at Harris. 'And another time in the hold, not long after we set off when I was dreadfully sick and my pail fell over and I thought you…' she indicated Crozier, 'had rumbled me for sure.'

'What about food?'

'That wasn't so easy. Sometimes I managed to steal

60

scraps from the galley, but mostly it was just eggs.'

'Raw eggs?'

'I'm afraid so, and biscuits. I was very hungry, but then, there are many in the world who don't have any food at all.'

'Weren't you bored?'

'Sometimes, but when it wasn't raining I'd open the cover on one corner so there was enough light to read a book. And I also knitted a scarf. A lot of the time I'd just lie and listen to you lot complaining about how much work you have to do.' (McGregor snorted.) 'You know, you really do go on.'

'And had you planned to keep that up for the whole voyage?'

'No, of course not. Just until we were clear of Scotland.'

'And then what? You do know we're on our way to the Arctic?'

'Yes, and it's not ideal, but I've decided you can drop me off at Reykjavik. I'll offer my services to the women of Iceland.'

'Your services?'

'In their struggle for equal rights with men.'

'Oh Holy Jesus, a f—ing suffragette!' McGregor yodelled. 'That's all we f—ing need.'

A breadcrumb ricocheted off his shoulder.

'Let me get this straight,' Rafferty said. 'I'm sorry, what did you say your name was?'

'Phoebe. Phoebe Sturgeon.'

'Let me get this straight, Phoebe.' He stopped. 'Wait a minute, *Phoebe Sturgeon*...' He frowned. 'I know that name. Weren't you..? Aren't you the one that..., Yes, I thought you looked familiar – you were in the

61

newspapers – wasn't it you that uh..?' He faltered, his face deepening in colour. '--That threw the, uh... "item of ladies clothing" at the prime minister?'

All eyes returned, wider and shinier, to the interviewee. She flushed a little also, lifted her chin a fraction higher.

'It *was* you,' Rafferty continued. 'Yes, *Phoebe Sturgeon*. You hid in a broom cupboard in the House of Commons for something like two days. And you got him right in the face with the, uh...'

'Yes, it's coming back to *me* now.' Fitzmaurice snapped his fingers. 'There was much speculation in the press as to what the "item" was. And you escaped – that's right – I don't remember how, but they were after you for a whole list of crimes and misdemeanours.'

Phoebe averted her gaze. The aforementioned ranged from routine mischief such as daubing graffiti on public buildings, cutting telegraph wires, pouring lampblack into post boxes, disrupting court sessions, and smashing windows (years playing cricket with her brother Philip in the garden of their childhood home had given her a powerful and accurate right arm, and she had scored multiple direct hits on the Home Office, the Treasury, the Privy Council, the Savoy Hotel, Harrods, Liberty's, the *Daily Mail*, Dublin Castle, the Custom House, and the General Post Office on Sackville Street, to name a few), to heftier outrages such as planting a bomb in the gallery of the Metropolitan Tabernacle, and burning down Yarmouth Pier.

Then, of course, there was the show-stopper, the *coup de théâtre* that had crowned, and ended, her career as a militant in England: the "item". She remembered how the background tiers of gesticulating men slowed to a blur in the final moment; how the hullaballoo receded, leaving just her and the frock-coated figure before the parliamentary mace in a perfectly focused, silent space; how his pupils dilated as her arm drew back -- there in the inner sanctum, close enough to smell each other's breath – his shocked recognition of the "item" just before impact, reeling back in vain from its silken embrace, its scalding, intimate rebuke.

'And you just *vanished*. Crikey, who'd have thought it! The most wanted woman in England, an enemy of the state, right here onboard the *Dolphin*.'

'Bugger me sideways...'

'Please, McGregor, there's a lady present.'

'...with a haddock, that's just f—ing lovely.'

'I went to a girls' boarding school, so believe me, I've heard much worse.'

McGregor looked at her uncertainly.

'So you were in Ireland the whole time?' Crozier said.

'Yes.'

'But wasn't there an amnesty for the suffragettes when the war started?'

'Yes.'

'So, why didn't you go back to England?'

'I had my reasons.'

She surveyed the men across the table from her, the hostile Scot, the grizzled Cockney, and the three younger ones, roughly her own age, who regarded her with such curiosity. The fop was a type she recognised from her own background (albeit from a rarer stratum), wafting around endless village fetes and interminable harvest fayres. But the other two were more difficult to place: the dark boy with the strange accent, quiet, a sense of something troubling him; the musician with the pale eyes huge behind the thick lenses. They had one thing in common though, they were all nonplussed by her presence.

'Is Ireland all sorted out then?' Crozier asked. 'I mean, for women?'

'Far from it.'

'So why leave?'

She paused, taking in the room's wood-panelling, the dimming sky through the brass-rimmed portholes, and pictured the view from her room at Ennisfree, the rain sweeping across the neglected lawns, pooling in the dormant fountains, the ancient trees dripping. Her Ladyship would be leaning on the service bell around now, and down in the kitchen the tight-faced housekeeper and her defeated husband would be slopping soup into chipped Wedgwood. Apart from occasional weekend forays to Dublin for protest meetings and window smashing, it had been a long and lonely two years as a 'lady's companion'.

'Well, it's all about Home Rule now, isn't it? Suffrage in Ireland is just a sideshow.'

There was a tinkling in the doorway and Victoor arrived with a tray. They waited while he arranged cups, biscuits and a teapot on the table.

'I'm curious,' said Fitzmaurice presently. 'Why didn't you travel like other people? Why stow away?'

Phoebe stirred sugar into her brackish tea.

'Simple. I have no money. My family disowned me and my employment in Ireland was – oh, it's lovely to have a hot drink again — on the basis of bed and board only.'

'I see. And what did you do?'

'I was companion to a wealthy dowager in a big freezing-cold house in County Cork.'

'Really? Name?'

'Enola Vestey-Colquhoun. *Lady* Enola.'

'Vestey-Colquhoun … never heard of them. I wonder if they're related to the Tryon-Vesteys? Mother would know.'

There was a lull while they sipped. Phoebe ate another biscuit.

'So does that horrible lizard belong to you?' she said.

'I beg your pardon?'

'It's hideous. I nearly died when I first saw it.'

'Her name is Bridie, if you don't mind, and she's a very fine example of a South American green iguana.'

Mention of the reptile caused McGregor's knee to hit the underside of the table. He slammed down his cup.

'It's a dirty wee f—ing fly-muncher and it should never have come aboard,' he yelled. He jabbed a finger at Phoebe. 'And neither should you. Women are bad f—ing luck.' He stood up. 'Mr Harris, prepare tae turn the ship about, we're going back tae Stornoway.'

There was a jangling silence and then Fitzmaurice spoke.

'Mr McGregor, may I have a word in private?'

The skipper held the younger man's gaze for a moment.

'As you wish.'

He nodded at the first mate, who rose and headed for the bridge.

7

A Sighting

Crozier opened his eyes and stared into the darkness. He was on the top bunk, Rafferty below. He raised his head and flipped his hard, flat pillow over to the cool side. The wind had strengthened and he could hear rain on the deck above them. The rain at sea, he decided, was different. Lonelier. More intimate. It tapped on the soul. He thought about Phoebe next door in his recently-vacated bed, scrubbed and fortified, her first night of relative comfort in some time. Bidding them goodnight she had been quite a different prospect to the mad-haired starveling that had reared up from the lifeboat: the sun-deprived pallor had lifted, her hair shone and her eyes, earlier fractured and bloodshot, had cleared to a sceptical gooseberry-green. Only her borrowed garb, rough breeches and a roll-neck pullover rootled from the Savage Newell collection, maintained something of the vagabond.

He said, 'What?'

Rafferty sniffed.

'I say, I'm just after wondering – what do you think the "item" actually was?'

'What item?'

'*The* "item". The "item" that Phoebe threw at the prime minister.'

'Oh, that.'

'Yes, that.'

'I have no idea.'

'Come on, you must have *some* idea.'

'Well of course I have *some* idea, but it could have been a number of things.'

'I know, but what do you think it *was*.'

'How long have you been mulling this over?'

'Not very long. Well?'

'I really don't know... A shift?'

'A shift? No, I don't ... a *shift*? No, it must have been something more...'

'Rafferty, enough of this salacious nonsense. Please won't you let me sleep?'

'Oh *excuse me*,' Rafferty's voice rose half an octave. 'Oh, I'm so sorry. I didn't realise you Protestants had such delicate sensibilities.'

Crozier rolled onto his side and wriggled around, trying to align himself with the motion of the ship. He knew Rafferty well enough but sharing such cramped conditions was not going to be easy. Nearly two thirds of the cabin was taken up by their steamer trunks and personal effects, leaving a margin of less than eighteen inches around the bunk beds to manoeuvre. He had already caught Rafferty using his hairbrush.

'She is pretty though, isn't she?'

Crozier sighed.

'Not exactly.'

'Well, I mean to say, not pretty as *such*, not in the conventional way, but attractive, don't you think?'

'I suppose.'

Crozier waited. His cabin-mate was evidently not ready to relinquish consciousness.

'Walter?'

'Yes.'

'What do you think Fitzie said to the Scot?'

'I'm not sure, but it doesn't feel as though we've turned about.'

'I hope we don't. I hope Phoebe comes with us. At least as far as Iceland. It would be mighty unfair to make her go back.'

'It would.'

'He's quite a nasty man, isn't he?'

'Fitzie?'

'No, McGregor.'

'He certainly has a temper.'

'He does. And the language out of him. Jaysus.'

'I know. Desperate.'

'I'm baffled as to how Fitzie puts up with him. He's a fully-fledged case of what we medics call *proctalgia fugax*.'

'Which is?'

'A horrible pain in the ar—'

'Thank you, Frank. Any possibility of sleep now?'

In fact, Crozier did not sleep immediately. The arrival of Phoebe had disturbed thoughts of another woman. And of home. He drowsed. He was back in his father's house, on its little hill overlooking the park, the church at its side, the hallway full of morning light through the door's sugared glass, the dust planes sliding endlessly into each other. He could hear the murmur of voices far off, his mother most likely, instructing a maid. He imagined drifting along the corridor towards the kitchen, entering its warmth: smells of porridge and narcoleptic fumes from the range, the table laid for breakfast. In the scullery, the air would be rich with the damp exhalations of just-washed linen, draped over racks and hoisted to the ceiling by squeaking pulleys. He listened. There it was, the sound he missed, that assailed him in his loneliest moments, that was lodged in the core of his memory. On the windowsill a line of doves, soft grey blurs through the pane, nestled together in the heat and light and – what *was* the sound? – it was a kind of purring. Contented, yet somehow wistful. They were always there. His father put out grain for them from a sack he kept in his potting shed among the tools, the bags of compost, the herbs propagated in long trays and labelled: Thyme, Mint, Lemon Balm, Hyssop.

Purge me with hyssop and I shall be clean. He remembered the dreams: the first time, waking in the early hours, convinced, absolutely certain that all his family had been taken *(Then shall two be in the field; the one shall be taken, and the other left. Watch therefore: for ye know not what hour your Lord doth come),* running through the blood-red dark along the never-ending corridor to his parents' bedroom. And later the fear, still jolting awake in a sweat, the hymn in his head: *God's house is filling fast / Yet there is room* (What if there *wasn't* room?) *Some soul will be the last.* (What if you were in the queue *behind* the last one? What then?) *Are you washed in the blood of the lamb?* Yes, he had been washed. Squeaky clean. Redeemed. Saved on his sixteenth birthday. In his father's church. Buoyed by the love from the carbolic-scented congregation. Salvation. Cleansed in the precious blood. And yet...

'What happened?'

He opened his eyes. He had said the words aloud, half conscious, and had half woken Rafferty, who mumbled something that might have been 'girdle', twisted in his creaky cot and was silent. Crozier closed his eyes again… *And now these three remain: faith, hope and love. But the greatest of these is love.* He thought of Jenny and the summer before he went up to Trinity *(will you wait for me?)*: picnics on the slopes of Cavehill and the view over the city, its red-brick terraces and pale green domes, the shipyard and the sweep of Belfast Lough to the horizon; her yellow dress, the heat of the earth and the hiss of the breeze through the dry heather. Climbing to the summit, gazing east beyond Belfast Castle towards the far coast of Scotland; the edge of the hill forming the basalt profile of a dreaming giant. And all the while, the war at their backs: the *Lusitania* torpedoed off Queenstown with twelve hundred souls lost; the Triple Offensive under way; Warsaw already wrested from the Russians; much, *much* death.

Why had he not gone? Selfishness? Fear? *Love?* What had his father said? 'People like us will be needed *after* the war.' An objector, yes, but conscientious? The men of the Ulster Division were already at the Front, some of them parishioners, or sons, husbands or brothers of parishioners. People he knew. And now he really had no excuse. And where was he? *(It happened so quickly… Please forgive me, Walter.)*

*

When the crew emerged from their bunks at daybreak, the *Dolphin* was on an unaltered course. During their

conferral the previous evening Fitzmaurice had put
a number of arguments regarding the stowaway to
McGregor, all of which he had rejected, settling finally,
and with ill grace, for the promise of a hefty cash bonus
at the end of the voyage. After breakfast a meeting was
held to allocate duties to the new arrival.

'Can ye sew, lassie?'

'Of course I can. Can't you?'

'There are sails tae be repaired and I daresay some of
the men's clothing.'

'Why don't you sew them then?'

'Ah, Jesus Christ.' McGregor raised his eyes to the
heavens. '*Your Lordship?*'

'Uh, do I take it you would prefer tasks of a more
robust nature?' Fitzmaurice said.

'I don't see why I should have to do the sewing just
because I'm a woman, that's all.'

'A perfectly reasonable position.'

Fitzmaurice thought for a moment, then his eyes
brightened.

'Well, if you're not afraid of hard work, I have just the
job for you.'

'Yes?'

'Do you know where the bilge is?'

To her credit, Phoebe tackled all the duties assigned
to her ably and without a murmur, even, when it was
her turn, the sluicing of the heads, a chore the very mention of which drained the blood from the faces of her
shipmates. The crew, disconcerted, despite her manly
attire, by a feminine presence, went out of their way to
treat her with courtesy (though their behaviour, generally
speaking, was governed less by inclination and more by

fear of McGregor). The exception was the cabin boy, who goggled with furtive intent at every opportunity, increasing the volcanic pressure beneath his adolescent skin to new and troubling levels.

Rafferty and Harris kept a running book on the boy's dermal turmoil, betting on the longevity of the more spectacular pustules and papules (including a side wager one evening on the likelihood of a live eruption during dinner) and attempting to predict – with lucrative accuracy in Rafferty's case — the site of the next disfigurement.

Apart from a night of gales and a morning of heavy swell, the *Dolphin* made good headway following Phoebe's appearance. The first sighting of *terra firma* was reported by Harris on the fifth day: a momentary glimpse of snow-capped mountains far off, quickly obscured by mist. It was a still afternoon and they were running on steam power. All had settled into their tasks with the dreamy acquiescence required for passages of tedium at sea, taking their leisure where they could. Fitzmaurice had found a favourite spot on the port side of the stern where, due to the position of a supporting beam in the wheelhouse, he could not be seen by the officer in charge, and here he smoked his pipe and coughed quietly into a handkerchief. In the evenings, after dinner, Phoebe set about teaching the Trinity men how to play Bridge, their progress slowed by Fitzmaurice's insistence on withdrawing early to update his 'expedition journal'.

Crozier found this document lying open on the messroom table one afternoon at the following entry, written in a curiously jerky, childlike hand:

... be a charming, if misgided young filly who seems to have caught the eye of both my colleegues. I have assured the Scott, who has been beastly about the entire matter, that she shall remain in Rakeyervick after our business their is concluded.

With idle fascination Crozier flicked back to the beginning:

Expedition Log (Being An Acount of My Artic Adventure)
  By Hugh Peregrine Balthazar Fitzmaurice
  Thursday, 30th of March, 1916
  Wayed anchor at first light and left Queenstown with strong wind. In all there are eleven soles aboard (thirteen including the expedition leaders igwana and the ships' dog, twentyone including the chicken's – note: do chicken's have soles? Ask Crozier). The ships' captain is a rough type but seems respectfull enough and very experiensed. His advise, and I have excepted it, is to avoid the Atlantic squawls as much as posible by sailing round the east coast of Ireland and via the Hebradees. This is estamated to take around five days.
  10:00 hours. We have incountered a heavy swell which is having, has casued (the following lines were scored out and only partly legible) *the novice sailors among us feeling the affects of* (three words unreadable)... *a garstly mistake. Beleive now death real posibillity, therefore* (seven words unreadable)... *and hereby bequeeth my worldly goods to Nanny Brannigan, excluding the collexion of rare books and steriograrfs in my bedside locker in chambers, and excepting my igwana which I*

73

intrust to Mr Frank Rafferty, and my pipe which I leave to Mr Walter Croz...

Friday, 31st of March.

Order has been restored and most of the company has eaten a harty brekfast. One disterbing note concerns allercation of ships' duties...

At this point the log's author was heard whistling in the corridor and Crozier hurried up the spiral steps into daylight.

A short while later he was leaning on the gunwale on the port side when the cabin boy, who was perched in the crow's nest, gave a cry. Crozier thought little of it, the cabin boy being given to frequent involuntary ejaculations due to his volatile skin, but there came another shout, more urgent, and footsteps sounded behind him. It was McGregor, hoisting a pair of field glasses.

'What is it?'

The question was ignored. Crozier scoured the horizon but could see only the usual rippling mass of ever-changing seams and shadows.

'Is it a whale?'

Harris appeared and stood, also silent, watching the waves. The skipper exhaled heavily through his moustache and turned to glare up at the lookout who was still squinting out to sea. Harris raised his arm.

'There! One o'clock.'

McGregor pressed the binoculars to his face.

'Holy s—e.'

'Skip?'

'A f—ing periscope.'

'You sure?'

74

McGregor passed the glasses to the first mate.

'No question. It's a f—ing U-boat.' He turned and signalled to the bosun in the wheelhouse to stop the engine.

Crozier could see something moving now, about two miles off, a solid black line trailing a foamy wake. He gripped the top of the gunwale. There was a thinner upright as well, and he imagined he saw a flash of reflected light.

'Have they spotted us?'

'Not sure.' McGregor took out a cigarette and tapped it on the packet. 'Surprising if they haven't, mind you, seeing as we're the only f—ing ship for a hundred square miles.'

'Hello, hello, what's happening, is it another whale?' Fitzmaurice and Rafferty joined them, followed by Phoebe, and all three fanned out along the rail.

'No it's not,' Harris muttered. 'It's our friend Fritz in his little *Unterseeboot*.'

'Bloody hell.'

'Have they seen us? Are we in danger?'

'Dunno.'

'Surely it's obvious we're not military? Or commercial, for that matter? They wouldn't dare target us... would they?'

McGregor growled long and deep and flobbed a mouthful over the side.

Phoebe frowned. 'How elegant.'

'What do we do, Skipper?' Harris said.

'If the wind gets up I suppose we might stand a chance of outrunning them,' McGregor surveyed the clouds overhead, 'but other than that I can't see we've many options. Keep track of them. I'm going below.'

A few minutes later Harris scuttled away in the direction of the wheelhouse, leaving the others adrift in their own thoughts. They watched until the light dimmed and the object, indistinct to begin with, evaporated into the grey.

8

'I'll Sing Thee Songs of Araby'

'Don't you think seven spades might be a tad ambitious?' Phoebe eyed her partner over the top of her cards.

'Not in the least,' Fitzmaurice replied. 'This one's in the bag.'

The four of them were at the end of the mess table closest to the fire. The lamps were lit. The rest of the crew had dispersed, except for Victoor, who sat at the other end spooning cold stew from a bowl.

'By the way…' Crozier glanced over at the cook. '… anybody know what the meat was we had for dinner?' He lowered his voice. '*Was* it, in fact, meat?'

'Tinned ham.' Rafferty slapped a card down. 'And that's our trick, I think.'

'I assumed it was chicken,' Phoebe said. 'Poor things.'

'Well, it certainly wasn't roast pheasant. Damn!' Fitzmaurice jerked his head back. 'I didn't see that coming.'

'Wouldn't surprise me if it was seagull.' Crozier threw down the ace of spades. 'Cook's always awake before anyone else. I bet he's up on deck with a net.'

'I've noticed there are fewer rats around the bilge pump,' Fitzmaurice murmured.

'Seagull, chicken, rat, what does it matter? — Hugh, what on earth? — If we're going to eat other living

77

creatures, it's arbitrary to distinguish — Hugh, for crying out...'

'I disagree,' Rafferty said. 'There are lots of reasons — thank you Fitz, keep them coming — for drawing lines. Take the seagull, for instance, one of nature's scavengers, its flesh is generated from the most awful rubbish and therefore likely to taste accordingly.'

'Only increases my suspicion,' said Crozier.

'I was speaking from a moral standpoint.' Phoebe glared at her partner. 'Hugh, for heavensake...'

'Trickier than you think, this game, isn't it?' Fitzmaurice surveyed his remaining cards. He selected one then changed his mind. 'Speaking of tricky game, I must tell you a story.' He slammed a surefire loser on the table. 'I was out shooting with Cousin Ninian one time up in Westmeath. It was the damnedest thing. We hadn't had a single sniff the whole day, it was freezing cold, we were hungry and miserable and just on the verge of giving up – crikey, not again, sorry Phoebe — and we came out of some woods and into rough grass and next thing Ninian steps on the biggest pheasant I've ever seen – size of a bloody turkey and glossy as a peacock, an absolute beauty – and breaks its neck, snap! Just like that—'

'Really Hugh, that was pathetic, why didn't you listen to me?'

'Sorry, Phoebe, I told you I wasn't good at the mathematical stuff... Anyway, where was I? Oh yes, old Ninian wants to show off to the girls back at the house that he's a real hunter and can handle a gun and so on, so he has me throw the blasted thing up in the air – make it look realistic — while he takes pot shots at it. Uses all our ammo and can't score a hit — closest to death I've ever come, I can tell you — and then, with the very last shell, he blows the bloody thing into the top of a chestnut tree...' He trailed off, staring at the fireplace. 'And that was the end of it. I still wonder how that bird would have tasted.'

Phoebe gathered the cards together. Fitzmaurice had reminded them of the bounty back on dry land, beyond the reach of Victoor and his dark culinary arts. Rafferty was thinking of the ivory-seamed steak at the Bailey, Phoebe of her mother's Victoria sponge, Crozier of fat trout pulled from the lough beside his grandfather's house in County Fermanagh. Roasted. With lemon and bay.

'Another round?'

'Not for me, Phoebe.' Fitzmaurice pushed back from the table. 'If you'll excuse me, my journal won't write itself.'

'You and your journal. It sounds very intriguing,' Phoebe said in an innocent tone. 'When are we going to be allowed to read it?'

'Haha, not any time soon I'm afraid. My publisher will be the first to have sight of it when our expedition is over.'

'You have a publisher?'

'Well no, actually, not as such, but I thought I might try Uncle Ernest's people in London. They're sure to be interested. Two heroes in one family? I anticipate a bit of a sensation.' And he left the room smiling to himself.

'What shall we do now?' Phoebe said. 'I wonder if Victoor would make up a four.' She peered into the gloom. 'Victoor?' She held up the deck.

'Nee. Dank u. Nee lucky.'

'I know.' Rafferty produced his banjolele from the shadows. 'Let's have an auld song.'

After a neuralgic preamble, he sang, in his high, clear tenor, *Sweet Rosie O'Grady*. Phoebe, Crozier noticed, having been poised to make her excuses, eased back in her chair and cocked her head to one side. The Dubliner followed up with *I'll Sing Thee Songs of Araby*, halfway through which the door opened and the twins, attracted by live entertainment, entered and took their places to either side of Victoor. *Love's Old Sweet Song* was next and Crozier couldn't help but think Rafferty was laying it on a bit thick. He had to acknowledge though that the vocals were good. Not quite top class (lacking the body weight perhaps), but rich in tone, and supple in melisma.

'Anyone else?' Rafferty said. 'Don't let me hog the limelight.'

'No, keep going Frank, you have a great voice,' Phoebe held out her hands, 'but give me that banjo—'

'Banjo*lele*.'

'And I'll have a go at that A-string for you.'

Doyle arrived carrying, much to everyone's surprise, a small accordion, and without a word sat to one side and raised his eyebrows at the singer.

'The bosun's a musician, who'd have thought it,' Rafferty cried. 'Doyle, you look like a man who might know a verse or two of *Tread Softly On Me Praties*.'

Towards the end of that song, McGregor entered carrying a bottle and poured everyone a jigger, and after an interlude, Crozier, emboldened by the grog, sang the only piece to which he knew all the words: *My Lagan Love*; and then they all joined in *Spanish Ladies*, McGregor providing a particularly disquieting baritone. The bottle passed around until it was empty, and eventually Rafferty was asked for a final one to seal the night. He was dithering, suddenly at a loss, until Phoebe said, 'In the public house near Ennisfree there was a man who used to sing a song called *The Lass of Aughrim*, a lovely tune. Do you know it?'

'I do indeed.' Rafferty was relieved. 'Though it's very sad. Will you sing it with me? For company?'

Phoebe smiled and shook her head.

'I'd only spoil it.'

Rafferty took back his banjolele and picked out the melody while Doyle swayingly provided bass colour, his eyebrows writhing in time.

'*If you'll be the lass of Aughrim,*' Rafferty sang, '*as I suppose you not to be...*'

He had closed his eyes but the dying fire reflecting in his spectacles gave the impression that they were preternaturally agleam.

'*Come tell me of that first token / That passed between you and me...*'

Crozier had heard the song only once before, late one Friday night: a man in a battered suit, with his hat in his hand, much the worse for ale on the corner of Wicklow Street, the half-remembered lyrics delivered in an anguished tremolo that hastened the step of every passer-by. This, now, was a different thing altogether. And then another voice, also sweet, but softer, less formal, as Phoebe joined in.

'*Oh don't you remember / That night on yon lean hill / When we both met together...*'

Rafferty faltered for a half-second before modulating his tone to accommodate Phoebe's lower pitch.

'*O the rain falls on my yellow locks*
And the dew it wets my skin,
My babe lies cold within my arms
But none will let me in.'

The harmonising was effortless, the singers anticipating, entwining, caressing. Crozier found himself disembodied, far beyond the space they occupied, picturing from above, the ship like a toy on the surface of the ocean, its tiny constellation of marker lamps moving through the darkness, and this faint sound from within: human voices, not talking, but singing; singing to each other of all the pity, all the sorrow of love, as though they could somehow inoculate themselves against it. The fragility of their predicament struck him yet again: nothing but a few planks of wood between them and the deep.

He glanced over at Rafferty and Phoebe, who were on the last verse, intently watching each other's eyes the way duettists sometimes do, and a sensation passed through him, a tingling along the nape of his neck, familiar from childhood. He imagined the two singers, on a day far in the future, in a Georgian drawing room, with long burgundy drapes, in front of a fire that crackled in the hearth of a black marble fireplace. And, just as quickly, the image was gone, and along with everyone else he began to applaud.

*

Next morning, the skipper announced that they were passing the Westman Islands to starboard, and that,

82

barring storms, they were only one more sleep from Reykjavik. After more than a week on the open sea this led to much excitement. 'You'll be on land soon enough,' grumbled McGregor, whose humour had never fully recovered from the U-boat sighting. 'There's still plenty of work tae be done.' He began dishing out tasks: Crozier and Phoebe were given sail-mending duty, while Rafferty and Doyle were ordered down to the hold to sort equipment for a landing party. Victoor made a lugubrious start on an inventory of supplies. ('Don't forget parsnips and apples for Bridie,' Fitzmaurice instructed. 'And plenty of greens to keep her regular.')

It was overcast but dry, and surprisingly mild, so Crozier and Phoebe sat on the deck forward of the wheelhouse and spread the sailcloth between them, working along the ripped seams with their stitching awls and lengths of catgut. Crozier required a little guidance to begin with but Phoebe dispensed it with good humour.

'Did you know,' Crozier said after a while, 'that the man who invented Braille blinded himself with an awl?'

Phoebe paused.

'Why did he do that?'

'He didn't mean to, it was an accident. He was a child and he was playing with his father's tools, trying to make a hole in a piece of leather.'

'I see. I mean... That's interesting.'

'No, the interesting thing is that he then devised Braille – you know, the raised dots? – *using* an awl.'

'How ironic.'

'Isn't it?'

'Mysterious ways.'

83

Bunion came around the corner, his big wedge head swaying from side to side. He brightened when he saw Crozier and plodded over for a rheumy-eyed nuzzle.

'Bugger off, Bunion, there's a good boy.'

'Don't you like dogs?'

Crozier shrugged. 'For some reason I don't like touching *that* one.'

Bunion settled himself on the wheelhouse steps, where he could keep a loving eye on his adopted master.

'I thought men of the cloth were supposed to love all God's creatures.'

'I'm not a man of the cloth.'

'Yes, but you're going to be, aren't you?'

'I doubt it.'

'Why not? I thought that was the idea.'

'It was at one time but...'

'But what?'

'I'm not sure I believe in God any more.'

'Ah. Yes. I can see that might be a disadvantage.'

'Indeed.'

'Any reason?'

'I beg your pardon?'

'What changed your mind? Look around you, all this...' She waved a hand in the air. 'Where did it all come from?'

'You mean what happened on the day without a yesterday?'

Crozier stopped what he was doing, took in the billowing sails, the webs of cordage and the big bowl of sky, felt the liquid friction of the ship's motion. The girl was watching him, the wind whipping strands of hair across her face.

'You tell me.'

Fitzmaurice was in his cabin struggling with the bible-thick instruction manual for the Magiflex Rectograph Imperial. He had managed to attach the extended shutter-release tube to the casing using the Deckel screw provided *(fig.199)* but, squeeze the rubber bulb as he might, there was no response. He swiped at the pages. From *fig.201* onwards the task of explanation seemed to have been given over to a drunk man working with an entirely different device, something that was possibly not even a camera. Strange new procedures and components were being introduced. Why did technology have to be so difficult, he wondered.

He regarded the scene he had carefully composed – the scattered books, the open journal, his pipe smouldering on its stand – and imagined how the photograph would show him deep in thought, pen on lip, frozen for posterity in contemplation of the silent wilderness within. He turned to the miniature looking-glass on the wall and rehearsed a variety of pouts. *So young,* he heard future visitors to his museum remarking, *to lead such an important expedition. And yet there it is already in his face, you can see it: the leadership, the heroism...*

Reinvigorated, he returned to the obstinate contraption and, after staring at its complicated rear-view for a minute, twiddled with the aperture dial. He squeezed the bulb. Nothing. He fiddled with the focus. Nothing. He flicked a tiny lever he hadn't noticed before, squeezed again, and this time the mechanism responded. Progress! He glanced over at the desk. The sun through the porthole was diffracting atmospherically through bands of pipesmoke. Perfect.

He checked the flash-gun tray, onto which he had shaken out the contents of a tin marked JOHNSON'S No. 2 FLASHPOWDER, and cocked the ignition hammer. Then he took the attached string in one hand and the shutter release tube in the other and, with a great deal of effort, fed them beneath the desk before settling himself in his chair. It struck him that he would have to drop the scholarly pen-on-lip touch, as synchronising the shutter and the flash would require the split-second cooperation of both hands, which would need to be out of shot. (He should really have sought assistance but hadn't been able to bear the thought of the ribbing.)

He set down the rubber bulb and clenched his pipe between his teeth. He believed this would add gravitas. Turning quarter-profile to the lens, he fixed his gaze on a knot in the wall and raised a quizzical eyebrow to destiny. Then, as he up-tilted his chin the better to emphasise his jawline, a vile puddle of tarry dottle ran back down the pipe-stem and into his throat and he choked, expelling a geyser of burning filaments from the end of the bowl. At the same moment he jerked on the flash string.

Up above, the explosion shook the wheelhouse, dislodging a compass from the wall and causing McGregor to upend a scalding beaker of Bovril into his lap.

'F—k me pink, we've been hit,' he cried. 'Mr Harris, sound the alarm!'

On deck Crozier and Phoebe jumped to their feet holding the sail between them and stared at each other in bewilderment as the ship's bell began to clang. Pounding down the steps from the bridge, one hand clamped to the front of his trousers, McGregor failed to see

Bunion sleepily raising his head. With a scream worthy of Geronimo breaching a Mexican battlement he flew, with incredible velocity, through the air, skidded across the sailcloth and over the top of the gunwale, and disappeared from view.

9

The Honorary Consul

The Icelandic coastline, with its jagged peaks and crags, had a raw, untidy look to it – the cataclysmic upheaval of its formation still oddly recent – that put Crozier in mind of the Giant's Causeway. Cliffs of crenellated basalt soared from beaches littered with shale and strewn with huge boulders, while out from the shore, grotesque in the dawn light, stacks of twisted rock rose from the water and seemed to stand guard.

Through the binoculars Crozier could see kittiwakes *(Rissa tridactyla)* and skuas *(Stercorarius skua)* cruising the heights, Atlantic puffins *(Fratercula arctica)* jostling for position along grassy ledges. He set the glasses down and breathed into his hands to warm them. It was thrilling to be so close to landfall again. He looked round at the others, all mute with anticipation. Ten minutes later, however, a thick fog descended and they were forced to lay to for a couple of hours.

By eleven o'clock they had rounded the southern horn of Faxafjord and by lunchtime Reykjavik began to materialise out of the mist, the masts of schooners and fishing boats swaying in the harbour, tiny figures moving on the dockside, the blurred geometry of the town itself just visible beyond. They dropped anchor some way from shore and the launch was lowered for the initial landing party, which consisted of the non-sailors and Bunion, rowed by the twins. Harris, Doyle, Victoor and the cabin boy would follow in the afternoon when the twins had returned with the first load of supplies. McGregor had retired to his bunk with a bottle of Wee Jimmy to help him over the severe chill that had resulted from his unplanned dip in the Atlantic.

'What a ghastly smell,' Fitzmaurice remarked as they neared the jetty.

'Rotting fish,' Crozier said.

'My God, quick, I'd better light my pipe.'

On the pier, amid broken boats and piles of nets, groups of men stood around talking and smoking, while women hauled creels of cod and herring, and loaded carts pulled by shaggy little ponies of various hues. The local dog-pack, a whipped, hungry-looking crew, was camped further back around a mound of lobster pots. Perceiving them dimly from his place at the front of the boat, Bunion flexed his nostrils and one of his eyes began to flicker.

The town was fronted by a row of white-washed, black-timbered general merchants' stores and it was towards these that the landing party gravitated, once they had tied up the launch and fended off a cackle of knick-knack-peddling crones. The shops, marked with proprietary names such as 'Hilmarsson' and 'Sigurds-son', were flanked by warehouses advertising salt, coal and chandlery. Ponies, their reins pulled over their heads and hanging down to the ground, waited outside, shifting from hoof to hoof and exhaling puffs of vapour. The twins disappeared to begin negotiations. Spotting a trio of women laying out fish for curing, Phoebe went off to interrogate them. Bunion, meanwhile, paced back and forth with his snout cocked in the direction of the pack.

'I'm surprised Uncle Crispin's not here to meet us,' Fitzmaurice said. 'I would have thought it part of his job to welcome every British subject on arrival.'

Rafferty bristled.

'Are *all* your relatives lions of the Empire?'

Sir Crispin Pimm, related to Fitzmaurice by marriage to one of his father's step-sisters, was the British honorary consul in Reykjavik, a post that had fallen to him after the previous title-holder – the only one among the half dozen longterm Englishmen in the country not unhinged by schnapps or homesickness – inadvertently discovered a new geyser while out for a ramble.

Fitzmaurice thought for a moment.

'No, not all, some of them work in the City. But now you mention it, my great-grandfather was Wellington's adjutant at Waterloo, my grandfather was Consul-General of the Mortlock Islands, and one of my great-uncles was Lieutenant-Governor of Uttar Bakavsa. But I'm not sure you could describe Uncle Crispin as – ah, here he is now.'

A tall man of indeterminate later years, still erect in carriage but fast running to seed, was striding towards them, looking about him with an imperious air. Sir Crispin Pimm was one of those men, abundant in the slipstreams of Empire, for whom the rules that constrain the lives of others are of scant concern. Behind the slow-motion wreckage of his face an unscrupulous energy burned.

'Hugh, my boy, how the devil are you?' he cried, seizing Fitzmaurice by the ears. 'I can't believe you're here. You haven't changed a bit.'

'Ow. Ow. Marvellous, thanks. Ouch. Neither have you.'

'How long can you stay?'

'Oh, just a few days, Uncle, as long as it takes to re-stock the ship.'

'Excellent. You'll have a chance to look around, and I've managed to swing a state dinner in your honour tomorrow night... Now, who are *these* chaps?'

Sir Crispin held his face very close — barely a couple of inches — like an incredulous sergeant-major, and Crozier found himself staring into intensely blue, strangely opaque irises, too shocked to recoil.

'This is Walter Crozier, Uncle, one of my chums from College.'

'Crozier, eh?' Sir Crispin said, maintaining proximity. 'A good Borders name.'

'Actually, it's of French orig—'

'And who's this?'

'Frank Rafferty, another College pal.'

Rafferty was blinking hard behind his glasses, holding his breath while Sir Crispin inspected his pores.

'I had a footman name of Rafferty once. Had to sack the bugger for thieving,' the honorary consul said. 'You're not from Cork are you?'

'Dublin.'

'Ah, good. Jolly old town. Haven't been there in years. I hear the natives are very restless these days.'

'The *natives*?'

Phoebe joined them, her face flushed.

'Much as I suspected, these poor women are doing all the work while the men loaf around drinking and smoking. I'm organising a meeting.'

Sir Crispin's head swivelled and his eyes bulged as he

took in Phoebe's outsize oilskins and sou'wester, courtesy of Savage Newell.

'And who, pray tell, is this young fellow?'

He moved in for a close-up but Phoebe skipped back smartly, her hands on her hips.

'Uncle, I'd like you to meet Phoebe Sturgeon who will be staying in Reykjavik for a while.'

'Phoebe? Isn't that a girl's name?'

'Yes, Uncle.'

Sir Crispin looked confused, but before he could seek clarification, a cacophony of yelping broke out nearby and they turned to see a shifting whirlwind of dog limbs, people scattering in all directions. A small mongrel hurtled through the air.

'Bunion!' the shipmates said in unison.

Alerted by shouting, the twins emerged from the doorway of J. Andersen Salt & Coal and rushed towards the gathering crowd. Three buckets of seawater failed to dampen Bunion's bloodlust and eventually Mikkel or Magnus seized him by the back legs and hauled him from the fray, tethering him to a buoy where he sat shivering and licking himself.

'Well,' Sir Crispin said. 'That was exciting. Welcome to Reykjavik. Follow me and I'll show you to your digs.'

The town was an unplanned jumble of buildings of square build and bright colours huddled together on the vast lava plain, with diamond-bright mountaintops in the distance to either side and a ridge of purplish hills to the rear. It was dominated by a large church of the pilgrim style with a short wooden clock-tower bolted onto the roof. Nearby, the red Danish flag, one of several visible on the skyline, twitched over the entrance to the parliament.

'Look at that,' Rafferty muttered to Phoebe, 'Danish flags everywhere. Will these people never be free?'

Sir Crispin marched ahead, alerting them to water-filled potholes and cairns of pony dung, spouting snippets of history, pointing out places of interest ('That was the town's first shop, opened just fifteen years ago. God knows how people managed... There's the Latin School...') In the main square they stopped while their host talked, in a mixture of Icelandic and English, to a silver-bearded man dressed in a Viking-esque leather tunic and matching helmet. After a few minutes the conversation escalated into an angry flurry and the Viking turned abruptly and walked away. Sir Crispin rejoined the others.

'Tricky blighters, the locals,' he said. 'I'd have him arrested but there are only three policemen and he's related to two of them. In the old days I'd have had him flogged.'

As they proceeded he explained that he had purchased two hundred Icelandic ponies from the man, intending to export them, at a tidy profit, to Britain for use in the coalmines, work for which he had imagined them well-suited given their compact size and legendary stamina. However, after the first shipment a snag had emerged.

'Turns out they can't stand being in confined spaces. You see, they're so used to the pure, fresh breezes of the fjords that after an hour underground the little bastards just faint dead away. Useless. You can't be bringing ponies round with smelling salts all day. Now the scoundrel won't take them back.' He paused to run a fingernail around the flared rim of a nostril. 'I'll probably have to pass them off as beef.'

Their accommodation was a ramshackle three-storey hotel of planks and corrugated iron where civilisation petered out and the desolation of the lava plain resumed. Visible from the perimeter of its muddy, fenced-off garden, a straggling collection of turf huts seemed to grow out of the earth, grass carpeting the walls and roofs. People in dark clothes moved between them, and goats and sheep grazed, some of them on the dwellings themselves. Further off, a large lagoon reflected the clear afternoon sky and the bleak gyres of the seabirds.

They were greeted at the desk by a squat figure of uncertain gender and no discernible teeth, who smirked horribly at Sir Crispin, then shouldered their bags and gruntingly led them to rooms under the eaves. Fitzmaurice and Phoebe were allotted a chamber each, while Crozier and Rafferty, due to ongoing repair work, found themselves thrown together yet again. Conditions were less cramped than on the *Dolphin* but nevertheless snugger than either would have preferred. Sir Crispin was staying on the second floor, in the hotel's only 'suite'. ('I had a nice house in the centre but there was a tiresome misunderstanding about rent,' he explained. 'Anyway, after Lady Pimm went home — she found the climate very disagreeable, poor thing – there wasn't really much point.')

It was too late for lunch, so they settled for an early dinner, which they took in the hotel's damp and echoing dining room. Over pickled herring and dried catfish Sir Crispin held forth on his adopted country and his fading hopes to exploit its resources.

'This business with the ponies is most unfortunate. It's set me back quite a bit,' he said, pouring himself an impressive measure from the bottle brought by the hostess (whose name, it was revealed, was Bjork). 'I might be able to turn them into pies, flog 'em off cheap to the Irish, but I'll be making a substantial loss. This stuff...' he held up a medallion of fish, 'has a big market, especially the salt-cod, but we haven't developed a taste for it in Britain and the Spaniards have their greasy paws on the rest of the trade. They can be very touchy about interlopers. Bloodthirsty lot. There must be metals and minerals here but the ground's frozen solid most of the time. Too expensive to get at. Plenty of hot water, of course, but how do you export that?' He dabbed at his lips with the edge of the tablecloth. 'I've actually got my eye on the puffins. Millions of 'em, you see, and really quite tasty. Puffin pie? What do you think? Go down well at Simpson's-in-the-Strand?'

After dinner, they took a stroll on the lava plain. It was a clear evening and skeins of milky green light were writhing across the northern horizon, smoke-like ribbons that billowed and twisted into fantastical shapes – animals, wraiths, ogres – unwinding as quickly as they formed, dispersing among the stars.

'Impressive, isn't it?' Sir Crispin said.

'It's wonderful,' Phoebe whispered.

The others expressed their feelings in a variety of grunts.

As they watched, the emerald vapours, which seemed blown on a wind from another world, were intersected by vertical striations of yellow and blue, then mauve, crimson and silver, until it looked as though a downpour of multi-coloured rain was headed their way. This evaporated and was replaced by a huge lenticular cloud, within which flashed and twinkled all the hues of an opal.

'I don't understand, though,' Phoebe said. 'Why does it happen? What's causing it?'

'Haven't the foggiest,' Sir Crispin said. 'The Scandewegians say it's the Valkyries' armour gleaming as they ride back and forth from Valhalla. The Eskimos, on the other hand, reckon it's the souls of their ancestors playing football with a walrus's head or something. By the way, you're not with child are you?'

'I beg your pardon?'

'It's just if you are, you should look away. The locals believe it will make your baby cross-eyed.'

'How interesting. But no, I'm not. At least, I don't think so.'

The other three turned to stare at her. Phoebe gazed up at the night sky.

'Just look at all the stars – is that Orion? — and it's not even completely dark yet.'

'Soon, it won't get dark at all,' Sir Crispin said, 'and in winter there's no light whatsoever. Poor Lady Pimm found that very difficult.'

They stood, tiny figures on the edge of the vast plain, contemplating the cold sparkle of the heavens.

'*The eternal silence of those infinite spaces affrights me,*' Crozier murmured after a while, but no one appeared to hear him or, if they did, could think of an appropriate reply.

*

The next day, after a breakfast of bread and herrings, the company dispersed to attend to various errands and interests: Sir Crispin to probe the logistics of large-scale puffin procurement; Fitzmaurice and Crozier to liaise with the *Dolphin*; and Phoebe, accompanied by Bjork, to round up and militarise the womenfolk of Reykjavik. Inspired by Phoebe, Rafferty announced his intention to seek out the local insurgents. They were walking in the direction of the harbour and had just passed a statue of the independence hero Jón Sigurðsson.

Fitzmaurice eyed Rafferty with suspicion.

'Since when were you a revolutionary?' he demanded.

'I believe all nations should have the right to govern themselves. I've never made a secret of it,' Rafferty said.

'And what exactly is it that you hope to achieve in two days?'

'I can pass on the lessons learnt in Ireland, for a start,' he replied. 'Anyway, I was thinking I might just stay here and join the struggle.'

'*What?*' Fitzmaurice and Crozier halted. Rafferty turned to face them.

'These people have been under the thumb of the Danes long enough. And besides,' he added, 'we can't leave Phoebe here on her own.'

His companions exchanged glances. After a pause they walked on.

'Wouldn't your own country be a better place to start?' Crozier said.

'Ireland will rise up with or without me.'

'Never,' Crozier said. 'It'll never happen. The Irish are too busy fighting among themselves.'

They had reached the top of the street that led to the port. Below, in the main square, they could see Phoebe standing on a crate, addressing a small crowd of bemused fishwives who had stopped to eat hunks of bread in the sunshine. Freshly recruited to the cause, her interpreter, Bjork, was marching to and fro in front of the makeshift podium, beating her breast and shaking her fists at the heavens as though auditioning for a Greek tragedy.

As they watched, Sir Crispin's Viking nemesis from the previous day entered stage right, walking briskly, noticed the activity and veered towards it, halting a short distance away. He folded his arms. Seeing him, Phoebe broke off. The women turned as one to stare at him. Not a word was spoken. The silence swelled. A paroxysm of fear passed across the Viking's face, and appearing suddenly to remember an urgent appointment, he scuttled away. Phoebe resumed.

10

A Feast

'Please, call me Steingrimur.'

The Under-Secretary for Natural Resources extended a plump, neatly-manicured hand which Fitzmaurice hesitatingly took.

'Stan—?'

'—grimur.'

'Pleased to meet you Stan Grimer.'

'And you are the *fáviti* nephew – your uncle has told me all about you. Can I say, I very much like your neckwear.'

Fitzmaurice's bowtie, lent to him, despite sustained protest, by Sir Crispin to complete his improvised formal attire, was large and green, and had been tied far too tightly. As the night wore on it would increase its grip.

'Thank you, it's—' Fitzmaurice began, but was pushed gently aside to make way for the next in line. This happened to be Phoebe, who had been decked out by Bjork in full traditional garb, including a black velvet tunic with silver buttons, a ruff, and a white, two-foot-high head-dress in the shape of a forward-curving horn.

Steingrimur surveyed her with some pleasure.

'Ah, the famous suffragette. We are indeed honoured,' he said, bowing low and clicking his heels. 'I hear you addressed the women of the town this morning. You must tell me over dinner how you found them.'

'Of course,' Phoebe replied, slightly nonplussed. 'I'd be glad to.'

The queue moved again and, accepting a glass from the hovering waiter, she joined the other guests, among them the bishop, the chief justice, the chief physician and the under-secretary's wife. Nearby, several other dignitaries were receiving the close-up treatment from Sir Crispin who, with his freshly-oiled hair and antique lounge suit, had the air of an undertaker with designs on the widow. The word 'puffin' hung in the air.

The reception was being held in a house built in high style for the country's colonial governors: enormous oil paintings, chandeliers, clusters of crystal glasses glittering along the length of a table hewn from primeval wood. Crozier found himself seated between the chief physician and the bishop, but barely had time to introduce himself before the toasts began, three in a row, generous helpings swiftly replenished, of a poteen-like spirit that tasted of pine sap. They drank to the young adventurers, wishing them Godspeed on their expedition, to the distinguished guests, and to Sir Crispin and the mutual trade benefits that would eventually result from his selfless endeavours.

'My word, that's bracing,' Crozier said after the first tumblerful.

The bishop nodded and smirked. The soup arrived. On the other side of the table Fitzmaurice, his eyes starting to bulge from the effect of the schnapps on his constricted jugular, was explaining to the chief justice the difference between an iguana and a basilisk.

'I believe they're related but the basilisk is much smaller

100

and can run across water – that's why it's known as the Jesus Christ lizard – and it has a crest on its—'

'And they are changing colour?'

'No, that's a chameleon. Completely different. If you'd like to come aboard the *Dolphin* I could introduce you to Bridie.'

'Thank you. That will not be necessary.'

Fitzmaurice clawed at his collar and mopped his puce forehead with a napkin. Glasses were refilled, discharged — *Skál!* — and topped up again. The soup bowls were taken away and replaced with platters of cold fish. The dress code for the occasion may have been formal but the atmosphere was relaxed and the babble of conversation soon rose to an almost festive pitch. Rafferty, his tongue already liberated, was apprising the under-secretary's wife of the ferment in his native land and empathising with the subjugation of her own people. Her expression, confused to begin with, graduated to one of haughty bemusement.

'Well yes, but there *is* a difference,' she said at length. 'You see, we've already had home rule for more than a decade.'

Rafferty's head jerked sideways.

'But the Danish flags. They're all over the place.'

'Pure laziness, I'm afraid,' she laughed. 'We put them out for the king's visit six months ago and we just haven't managed to take them down yet.'

'But you don't have full sovereignty?'

'Not yet, but soon. It has been agreed.'

Rafferty stabbed a herring with his fork.

'Your English is excellent,' Phoebe was saying to Steingrimur. 'Really quite faultless.'

101

'Thank you. Yes, I was educated in England – in Copenhagen also – but mainly in your country. But you'll find that most of us have the language to some degree. Now, tell me, how was your speech received?'

Phoebe adjusted her horn-hat, which was listing to one side.

'It went very well. They seemed genuinely interested in what I had to say—' She paused while the waiters removed the plates and set down the next course.

Sir Crispin turned to Fitzmaurice. 'Roast puffin, Hugh. See what you think. I'll be talking to Steinie's people later about an export licence.'

Fitzmaurice contemplated the burnished carcase in front of him. He was beginning to feel odd. Oaky purple wine was poured into goblets.

'It's important that women are kept abreast of the suffragette struggle,' Phoebe continued. 'No matter where they are—'

'They did tell you that women here already have the vote?'

'Yes, but only over the age of forty. That's not good enough—'

'It's better than Britain.'

'True, but—'

'And America.'

'Yes, but—'

'And Germany and Russia.'

'Granted, but—'

'And, in fact, most of the rest of the world. Women are strong here, you see, because we are a seafaring nation. While the Vikings were away raiding and pillaging, women were holding the fort, running the farms, taking care of business, and that has paid off. How do you like the puffin?'

'It's very good... Are you supposed to eat the beak?'

Further along the table, the bishop, whose upswept eyebrows and unblinking amber eyes gave him the look of some form of raptor, was regarding an oblivious Rafferty with some interest.

'And you say he worships the statue every day?'

'Oh yes,' said Crozier, who was unused to large quantities of strong liquor. 'He keeps it wrapped in a shroud under his bed.'

The bishop shuddered.

'Along with his relic,' Crozier added for good measure. 'A length of St Celia's shin-bone.'

The bishop gave a woof of disgust.

'You are aware that it was outlawed here for many years?' he said.

'So I believe.'

'Yes indeed. No Catholic priest was permitted to set foot on Icelandic soil for more than three hundred years.'

'Quite right,' Crozier said, tearing off a puffin leg.

'It's all changed now, of course. Now we have two Catholics on the island. We did have three but one converted. Loneliness, I think.'

'How interesting,' Crozier said, taking a noisy slurp of wine.

'We've done our best,' the bishop continued, 'to dispel mistaken beliefs, but it's disappointing how much superstition still persists among the islanders.'

'What do you mean?'

'Has Sir Crispin not spoken to you of the *huldufólk*?'

'The which?'

103

'The *huldufólk*? The hidden people?'

'I don't think so.'

The bishop appeared surprised.

'Really? It's all nonsense, of course, but it goes back a long way in our folklore. Tales of supernatural beings – spirits, elves, trolls — who live in the rocks, and beneath the hills. It's part of everyday life.'

'How can people believe in things they can't see?' Crozier mused.

'Oh but many claim they *have* seen them *and* talked to them, and in some cases even to have... well, never mind. The point is that such convictions are not compatible with Christianity.'

'*Up the airy mountain, down the rushy glen,*' Crozier sang, '*we dare not go a-hunting for fear of little men.*'

'What's this about *huldufólk*?' Sir Crispin demanded, leaning forward.

'I was just saying,' the bishop said, raising his voice, 'how we must eradicate this absurd belief in the non-existent.'

A hush descended. A piece of cutlery hit the floor. The waiters came to attention, decanters of wine suspended in mid-air. The moment elongated and then ballooned. At last, someone coughed.

'That's as may be,' Sir Crispin said. 'All I know is they've frightened off my workers and stopped me building my bureau.'

'Sir Crispin, I assure you,' the under-secretary broke in, 'that matter is in hand. You shall have your bureau.'

'I'm also pretty sure they put a spell on my bloody ponies.'

Conversation resumed. Someone further up the table did an impression of some kind of farm animal.

'That sounds intriguing,' Phoebe whispered. 'What's he talking about?'

Steingrimur sighed.

'Sir Crispin has fallen foul of local superstition. Despite repeated warnings he is insisting on having his consulate on land where some *huldufólk* are believed to live.'

'Sorry, but what exactly are *huldufólk*?'

'You would probably call them elves.'

'Are they like leprechauns?' Fitzmaurice said. 'Mother caught a leprechaun once, at least she thought it was, at the bottom of the garden eating her raspberries. Managed to trap it under a tarpaulin and knock it out with a spade, but, quite embarrassing actually, it turned out to be just a particularly ugly child from the village.'

'...Yes,' Steingrimur continued, 'otherworldly beings. They remain hidden most of the time but when they're threatened or their territory is damaged they can be very troublesome. Vindictive even.'

'And what have they done this time?'

'Sabotaged Sir Crispin's plans.'

'Oh?'

'Yes, it was all fine to begin with. The foundations went down well enough but then,' he shrugged, 'missing equipment, strange noises, mysterious ailments. And then one day, for no reason, the scaffolding collapsed and the foreman's legs were broken. That was it, the workers downed tools.'

'Blimey. So what happens now?'

'We must bring in a mediator, a clairvoyant of sorts, to communicate with the *huldufólk*, to placate them and secure their blessing.'

'What do these "hidden people" look like?'

The under-secretary laughed.

'I've never seen one myself actually, but they are reputed to dress in green and come in various sizes: some are as big as humans, others – the flower elves, for example – are only a few inches tall.'

'How extraordinary.' Phoebe thought for a moment. 'Where did they come from? Have they always been here?'

'There are various stories. My grandmother, for instance, told us they were the unwashed children of Eve. She said that, one day God decided to visit Eve, who, as you might expect, being the mother of creation, had many offspring. It was short notice and she flew into a panic trying to make them presentable, but she ran out of time. So what did she do? She hid the dirty ones so they wouldn't offend her special guest. He duly arrived and inspected her brood and was pleased. He then asked if there were any more but Eve, for shame, denied their existence. God, being of course omniscient, found out about them and determined that whatever humans tried to hide from him he would hide from humans.'

Trenchers of smoked mutton were set down, glasses recharged. The light outside had dimmed so extra candles were brought in and lanterns lit. Shadows chased each other across the ceiling beams.

'*You* don't believe in this stuff, do you?' Phoebe continued.

'Of course he doesn't,' the bishop interjected. 'Only a *fáviti* would take such nonsense seriously.'

'Only a *what?*' Fitzmaurice said, looking up.

'Real or not, Reverend,' Steingrimur said with a smile, 'tales of ghostly creatures and trolls keep our children

106

from wandering too far.' He lifted his glass. 'A toast, ladies and gentlemen,' heads turned, 'to the *huldufólk* . May we live in peace with them.'

Sir Crispin and the bishop both muttered under their breath but drained their drinks nonetheless.

After rice pudding and another round of toasting, quiet was called for and an immensely old, goat-faced man in a grey cloak was ushered in and helped onto a high stool placed at the top of the room. He surveyed the company with mild disdain and then, in slow, narcoleptic Icelandic, proceeded to tell a story that seemed to Fitzmaurice, whose bowtie had now become a garotte, to last several hours.

At last, the old man's voice faded to a croak and the saga came to an end, prompting a cheer of relief. The waiters darted forward with refills.

'A toast!' Rafferty cried. 'To the people of Iceland.'

More salutations followed: to the King (no one was quite sure which); to women's rights; to the rebels; to the Kaiser; to the one true faith; to the Holy Trinity; to God; to cod; to Home Rule; to the King, again; to Icelandic sovereignty; to victory in Europe, and last (and, coming from the bishop, most controversial) to the under-secretary's wife's eyes.

Sir Crispin climbed unsteadily to his feet.

'Time for wrestling,' he announced.

A shadow passed across Fitzmaurice's sweaty visage.

'Oh no,' he moaned, holding his head in his hands. 'Not wrestling. Not now.'

'Come on, boy. Me and you. Just like Christmas in the old days.'

The honorary consul shrugged off his jacket and began rolling up his sleeves. He slapped his nephew on the back.

'Up you get, you rascal.'

'Please, Uncle, I don't want to. I don't feel well.'

'Don't give me that. Let's show them how it's done.'

Fitzmaurice looked to Crozier and Rafferty in desperation but they merely grinned and nodded encouragement. With great reluctance he rose from the table, turning just as his uncle rushed at him, and the next moment the two men were grappling in the manner of a couple of orangutans trying to pass each other in the galley of a pitching ship.

Despite the age difference, and Fitzmaurice's height advantage, they were surprisingly well matched and much grunting and swearing followed as they crashed from side to side. Waiters leapt out of the way. A trolley laden with crockery was knocked over. The under-secretary started to protest but unsure of the protocol, lapsed into baffled silence. Then, just as Fitzmaurice appeared to have gained the upper hand, catching his uncle in a head-lock, his neckwear finally got the better of him and he collapsed on the floor, gasping for air like a dying moose. As the diners debated whether or not to applaud, the chief physician, setting his cigar down, knelt beside the apoplectic wrestler and cut the string of his bowtie with a cheese knife.

'Who's next?' Sir Crispin bellowed, as Fitzmaurice was helped back to his chair. 'What about you, Bishop?'

The churchman demurred.

'...Perhaps not. Hey, you two young fellows,' Crozier and Rafferty started in alarm, 'let's be having you.'

Steingrimur attempted to intervene.

'Just a suggestion, Sir Crispin, but this may not be the time nor...'

'Nonsense,' the gladiator shouted, snatching a drink from the hand of the nearest guest. 'It's our custom, Steinie. Don't try to stop us.'

He downed the beverage and tossed the glass over his shoulder (narrowly missing the old storyteller). In the next instant, his shirt was off and the first verse of *Rule, Britannia!* was reverberating through the glassware.

As he slid from his chair, some time later, Crozier's final perception, from the vantage point of the floor, was of a full moon glimpsed through the window, high and bright, and ringed by a halo the colour of a bruise.

11

Fate Catches Up With Sir Crispin Pimm

Early the following morning the revellers assembled, as arranged, at the stables near the hotel, where their ponies were saddled up and waiting in the paddock. Only Phoebe had failed to show. (The first knock on her door had elicited a faint groan of anguish, the second an outburst of swearing so savage Fitzmaurice had to catch his breath. 'I think we'll leave her,' he told the others. 'She's going to have a bit of a lie-in.')

Sir Crispin, who was engaged in discussions with the stable-master, had arrived at breakfast with a brisk and cheery demeanour starkly at odds with his appearance. His face was cadaver-white, his mouth a crimson gash, while behind the electric blue of his crackle-glazed eye-balls an erratic pulse thudded visibly. He was dressed as though for a day's grouse shooting, in a tight tweed jacket and yellowing jodhpurs, his feet shod in creaky walking boots.

'Righty-ho,' he announced, rubbing his hands together. 'We're all set. This is Bjarni, our guide.' A short, bearded Icelander in a bowler hat appraised the party with a sceptical eye. 'His sons will follow behind with the equipment and the lunch hamper.'

The previous day Fitzmaurice and Crozier had ferried

the Magiflex and a trunkful of Savage Newells from the *Dolphin*. The camera, the apparel they were not already wearing, and provisions for the trek were strapped to two of the sturdier ponies. After a brief tutorial on equestrian etiquette and a couple of minor mounting errors the party trotted out onto the lava plain. It was a clear spring day and the light was not sympathetic to their condition. Fitzmaurice was feeling particularly ill. Somehow he had been allocated one of the smaller ponies and, his long legs hanging low, every so often his toes would scuff on a rock, sending sparks along his spine and setting another firework off in his skull.

'My God, I can't believe they made us drink so much,' he moaned.

'They were just being hospitable,' Crozier said. 'It was really very nice of them.'

'That wasn't hospitality. It was attempted murder.'

'No one forced you.'

'Oh, I think they did.'

'Please,' Rafferty called over his shoulder. 'Please, you're making it worse. Why don't you just relax and enjoy the scenery? Look over there. Is that a volcano?'

The plain stretched away from them in all directions under a huge azure sky, the horizons bounded by oddly-shaped mountains gleaming with snow. The scrubby earth, rippled by aeons of subterranean turmoil, was punctuated by humps and spikes of malformed stone. Apart from the occasional bird whistle – Crozier quickly identified a whimbrel (*Numenius phaeopus*) and a snow bunting (*Plectrophenax nivalis*) — the landscape seemed empty of life, silent beyond the thump and skitter of the ponies' hooves (and the odd tormented appeal by

111

Fitzmaurice to a higher power). The track they were on was primitive, little more than an expanded rabbit trail that kept them in single file for much of the way, but eventually they came to the foot of a high volcanic ridge and began, after some expressions of alarm, on a meandering path towards the summit.

Despite the increasingly sharp air, Crozier was perspiring freely beneath his Savage Newell 'Frontiersman' cape, the droplets tickling as they rolled down his back. His head was pounding, his guts bubbled and griped, and his limbs were burning, partly from dehydration, partly from the exertions of the night before, but the malfunction preoccupying him most was visual. Over several miles he had become convinced of the impression that creatures of some sort were moving among the rocks. His immediate thought, at the first inky flicker, had been of a reptile, of the whiplash tail of a lizard scuttling for cover, but then he remembered where he was. When it happened again, he assumed rabbits, even though the character of the movement was not quite right. Perhaps some order of shy, flightless bird?

On the lower slopes of the ridge, the frequency increased but, as before, when he looked directly there was nothing; all was still. And yet, the margins teemed... Once, when he turned his head particularly quickly – the result of an involuntary muscle twitch – he was sure he'd caught the after-trace of a pair of eyes, intent and watchful among the boulders. A short time later he had the sensation of something trying to claw a purchase on his trouser leg and almost fell off his steed in a flailing panic.

He glanced back. Following up the rear, the sons,

Bjorn and Bjenny, were oblivious. He maneouvred the water-flask from his pack, took a drink, and wondered whether it was possible that he had sustained permanent brain damage. Up ahead, Fitzmaurice seemed absorbed in the landscape, while Rafferty, further along, was singing, snatches of a plaintive melody floating back down the line. Sustenance and a little rest and the hallucinations would cease, Crozier told himself.

At last the gradient eased and they found themselves on the top of the ridge. The Icelandic interior lay before them: ice-floes, crevasses, miniature deserts, nunataks; the darkness of the lava fields as though a vast shadow was being cast from above. Mountains ranged into the distance on either side, their upper crags encased in dazzling ice. Below them, at the centre of a raised plateau, was a small lagoon that glowed an unearthly blue. Around it were several smaller pools from which spurted gouts of steam that drifted like the aftermath of cannon-fire. The travellers rested in their saddles for a while in silent wonderment until a faint rumbling from the plateau drew their attention. Sir Crispin consulted with Bjarni. 'Down there,' he cried, pointing. 'Something marvellous.'

As they watched, one of the pools began to fizz and bubble and the next moment a thick plume of seething water erupted some ninety feet into the air before collapsing to earth in an explosion of vapour. Tiny rainbows shone in the dispersing mist. A few seconds later it happened again.

Sir Crispin showed malacca-coloured teeth. 'Well chaps? That's not something you see every day.'

Rafferty sighed. 'I wish Phoebe could have been here.'

113

'Yes,' Crozier agreed, 'she would have liked that.'

'Come on,' Sir Crispin said. 'A nice hot dip before lunch.'

The descent was steep, the path slippery with scree and tortuously diverted here and there by huge boulders, some of which overhung precariously. At the bottom they made their way across a lunar landscape of sticky grey mud to the lagoon where they dismounted and the guide and his sons began to unload the packhorses.

'Devil of a thing,' Fitzmaurice remarked to Crozier. 'Had the strangest sensation along the way that something was trying to climb up my leg.'

Before Crozier could respond, a naked Sir Crispin, shockingly slabby and veinous, lumbered past them and plunged into the water, rolling around with great howls and yelps of pleasure. The Trinity men rummaged in the Savage Newell hamper for bathing costumes – heavy wool and shaped like short dungarees – and entered more cautiously, sniffing at the sulphurous fumes.

'My God, it's hotter than the College baths,' Rafferty exclaimed. 'You could poach a chicken in here.'

'I think I just poached *something*,' Fitzmaurice said.

'Oh, that's so good,' Crozier eased back and gazed at the sky. 'I thought I was going to die earlier.'

'Speaking of College, I wonder what's on the dining hall menu today,' Rafferty mused. 'Is it lamb chops? I think it is. God, I could just eat one now. With mint sauce.'

'It's Saturday. Dining hall's closed.'

'No it's Friday, isn't it?'

'Saturday. Definitely.'

'*Feels* like a Friday.'

114

'I miss College,' Rafferty said. 'I miss the routine, I miss...'

Sir Crispin wallowed close by.

'This water cures all ills apparently. Full of magic minerals,' he burbled. 'If only I could find a way to extract them.'

The lagoon was alive with gentle, swarming currents that caressed and buffeted; its surface shimmered with yellowish vapour. Underfoot the floor was uneven and textured like fine sandpaper. Crozier had the impression, looking down through the ripples, that his legs were outlandishly long and thin. Bones without flesh.

'I've been thinking about our giant,' he said.

'What about him?' Rafferty was floating on his back with his eyes closed.

Refracted through the wavering water, Crozier's feet were a fathom down. He wiggled his toes and to his mild surprise they responded.

'Well?'

'What? Oh, yes. I was wondering, and of course this depends on if we can actually find the spot, whether we should be...'

'Yes?'

'Well, taking a dead man's bones, you know, without his permission.'

Rafferty laughed. Fitzmaurice smoothed his wet locks back with both hands.

'First of all, we *will* find him. Secondly ... a dead man's *permission?*'

'You know what I mean. Isn't it tantamount to grave robbing?'

'Not in the least. That only applies to... to hollowed ground. Doesn't it, Rafferty?'

115

'Hallowed. Yes, I believe that's correct.'

Crozier said nothing.

'More importantly,' Rafferty continued. 'What are we going to do about Phoebe? We can't leave her here.'

'I'm afraid we've no choice,' Fitzmaurice said, 'McGregor won't let her back on the *Dolphin*.'

'Rafferty's right, she must come with us.' Crozier kicked his feet, splashing water into the air. 'She's part of the team now. Anyway, who's in charge of this expedition, you or McGregor?'

Fitzmaurice squinted up at the sky.

'...Fitz?'

'We'll see.'

The earth growled again and another column of scalding water blasted from the nearby geyser with a deafening hiss, showering them with hot rain. Sir Crispin surfaced beside them.

'I don't know about you fellows, but I could eat a burnt monkey on a stick. Spot of lunch?'

On some lichen-coated rocks a safe distance from the spring, Bjarni and the boys had laid out beer and a brace of cold birds. Gradually, they felt their spirits revive. Even Sir Crispin regained some colour and began to look a little less insane around the eyes. When they had eaten and rested, Fitzmaurice fetched the Magiflex.

'Right chaps, coats off and over to the pond,' he said, grappling with the tripod. 'With any luck we'll have a geyser in the background as well. And remember to show off those muscles.'

As he began working his way through *figs. 1-7*, his companions discarded their outer layers and stood shivering and grumbling at the edge of the lagoon, the waterlogged

116

gussets of their Savage Newells swinging low. Sir Crispin, having declared himself 'a new man', was already bobbing around in the spring, his face blurring pinkly in the steam. Fitzmaurice inserted a plate and, pulling a picnic blanket over his head, twiddled the viewfinder until the scene came into nebulous definition.

'Positions, gentlemen, please,' he called.

Crozier remained upright, pointing at the sky while Rafferty hunkered down, peering at the ground like a master tracker examining the spoor of some nameless quarry. From beneath his focusing cloth, Fitzmaurice became aware of a muffled rumbling and his pulse quickened. The geyser! He cocked the shutter *(fig. 193)*. In the viewfinder he noticed that both his subjects had turned and were staring at the mountainside.

'No,' he shouted, 'back the way you were. Wait for the geyser.'

He adjusted the depth of field *(fig. 196)*. He could hear raised voices and several sets of footsteps behind him. Now what? Damn. They were going to miss it. He leant forward, groping for the aperture dial *(fig.197)* and knocked the lens off-centre. It was hot under the blanket and his face was moist. With effort he twisted the device back into position and began to refocus. There was a sound like a thunder-crack and a moment later he was brought to his knees by the weight of a deluge from above. The plain seethed all around and the camera was snatched away like driftwood.

He emerged, gasping, into the air and stared in bewilderment: Crozier and Rafferty lay on their backs on the mudflats; Bjarni and his boys were standing at the edge of the hot spring – or rather, where it had once been, for now it was more or less empty of water. In its place, and he noted in passing the changed profile of the mountainside, was an enormous boulder, ice-bound and monumental, under which, for evermore, lay the obliterated remains of Sir Crispin Pimm.

12

Dead Calm; Tensions Rise

'There you are, that should hold now. It's not too tight, is it?'

Phoebe leant back and scrutinised the strip of black cloth she had re-fastened around Fitzmaurice's upper arm. He sniffed; grunted.

'How long do you think I should keep it on?'

'I'm not sure. As long as you're in mourning, I suppose. A week?'

'A *week?*'

In the three days since the *Dolphin* had sailed from Reykjavik bound for Greenland, Fitzmaurice had indulged in a bout of self-pity that had surprised even himself: drifting round the ship like a wraith, staring out to sea for hours on end – even, on occasion, refusing food. The sudden elemental violence of his uncle's death, and the lack of a corpse to consign with the usual propitiatory incantations, had shaken him – it had shocked them all – but he was beginning to run out of steam on the grief front. Fond though he had been of his uncle, even Fitzmaurice (by his own admission not the most astute judge of human nature) would have to concede that Sir Crispin had not been a paragon of moral rectitude.

'Actually, it is a *little* tight. Would you mind?'

All in all, Fitzmaurice felt he had done as much as he could. With Steingrimur's help he had contacted his uncle's business partners in Reykjavik, settled the bill at the hotel (Bjork seemed inordinately distraught), and wired the British authorities in Whitehall to let them know they required a new honorary consul. The telegram to Lady Pimm had been more difficult. A spell of poignant pencil-gnawing eventually resulted in the following dispatch: BAD NEWS STOP SIR C SQUOSHED BY ROCK STOP NO BODY STOP SORRY.

They had arranged for the deceased's worldly goods to be shipped back to England and for the sale, at a significant loss, of his band of ponies to an agricultural collective. Steingrimur also sent the town's trio of policemen out to the lagoon to assess the possibility of lifting the boulder, but they concluded that it was far too big and heavy and, perhaps more saliently, that no one really wanted to see what was underneath. On the morning before the *Dolphin* weighed anchor a sparsely-attended service was held at the cathedral where, the bishop being mysteriously unavailable, a flustered commissary stuttered his way through edited highlights of Sir Crispin's chequered career. Afterwards Fitzmaurice said a few words, literally, finding himself at a loss for tributes after 'My uncle was a man...'

Back at sea, McGregor was impatient to make up for lost time, and with a fair wind they made substantial progress to the southwest. The skipper had recovered from his chill but remained subdued, putting up only token resistance to Phoebe's reappearance. The crew, similarly, were docile, having taken full advantage of Icelandic hospitality during their extended shore leave. The cabin boy was in a particularly dreamy state, mooning around the ship with a sickly smirk on his face, due to a brief but transformative late-night encounter with one of the harbour crones.

In their coffin-sized cabin under the fo'c'sle once again, Crozier and Rafferty were finding life at close quarters a challenge. Minor trespasses were accumulating: Crozier's snoring, Rafferty's disregard for private property (there had been a nasty row about some shoe polish), but other tensions were also coming into play. Phoebe's crusading zeal had awakened in the Dubliner a fresh sense of injustice. Why, he wondered, was he not back at home helping to free his country from oppression rather than consorting with agents of the Ascendancy? On a hare-brained scheme that would do nothing to further the cause of Ireland?

The more he thought about it the more he smouldered. A faint paranoia crept in: fair enough, they treated him as an equal but did that not just point up their complacent superiority? He found himself listening for slights, for double-bluff condescension, for slips of assumed authority. Fitzmaurice he discounted to a degree, as being not only irredeemably mired in privilege but more or less incapable of coherent thought. Crozier, though, was different; he was intelligent, and versed in moral truth, and surely knew the writing was on the wall.

There was another source of friction under the fo'c'sle, however: Phoebe. Rafferty suspected Crozier had his eye on her. Little things: comments, the odd curious glance, manoeuvrings for proximity. And this troubled him. For the fact was, he was falling in love.

*

On the fourth morning, which happened to be Good Friday, the wind dropped and a freezing fog enveloped them. Under engine power the *Dolphin* proceeded at a cautious three knots. By the afternoon of the following day the ocean was dead calm and there was little more than ten yards of visibility. McGregor was becoming anxious about conserving fuel for heating and cooking. A feeling of unease began to grip the crew.

'It's very unusual,' McGregor told Crozier. 'Conditions like this shouldn't persist in these parts for more than a couple of hours.'

They were standing near the mizzen-mast gazing out at the wall of murk, which seemed to rest like a solid object on the surface of the water. Above them the tops of the masts were obscured by pewter mist. Apart from the distant rumble of the ship's propeller and the slow shoosh of the bow, all was quiet. Crozier was aware of the icy damp on his face. He gritted his teeth to stop them chattering and blew into his gloved hands.

'I don't know. I've never been to sea before.'

'Well, take my word for it, it's very f—ing odd,' McGregor said, 'and if things don't change soon I wouldn't be surprised if there was an offering on the cards.'

'A what?'

'An offering. You know, a sacrifice? The men are very superstitious.'

'Are they?'

'Oh aye. Never set sail on a Friday. Or the first Monday in April. Or the second Monday in August. Panic if they see a redhead before a voyage. Don't like anyone whistling. That kind of thing. Won't have bananas onboard.'

'Bananas?' Crozier had the sensation that his skull was starting to freeze.

'One time, on a spice run out of Zanzibar, they found

a crate of them in the hold.' He shook his head. 'We had to sacrifice all the f—ing chickens and throw them over the side. Ate nothing but f—ing rice for a month.'

'That's horrible.'

'And you've probably noticed that nobody, and I include myself, is happy about there being a woman onboard.'

Crozier swivelled.

'Are you saying we'll have to sacrifice Phoebe?'

McGregor snorted.

'No, nothing like that. Jesus Christ, it's the twentieth f—ing century,' He coughed and spat. 'No, not Phoebe. Something else. Another living creature.'

'A chicken?'

'Not a chicken.'

'Bunion?' Crozier's tone was hopeful. He received a glare.

'Hang on... You don't mean,,?'

'Let's face it,' McGregor said, 'nobody likes that f—ing thing.'

'Crikey.'

'Don't worry, it would only be a last resort.' The Scot turned to leave. He paused. 'Probably best not mention it tae "his Lordship" though.'

Crozier continued to lean on the handrail, staring into the mist. He tried not to think about the consequences of what the skipper had just outlined but it struck him how removed a ship at sea was from the weight of consensus, and how easy it would be to drift beyond judgment and law. Beyond reason. What was life onboard after all, but a form of dictatorship? Was McGregor a dictator? He certainly had tendencies. But then maybe they all would, given the opportunity. The chance to play God. Come to that, was *God* a dictator? He liked His own way, that was a given, but...

A sound in the distance interrupted his reverie. A muffled cry deep in the sea smoke. Human? He tightened his grip on the gunwale. Again, more distinct this time, a definite tone of distress. His heart quickened and he wondered if he should alert someone. It came twice more – difficult to tell the direction but closer by – and, after an interval, another, but further away this time, and with a dying fall. And then nothing. He listened, motionless, for a few more minutes before straightening up. He opened and closed his stiff hands to restart the circulation. He replayed the sound in his memory and then began to wonder if he'd heard anything at all. If it *had* been real then it was most likely a seabird: a storm petrel *(Hydrobates pelagicus)* perhaps, or a Manx shearwater *(Puffinus puffinus)*. Both were common around the Icelandic coast, and now he thought of it, shearwaters were known for their eerie cry. Lost souls, some called them.

The fog had not lifted the next morning. In fact it had become denser, darkening the crepuscular shroud around the ship. The order was given to shut down the engine, and the ensuing stillness and silence added to the gloom. The crew went about their tasks as usual but, there being no sailing technicalities, the work was largely completed by lunchtime. McGregor locked himself away in his cabin to study charts; Harris and Doyle moped in the wheelhouse drinking tea. In the galley, by the glow of an oil lamp, Victoor clanked back and forth while Phoebe peeled vegetables for the evening meal. Bridie, unsettled by the lack of daylight, twitched and glowered in her cage.

Under the fo'c'sle Crozier, tired from deck scrubbing and intent on a nap, was breathing heavily, his face hot. Despite repeated pleas and warnings, Rafferty had failed, yet again, to secure the door against the ship's dog. Usually this resulted only in the beast somehow ascending the rudimentary bunk-ladder and making itself flatulently comfortable in Crozier's bed. This time it had shown more initiative. It was stretched out in the middle of the room, its great chest rising and falling in agitated slumber, on a nest composed of most of his belongings. Crozier's steamer trunk, extensively scraped and gouged, lay open, a ripped shirtsleeve hanging from one corner, a detached trouser-leg from another. Between its twitching paws the monster clutched a half-eaten brogue, while scattered around its head, Crozier noted with some distress, were the confetti-like remnants of some of his most prized books.

Dinner that evening was a subdued affair. Neither Victoor's token attempt to celebrate Easter Sunday with boiled eggs and hot cross buns, nor Phoebe's impression of Sir Crispin choking on a puffin leg (Fitzmaurice was in his cabin), could dispel the atmosphere of foreboding. McGregor said little and rose from the table early, Harris and Doyle drifting in his wake. When Victoor and the cabin boy had cleared away the dishes, Phoebe suggested a game of gin rummy but Crozier was still angry with Rafferty and excused himself to go and read *Treasure Island*, which he had pillaged from Fitzmaurice's meagre library.

Sometime after midnight he stirred in his sleep. The *Hispaniola* was anchored in the narrow passage between the mainland and the islet marked on Captain Flint's map as 'Skeleton Island'. Through his spyglass Crozier could see the pirates – among them two burly blond twins — moving in the swamp behind the trees. There was no sound but for the distant boom of surf and there was no breeze, the hot air heavy with a peculiar, stagnant smell. Rafferty, at his shoulder, sniffed. 'I don't know about treasure,' he said, 'but I'll stake my wig, there's fever here.' Before Crozier could reply, the ship was shaken by a volley of cannon-fire and everyone began shouting at once. 'Damn your eyes, McGregor,' Crozier yelled. He woke up. Rafferty was already standing, pulling on his jacket. 'Something's wrong,' he hissed.

Crozier swung his legs over the side of the bunk and sat, trying to make sense of the sounds overhead: chaotic thumping, urgent voices, the clanking of an untethered metal object. Intruders? *Pirates?* He jumped down, located his boots in the darkness, and hurried after Rafferty. The door to Phoebe's cabin opened as he passed. 'What the hell's going on?' she demanded. 'Trouble,' he told her. 'Stay there.'

At the top of the ladder leading to the hatchway, he paused. The commotion had died down and he could hear someone talking in a soothing voice, as if to a child. He pushed at the swing-doors and peered out. Rafferty was nearby with his back to him. Beyond, in the trembling light cast by a hurricane lamp, was a strange scene. Perched on the lower yard of the mainmast, side by side, their eyes wide with terror — they were staring at something blocked from his view — were Harris and Doyle.

The first mate's hands, he noted, were bloodied, and one of the bosun's eyebrows was missing.

'Just keep calm and don't make any sudden moves,' Rafferty was saying. Crozier felt the weight of someone on the rungs below him and clambered out of the hatch. As he straightened up he saw what the others were looking at and all became clear.

Tensed on the deck, dorsal spines erect and mouth agape in a silent scream of rage, was Bridie, her tail whipping around like a loose electric cable. Rocking on its side nearby was a large metal bucket. 'What's happening?' Phoebe said, appearing at his shoulder. Crozier held up a warning finger. Rafferty knelt down, proffering his hand. 'Here Bridie, good girl.' The lizard, its attention fixed on the mainmast, registered his movement. 'Bridie, everything's going to be grand.' He reached for the bucket. 'I'm just going to pop this over...' The lizard started to hiss. Rafferty paused. '...just going to...' A low, phlegmy rattle replaced the hiss. Rafferty waited for it to stop. 'Bridie, there's nothing to worry about, I'm only...'

There was a sound like the screech of locomotive brakes and Bridie lunged sideways. Rafferty dropped the bucket and leapt into a prancing run in the direction of the others, the lizard skittering after him. Someone screamed — Crozier wasn't sure whether it was him or Phoebe — and all three of them raced towards the stern where they scrambled onto the poop deck and lay in a tangle gasping for breath. Bridie, prioritising her revenge, doubled back to where Fitzmaurice, attired in a Savage Newell tweed nightshirt and reindeer pampooties, was staring in bafflement at the two sailors clinging to the mainmast.

'So Bridie, for no apparent reason, broke out of her cage, made her way up through the ship – climbing several sets of ladders, mind – forced her way into the wheelhouse and viciously attacked you and Doyle? Is that what you're telling me?'

'That's about the height of it, yes "your Lordship",' Harris said, examining his savaged hand. Beside him, the bosun dabbed at the bald strip of skin above his eye, marvelling at its coldness.

'Then you managed to get away from her but she pursued you and you only escaped with your lives by climbing that mast. Is that correct?'

'We were in fear of our lives, that's right, "your Lordship".'

Fitzmaurice stood for a few moments in puzzled silence, then leant down and gathered the iguana up in his arms.

'Don't worry, sweetheart, daddy's got you,' he crooned. He looked back up at the mast, but the two men were no longer paying attention to him or his pet. They were gazing around at darkness visible once more, jaundiced clouds and prickling stars, the fog flying away like smoke from a bonfire. And they were feeling the wind shivering through the rigging and hearing the first fat drops of rain spatter on the deck.

13

A Storm

The storm arrived with an abrupt, pent-up fury, as though it had grown frustrated searching for them. No sooner had Harris and Doyle climbed down than the sky convulsed and thunder shook the *Dolphin* from stem to stern. Within seconds the rain had become an icy monsoon and a gale was roaring overhead. The ship began to pitch and roll on drumlin-sized waves. 'Harris, reef that sail,' McGregor yelled, emerging from the hatchway. 'Prepare to heave to.' He hurried towards where Crozier, Rafferty and Phoebe had joined Fitzmaurice. 'Go below all of yis and tell the crew tae get up here,' he told them. 'But stand by – I might need yis.'

Down in the mess, Fitzmaurice swaddled Bridie in a blanket and dandled her on his knee while Rafferty attempted to revive the embers of the fire. Crozier crashed around in the galley, eventually emerging with a pot of tea which he sloshed into cups and handed round along with pieces of hardtack. Above them they could hear, amid the howling of the storm, shouted commands and the bangs and clankings of what they imagined were hatches being secured and halyards tightened. Phoebe had retreated to her cabin.

'Bit of a change in the weather,' Crozier observed.

'What I want to know is, what the bloody hell they were doing with my iguana,' Fitzmaurice muttered. 'She was in a fearful rage.'

He hugged her closer and she peeped up at him like a tiny beshawled crone. He rubbed her under the chin. Crozier choked slightly on a shard of biscuit.

'I mean, what if she'd slipped overboard?' Fitzmaurice said.

'Oh I'm fairly sure they can swim,' Rafferty said.

'What?'

'Iguanas. Good swimmers. I read it in Darwin.'

Fitzmaurice glared at him. He was frisking the lizard along its length.

'My God, she's shaking like a leaf, she'd better have her hot water bottle. Here, Rafferty, take her while I fetch it.'

'I will not.'

'Crozier?'

'I haven't finished my tea. Just set her down, she'll be fine.'

'Oh, for Godsake.'

The ship pitched and Fitzmaurice was propelled into a stumbling run towards the galley. After he left the room the other two gripped their chairs and sat without speaking. The *Dolphin* was groaning deep in her timbers, and each plunge into the trough of a wave produced a jarring thump from the bow. The wind whistled in the pipes. The fire guttered.

'Doyle's going to look very silly with only one eyebrow,' Crozier said.

'I know,' said Rafferty. 'And did you see the state of the first mate's finger?' He shuddered. 'That really should be stitched. What on earth were they thinking?'

'I told you what they were thinking. I just didn't believe they'd try it. But remember, Fitz mustn't find out. He'd go mad.'

Fitzmaurice leaned out of the galley. 'Who'd go mad?'

'Just saying, Doyle will be furious when he sees his missing eyebrow.'

'Serves him bloody right,' Fitzmaurice sniffed. 'They were up to something very rum, the pair of them, and I mean to find out what it was.'

He disappeared again. Overhead, the booming of the wind was like the erratic beat of a monstrous drum, counterpointed by the rumble of huge weights of water falling on the deck.

'For Godsake, Crozier, be a good fellow and give us an auld prayer or something.'

Crozier was staring into the faint glow of the hearth.

'Why don't *you*,' he said, 'give us "an auld prayer"? Or something.'

'Don't know any.'

'Really?'

'Not off by heart, no.'

'Not even the Lord's Prayer?'

'Of course. But we're not at that stage yet. I hope.'

Crozier flicked a crumb from the table into the fire-place.

'Well, you know, if someone hadn't left the cabin door open – *again* -- and a certain dog hadn't eaten my books, I could've read to you from Psalms about the people that go down to the sea in ships and behold the Lord's wonders in the deep.'

'You're not *still* moaning about that, are you?'

131

'Not at all, simply stating a fact.'

'Sounds like moaning.'

'There's only one whinger around here.'

'Really? And who would that be?'

'You.'

'Is that so?'

'Yes. You're never done whingeing and whining.'

'Really? About what exactly?'

Crozier could see the gleam of Rafferty's spectacles in his peripheral vision.

'Nothing.'

'Come on. What about?'

'Nothing.'

'Go on, spit it out.'

'Oh, for Godsake,' he twisted around so he was square on. 'You know what I'm talking about: about how the British Empire abused and oppressed you and stole all your potatoes, and how you'll never be free and nothing's fair.'

'Sound like legitimate complaints to me.'

'Says young Master Bourgeois of Phibsborough, studying medicine at Trinity College.'

'Sorry, that's relevant how?'

'Well, you don't appear to me to be overly oppressed.'

'My personal circumstances have nothing to do with it, the problem lies with centuries of colonial exploitation.'

'Ireland isn't a colony. How many British colonies have representatives in the English parliament?'

'I don't want representation, I want an *Irish* parliament.'

'That's nonsense. You know as well as I do that if

England didn't exist... hadn't existed... it would be... would have been necessary for Ireland to invent... England.'

'*What?*'

'Never mind. Look, you took my hairbrush.'

'You used my toothbrush, that's worse.'

'That was an accident. You left the cabin door open and Bunion...'

'It was my cabin in the first place and, now we're on the subject, I don't remember actually inviting you...'

'Ha! I knew it! I knew you didn't want me in there.'

'Why would I? You leave your things all over the place.'

'You're the untidy one.'

'*And* you snore.'

'I do not snore.'

'Yes you do, you sound like a f—ing grizzly bear.'

'Take that back.' Crozier was on his feet, leaning on the table, his chin jutting.

'No, I won't. And while we're at it, perhaps you should also try adjusting your attitude.' Rafferty pushed *his* chair back and stood up.

'What's that supposed to mean?'

'Well, let's face it, you're a bit holier-than-thou.'

'I am not.'

'Yes, you are, you're always acting as though you know best.'

'Nonsense. *You're* the one that thinks he's always right and the rest of the world is wrong. You're incapable of seeing beyond your own opinion, just like every other armchair nationalist I've ever met.'

Rafferty was breathing noisily through his nose.

'It's her, isn't it?' he hissed. 'You're jealous.'

'Who? Jealous of what?'

'Phoebe. You're after her, admit it.'

Crozier stared.

'What if I was? What's it to you, you don't stand a chance any...'

Rafferty struck the first blow, catching Crozier on the ear with a knuckley half-fist that hurt them both equally. Responding by instinct and through blurred lashes, Crozier landed a straight right to Rafferty's chin that sent the Dubliner reeling backwards. Bridie raced past him in the opposite direction. Rounding the table, Crozier met Rafferty as he bounced back off the wall and the pair of them, neither used to physical combat, began slapping and flailing at each other like outraged dowagers.

Their bout was not made any easier by the motion of the ship, which caused them to totter at speed first one way then the other, temporary advantage being given to whoever was at the top of the slope. Fighting words were exchanged. Cups were knocked off the table. Bridie darted back and forth, dodging out of the path of their stumbling feet, at one juncture halting proceedings with a raised palm while she discharged a startlingly loud sneeze. Fitzmaurice reappeared and, wedging himself in the galley doorway, watched as two grown men attempted to conduct a boxing match on a giant see-saw, refereed by a lizard in a hairy cowl. Before long the struggle to stay upright was lost and they collapsed to the floor in mid-grapple, rolling over and over in a flurry of cold sweat and snot.

'What the hell?' Fitzmaurice reached down and detached Crozier, jerking him to his feet and pushing him away. He helped Rafferty up.

134

'What do you think you're playing at, you bloody eejits? Don't you realise we're in the middle of some kind of hurricane?'

Crozier and Rafferty scowled at each other, the latter reattaching his mangled spectacles, which were dangling from one ear. Fitzmaurice scooped Bridie up and whisked her off to the galley; at the same time Phoebe entered by the main door, wrapped in many layers of Savage Newell, a rough woollen scarf around her neck.

'What's been going on here, boys?'

'He started it,' one grumbled.

'Bloody didn't,' said the other.

Phoebe regarded them through one half-closed eye. They reconvened at the table and sat in silence, the pugilists probing various abrasions. Fitzmaurice returned, examining a large pocket watch.

'Damn, it's stopped. I wonder what time it is.'

'What does it matter?' Phoebe said.

'It matters,' Fitzmaurice pouted, 'to the meticulicity of my expedition log.'

'*Meticulicity?*'

'Yes. It's important that historical documents are accurate.'

'Isn't that Sir Crispin's watch?'

Fitzmaurice looked momentarily shifty, then recovered himself.

'It is. It's a memento. He would've wanted me to have it.'

'It's very tasteful.'

'Yes.' Fitzmaurice peered at the timepiece, which had on its dial a hand-painted depiction of a nymph and a satyr engaged in indistinct but unmistakable congress, and became teary. 'Poor old Uncle, he always…'

The door to the mess was flung open and Harris stood there, glazed and dripping.

'Skipper wants all hands on deck.'

14

'Their Soul Is Melted Because of Trouble'

Above, all was tumult: a reckless, destructive force broken loose from some great vault of inner space, warping the masts, ripping at the cordage, snatching away anything that wasn't lashed down and flinging it into the foam-streaked darkness. High banks of black water surged about the ship. Waves were thrashing against the bridge, the mid-deck awash in seething foam. With each pitch, the vessel toppled into enervating emptiness, each time meeting another solid wall of sea.

The four of them, having forced their way out of the snapping hatchway, stood clutching each other for support, blinded by the onslaught, unable to hear anything above the shrieking of the gale. Rain flooded in at the necklines of their Savage Newell oilskins, chilling their flesh. McGregor materialised out of the murk and put his mouth to Fitzmaurice's ear. Even at such proximity his words were swallowed by the wind.

'I want you tae… go tae Kinsale… get me a ham sandwich,' he yelled. 'And stop f—ing around.'

Fitzmaurice searched the skipper's eyes, which were pink with brine and gleaming with an odd light.

'A… *ham sandwich*?'

McGregor again pressed his lips close.

'I want you tae brail up that sail with a Buntline hitch,' he screamed, '...stop it flogging around.'

He put a length of rope into Fitzmaurice's hand and pointed at the foremast. He seized Crozier by the shoulders and, leaning in led him to understand, after a hoarse and prolonged to-and-fro, that he and Rafferty were to relieve the twins in the engine room. Phoebe was sent down to man the bilge-pump.

Making their way through the ship, Crozier and Rafferty were flung from side to side, grasping at guardrails and doorhandles to steady themselves. Water had entered through a loose hatch and was rippling the length of the main alleyway like a miniature tidal wave. At the foot of the staircase to the lower deck they encountered the cabin boy cowering under a bench, babbling to himself. He barely noticed them as they passed. 'Poor kid,' Crozier said, but Rafferty didn't hear him over the thunderous pummelling on the hull.

The ladder down to the engine room was slippery and, as Crozier stepped off it, Rafferty arrived behind him with a clang and rolled sideways across the iron-plated floor. The twins turned from the crimson glare of the boiler, the coal dust on their faces giving their eyes an unnatural whiteness, and seeing reinforcements, leant on their shovels and swabbed sweat from their foreheads. There was steam leaking from the cylinder housing and it gave the air a harsh metallic taste. In all the dark corners there was a sense of movement, the clattering motion of the piston rods stirring up the shadows like glar in a pond. Mikkel or Magnus took Crozier by the arm and led him to a cluster of dials affixed to a plate above the boiler. 'This one,' he shouted, indicating with a sooty finger the needle on the steam gauge. 'He must stay here. Not to go below. If he here, no good.' He was nodding – 'Ja?' -- his expression half-crazed, sweat dropping like beads of solder from his oily beard. Crozier nodded back. The Norwegian pointed again at the left-hand side of the dial and made a throat-cutting sign.

Fitzmaurice's hands were shaking so much he could hardly hold the rope let alone tie a knot. The sea was at ankle-level on his rubber Savage Newells as it boiled through the scuppers, and the buffetings of the gale were like flurries of punches from an invisible assailant. He managed to get a grip of the wildly flapping sail but then couldn't differentiate in his mind between hitches: Buntline, Clove or Boom? Or Camel? He glanced back over his shoulder towards the glimmering light of the bridge hoping for guidance and noticed Bunion's head poking round the side of the hatch door. It was followed, after a struggle, by the rest of the mutt's bulbous body. Disoriented, his little ears flittering like pennants, he clumped out onto the deck and stood peering around. At the wheelhouse window McGregor spotted the dog and began to open and shut his mouth in Fitzmaurice's direction. 'Bunion!' Fitzmaurice shouted but he knew it was futile. He let go of the yardarm and started towards the animal, keeping low and angled into the wind. Bunion shook himself and sat down, froth eddying around his haunches.

As he edged up the rolling slope, Fitzmaurice felt himself slipping into a dream-like state of detachment, his whole consciousness folded into a tiny chamber of calm within the rushing din of the gale. He looked up to check his progress, blinking away the rain, and in the next moment his legs were swept from under him and he was hurtling across the deck in a torrent of ice-cold sea. He landed with a smack against the bulwark and, hoisting himself upright, soaked to the skin, struggled to catch his breath. The remains of the wave that had caught him careered on towards the bow, the bulk of it having sloshed up and over the gunwale, taking the ship's dog with it over the side.

Down in the belly of the *Dolphin,* alone and in scant lamplight, Phoebe listened to the ocean's unfathomable threats through the timbers and contemplated for the first time the possibility of death. She had faced danger before – some of the stunts she had staged for the suffs had put her in the path of serious violence – but the odds this time were beginning to look grievous. The prospect struck her matter-of-factly. They would be just another vessel swallowed by the sea, another news item. She conjured a headline -- ARCTIC EXPEDITION SHIP FEARED LOST WITH ALL HANDS – and pictured their photographs in a row before she remembered that she wasn't even officially on board, hadn't in fact officially existed for several years.

How long would it take for her name to emerge? Would her family miss her, she wondered. *Were* they missing her? She'd had only one letter from her mother since she left England, most of it a fret about her brother's travails with the beleaguered 9th Essex Battalion on the Western Front, the rest cool in tone and freighted with rebuke. Disappointment, sadness, that was all she had given them, after all they had done for her: the love, the happy home, the education. She'd wanted for nothing and had the best of everything. And she *was* grateful – she really was – for what she had received. But it wasn't enough. What they wanted in return for their gifts she hadn't been able to give: she could not keep from shaking the bars of her cage.

She realised that she had stopped pumping and the water in the well had risen again. It was higher than she had ever seen it. Black and glittering, and choppy from the lurching of the ship, it smelled of sulphur and urine and all manner of evil. It was fortunate that Doyle had repaired the pump's valve claque the previous day (using a particularly leathery leftover from one of Victoor's stews) because the bucket would have been useless against such volumes. She heaved on the handle, the downstroke requiring most of her weight and strength, and the mechanism gurgled and wheezed like a corrupted lung. Beyond the gleam of the lantern, running water ticked and popped all around the hold, heavier splashes hinting at bright little eyes in the darkness. She shivered. If *she* had created the world, she thought, she would probably have left a few things out — just off the top of her head: rats... smallpox... Brussels sprouts. She wondered whether a female creator would have made the universe a simpler or more complex place, then chided herself for patriarchal thinking.

Another jarring blow, as of the impact of a huge body throwing itself from a height, shuddered through the hull. She could hear the run-off sizzling through the scuppers even at this remove. Surely the *Dolphin* couldn't withstand seas of this size? How was the rudder even still attached? All it would take, she thought, was one big wave over the top, and that would be the end of everything. She saw all the faces of her past float by in close-up and then those that would join her on the spiral into the dark, and an ache of tenderness passed through her at one face in particular...

'*For he commandeth and raiseth the stormy wind, which lifteth up the waves thereof,*' Crozier intoned. '*They mount up to the heavens, they go down again to the depths.*'

'What are you *saying?*' Rafferty shouted.

Crozier shook his head. He stepped back from the furnace and wiped sweat and grit from his brow. Were they in hell? The darkness, the heat, the noise. They had been cast down. *Their soul is melted because of trouble.* Where were the twins? Someone was needed to trim the coal, narrow the gap. His lower back ached and his lungs burned from the fumes. He glanced at the gauge which had fallen and listened to the systolic thump of the engine. Was it slowing? The ship heeled and both he and Rafferty staggered backwards. *They reel to and fro, and stagger like drunken men, and are at their wit's end—* As they picked themselves up, the ladder shook and one after the other, the twins dropped out of the ceiling. 'Not to be going below!' Magnus or Mikkel yelled, pointing at the gauge and holding a shovel aloft.

As Fitzmaurice lay panting against the bulwark he could see, even through the deluge, the anguish on McGregor's face as it flickered in the wheelhouse window. Fitzmaurice himself was shocked, and a little sorry, about Bunion, but he had more pressing concerns: namely the rapid encroachment of hypothermic death. He began hauling himself with clawed hands along the gunwale. His limbs were numb and the muscles so tight across his chest he could barely breathe. His heartbeats, and he could hear each one, sounded like rocks dropped into a well. He felt hot and sleepy. He edged along, his legs almost beyond his control. Turning to assess the distance to the hatchway, he girded himself: these were his last reserves. The ship was listing. Sea was slopping over and running in torrents. He put a boot forward and tested for grip. Everything was slippery. And *hot*. So very hot. He squinted up at the masts. Like palm trees swaying in a tropical breeze. Was that the screeching of parakeets? And this sweet summer rain, so refreshing...

McGregor tightened the cord of his sou'wester and shouldered his way out of the wheelhouse. Towards the bottom of the stairs he held onto the rails and braced as the ship righted itself. Fitzmaurice had slumped to his knees with his eyes shut and appeared to be singing. Or asleep. McGregor stepped down, and as he did so, another crest curled above the starboard gunwale and tipped forward, launching a torrent across the deck. Such was its velocity most of the wave left the ship almost immediately, surging up and over the port side. Deposited, however, on the planking in its wake was a spinning object that McGregor at first took to be a large white fish. As it came to rest, he shook his head and swiped at his eyes with a gloved hand. The thing twitched, spasmed. He blinked. With a wriggling, writhing motion, it twisted itself abruptly into a standing position. He stared. 'Bunion, you wee bugger,' he breathed. 'Even Davy Jones disn'ae want ye.'

Between them, the skipper and the first mate managed

to drag Fitzmaurice down to his cabin. On the way they met Crozier and Rafferty who had been dismissed by the twins. Rafferty took one look at Fitzmaurice – raving through chattering teeth about the heat and struggling to discard his clothes – and ordered a hot water bottle and sweet tea. Harris had sustained a head wound which required dressing. Bunion was helped into Crozier's bed ('That really *is* a Stiff Dog') while Victoor was located – in the galley trying to bake bread – and, after he had brought tea, was sent down to relieve Phoebe at the pump.

On the bridge Doyle was locked in combat with the wheel, his face sick and exhausted above the ivory light of the binnacle. He turned as Crozier and McGregor entered, his missing eyebrow making him look oddly clown-like. Several panes of glass had been knocked out and the wind was driving spray through the gaps. The floor was wet. Crozier leant against a ledge that ran along the back wall and braced himself with a hand on either side.

The ocean seemed even more mountainous than before, the ascents steeper, the plunges more vertiginous. On the way up the view was of dark sky, low and starless, on the way down, of black water and explosions of flying spume. Huge volumes of sea were battering the wheelhouse and Crozier began to fear the whole structure would be washed away. *Then they cry unto the Lord in their trouble and he bringeth them out of their distresses.* What was the next part? *He maketh the storm a calm, so that the waves thereof are still.* Some hope. He pictured Rafferty clutching his rosary beads on the floor of the engine room: making his peace with God, securing passage. What comfort, Crozier thought, to believe in the hereafter, in continuity, in perpetuity. To be able to put it beyond doubt. To make the leap of faith. He had several times heard people declaring that they were not afraid of dying. This, he decided, was rubbish. They were fooling themselves. Or lying. Or they just hadn't thought about it hard enough. Terror, surely, was the only rational response, there was no...

He became aware of a change in the motion of the ship. She was still moving forward but with a smoothness that was strange after the hours of wild pitching. Something else was different too: the gale had ceased its howling and there was an unearthly quiet that his ears were having difficulty comprehending. Was the storm spent? The two men in front of him were standing stock still, transfixed by the middle distance. And then he saw it, having to glance away and back again to be sure: an enormous ridge of sea higher than anything that had come before, building and swelling as it approached, the foam on its crest like a luminous white seam unravelling at speed along its length.

McGregor and Doyle looked at each other and a word-less exchange took place. For a moment the only sound was of dripping water and the creak of the steering gear. McGregor reached forward and wrenched at a lever and a faint clanging came from deep within the ship. 'Hold hard, Mr Doyle,' he cried. 'If she stalls we're f—ing done for.'

The black mountain toppled towards them and the *Dolphin* rose into the face of it, surging upwards at an impossible angle towards a peak that would not come, seeming to tremble on the edge of gravity. Untold tons of sea crashed over them, shattering the glass in the

145

pilothouse windows and dousing the last of the lanterns. The skipper and the bosun were both at the wheel, straining to steady it, McGregor yelling through mouthfuls of brine. The ship cleared the apex of the wave – Crozier had the impression they hovered for an instant in mid-air – then plummeted headfirst into the trough.

15

Above It All

The gull *(Larus glaucoides)* appeared as a spot, a trick of the light on the horizon, beating a straight, high path towards the southwest. The sky in which it flew was a wash of pale grey and the sea, though in pensive mood, was largely untroubled. Apart from a throb of fresh wing-strength as it entered the cleansed air of the storm zone, the bird registered few signs of the recent violence. The ocean's surface was empty in every direction, rolling away to the edges of the world. The buffeting of the wind at this altitude made a rhythmic sound that was lulling and the gull had fallen into a kind of trance. Now, its attention was caught by an object in the distance and after a moment, almost imperceptibly, it adjusted its flightpath.

Sliding sideways on an updraught to maintain position, the bird surveyed the devastated vessel below. White with encrusted salt from the overwash of the tempest, the *Dolphin* drifted on the waves, her torn sails flapping in the grip of her bedraggled rigging. A sheared foremast, the wreckage of it tangled in the cordage, had destroyed her symmetry; the creaking of her timbers, as she rolled with the current, sounded like faint groans of despair. Nothing moved on her ruined decks. The gull jockeyed on the wind for a different view but, detecting no vital presence nor potential for food, relaxed into the breeze, dropped a fraction, and locked into a glide back on its original course.

Some four hundred leagues to the southeast, another of the gull family, *(Larus argentatus)*, was perched on a ledge above the main portico of Dublin's Custom House, a yellow eye fixed on the restless surface of the River Liffey below. In recent days the city's migration patterns had changed; unusual activity was taking place. The cargo ships and fishing smacks, touchstones of the scavenger's routine, were not where they should be. The street hawkers were absent. The alleyways behind the grocery shops and bakeries were devoid of scraps. The air was pungent, and it rippled at intervals with sudden gusts of turbulence that made for uncertain flying.

Nearby, a boat was anchored at an angle to the river, her upper works reflecting darkly in the water, and at that moment a loud report issued from her bow. Startled, the gull launched itself from the parapet and flew towards the far bank, soaring above the quayside terraces and leaning into an arc towards the centre of the city. In the streets below, large clusters of people formed ever-changing shapes, like agitated shoals of fish: first one way, then another; surging forward, falling back. Lines of men on horses snaked among them. A rumbling sound rolled across the river and great billows of dust began to fill the sky above Liberty Hall.

In the grounds of Trinity College the bird came to rest on the dome of the campanile. In the front square, men in uniform marched back and forth, their boots clacking on the cobbles; others hurried between doorways, carrying boxes. On the rooftop opposite, more men were ranged about, some kneeling or lying down, others moving in an awkward crouch. Every few seconds there were cracks and thuds followed by puffs of blue smoke. There was shouting.

The gull swooped at a diagonal across to the sill of a high window and plodded along it. Within, three figures in black robes were peering out, goblets in their hands. One of them leaned forward and rapped on the pane with his walking stick and the bird set off again, this time in a straight line, heading for the tranquility of the duck pond on Stephen's Green. But here also was strangeness: no crumb-rich people taking lunch on the grass or scattering bread on the water, no children running among the flower-beds, no background gauze of human voices. And the ducks were gone.

The gull landed with an untidy splash, sending ripples into the green shadows beneath the weeping willows. It cruised around for a while, nipping at the surface, but there was little to be had. It was finding the absence of other pond life, and the silence, unnerving. There was another lake in a park not far away, and with memories of an afternoon of abundance, the bird took off again, emerging above the trees and veering southeast along the curve of Baggot Street.

Crossing the Grand Canal, it spotted a raft of ducks paddling upstream and stalled briefly, considered joining them, but there was a noisy commotion at the next bridge along and it pressed on towards the park over the Georgian rooftops of Waterloo Road. At number sixty-two, the lady of the house was arranging a bowl of red tulips on the breakfast-room's gleaming oak table and listening for the arrival at the door of her sister-in-law.

Mary Rafferty, who had set out from Phibsborough on the other side of the river two hours earlier, was a brisk walker but her journey had been complicated by successive deviations away from the boom of artillery on the main thoroughfare and the stutter of gunfire further along the quays. At that moment she had made it as far as Great Brunswick Street, which was unusually quiet, and in between the Ionic columns of the Antient Concert Rooms she sat down on the steps to catch her breath. She watched black smoke drift on the skyline from the direction of Sackville Street and felt a hot stab of anger. This whole affair would be put down in double-quick time, her husband had said. Nothing to worry about, just a shower of chancers with rusty guns. Well, it hadn't been, and now it was out of hand. Who did they think they were, holding the city to ransom, stopping people going about their business?

Another volley of shelling, from Trinity College, reverberated through the streets. She wondered where her husband was at that moment. Safe in his office, with any luck, away from the shenanigans. Cup of tea and a nice scone. There was a time when he would have been well able for the rough stuff – enthusiastic even (if truth be told) – but he was slower now: creaky knees and a clickety hip. The groans out of him sometimes in the morning. She smiled. Silly old goat. Realising she was hungry, she rummaged in her bag for a mint and tried to picture what Florrie might be planning for lunch. She hoped not soup. Florrie wasn't a bad cook – her shortcrust, for instance, was decent enough, and she could turn out a passable sponge – but her soup! God have mercy. That chicken broth last time, fat half an inch thick on the top of it. Just about kept it down.

She took out a handkerchief and dabbed her face. Wrong choice of coat for the weather. Unseasonably warm. She thought of Frank up there in the snow, her mind struggling, as it always did, for a point of reference. So unimaginably distant. She dimly remembered a plate in an issue of *National Geographic* skimmed in a waiting room: bleak figures etched against mountains of ice; wastelands of frozen sea. But mostly it was just a big blare of whiteness. What had they been thinking? Their only boy out on the wild ocean. And him terrified as a child of water, could hardly get him in a bath until he was ten, screaming the place down, Mrs Hennessy banging on the door once, convinced there was murder. And little Frank with his eyes all pink from the soap and the crying, his hair all spiked up like a drowned kitten. Poor little chiseller. She blinked away the blur that had welled up. They should never have let him go, his head filled with nonsense by that dandypratt Fitzwhatsisname. She intoned a brief plea to God, crossed herself and stood up.

A man was approaching at speed. His brown suit was dusty and he was holding his hat in place as he ran, the heels of his boots ringing out in the empty street. She began to walk. The man slowed a little as he came near and she tightened her grip on her bag. He was looking at her as he passed: a quizzical expression. His face was streaked with dirt and he had a cut across his nose. She averted her eyes.

She turned right and then left onto Grand Canal Street. Not far now. Fifteen minutes and she would be sipping lemonade behind the tall windows of number sixty-two, with its vases of flowers and perfume of beeswax polish. Not that Florrie ever did a hand's turn, mind you. Married well, the girl. Surprising, seeing as she hadn't much going on upstairs. No, that was unfair...

She had reached Macquay's Bridge and, stepping down into the shade of the towpath, she was assailed by the cool breath off the water, the sweet stink of vegetation. So peaceful by the canal. She always enjoyed this part of the journey. As she proceeded she became aware that someone was yelling and she glanced up at the buildings across the road. A man was leaning from an open window. She looked around. Was he addressing *her*? She couldn't make out what he was saying but there was definitely foul language involved. *Ruffian*. She marched on. At the end of the path there was an upward slope and some exposed rocks and she had to take care not to lose her footing.

Emerging onto the next bridge, she stopped. Streaming along Northumberland Road towards her, still some way off, were hundreds of soldiers, four abreast, in full kit. She had to hold her hand up against the sun, but she knew by the glint of tunic buttons that it was a British battalion, and not, by the look of them, from one of the usual regiments. She nodded to herself. Not before time. Have a bit of law and order back around here. She checked to her right for traffic – apart from three men standing in a doorway, the junction was deserted – and crossed at a diagonal towards the continuation of the towpath. It occurred to her that she was late and that Florrie might be worrying, and she quickened her pace.

Just then, rapid footsteps sounded behind her — the

men from the doorway — and at the same moment shots rang out on Northumberland Road. She saw the soldiers scattering in disarray, heard shouting, and shrill blasts on a whistle. More guns crackled nearby, a volley of rifle-fire and the boom of something heavier, and she broke into a run. Figures were appearing now from several directions (she thought she recognised one of her neighbours, pistol in hand, a bandolier across his chest). If she could just dart between them onto the canal path, it would lead her to safety. There was a man in the way, squinting along the sights of his raised rifle, and she tried to push him aside but he was immoveable and the effort threw her off balance. She went down. Bullets ricocheted off the side of the bridge. Twisting in the air, her impression was that someone punched her in the back as she fell, a sharp, hard blow to the ribcage that knocked the wind out of her.

Lying there, her cheek against the cold granite, she looked up at the trees, the sky robin's-egg-blue between the branches, the leaves translucent jade. So lovely to see the new growth, she thought. So pale and delicate. She and Jack should take a drive in the Phoenix Park soon; the horse-chestnuts would be beautiful around now. A couple of faces peered down at her. Their mouths were moving but she couldn't hear their words. In fact, she couldn't hear anything. Had the guns stopped? Her back felt very warm. It was comfortable here. She hoped no one would try to move her. Although, she was very thirsty. Above her the leaves were shaking as though a long breeze was passing through them and the sunshine danced and sparkled, a blizzard of tiny lights. She pictured bubbles racing up through lemonade and imagined herself rising with them, up into the leaves, fizzing out through the treetops and into the broad expanse of blue. And, as the thought dissolved, Mrs Rafferty was gone.

Later that day, outside the mining village of Hulluch in northeastern France, a murmuration of starlings *(Sturnus vulgaris)*, disturbed by a stray mortar shell from behind German lines, rose from a birch wood and, in a flexing, warping cloud of wingbeats, vanished across the flatlands towards the west, skirting the fetor of the trenches. All but one, which slowed after a quarter of a mile and peeled off, descending to a slagheap where it ambled about for a while, pecking at the scrub. For the first time that afternoon, the artillery fire that had been a continuous din, like a frenzy of bass drums, had ceased, though smoke was still undispersed above no-man's-land. All around, the ground was churned and scarred, and littered with mounds of refuse. In the distance, two towers squatted on either side of an abandoned pit head, the wheels and spokes of the winding-gear black and intricate against the sky.

The bird paused to gulp down a beetle. Below the hillock where it foraged, a large crater yawned, two bodies sprawled on the lip of it, a third thrown clear. The bloodied carcase of a horse, its teeth bared to the heavens, lay on its back amid the mangled remnants of the machine it had been pulling. The starling made a short fluttering flight down the slope and waited. Nothing moved. Performing a series of airborne leaps, it arrived at the corpse furthest from the impact point: a man reclining on his side with his head resting on his arm, as though just taking a nap after a good picnic, his body unmarked apart from a missing left foot.

154

The bird bustled forward and made a tentative lunge at the spilled contents of a mess tin. Still nothing. There were a number of other objects in the mud: a pistol, half submerged; a crumpled helmet with the ace of spades — insignia of the 9th Essex – painted on it, and a silver cigarette case, engraved in one corner with the initials '*P.S*'. The starling hopped onto the man's hip and stood there, steadying itself with an occasional twitch of its tail. The breeze as it came gusting across the plain made a thin whistling sound and it ruffled the bird's feathers. A minute passed. And another. Then the guns started up again.

16

A Conversation

The *Dolphin* limped westwards. There remained just
enough coal to keep the galley stove lit for the four or five
days McGregor reckoned it would take to reach a suit-
able port (given a favourable wind), but another setback,
it was clear, would test them. The day after the storm,
Crozier overheard the skipper and the first mate talking
in the wheelhouse. Both were of the opinion they'd survived 'a shave even closer than Molasses Reef' (whatever
that had been). Harris and Doyle had earlier received a
severe dressing down for neglect of duty, namely failing
to notice the plunging barometer due to their antics with
Bridie.

The crew set about patching up what they could,
stitching sailcloth, replacing splintered yards, caulking
leaky deck seams, but the major repairs would have to
wait. Down below, in all the rooms and cabins, every
object was out of place, as though they were just parts
inside a toy that had been shaken by a rough child.

Fitzmaurice, his iguana, and the ship's dog were confined to quarters on regimens ranging from sweet tea and
blankets to full human body contact (though Crozier
curtailed the latter after a particularly invasive bout of
ear-licking). Fitzmaurice, despite calling petulantly for

his pipe (and his bowl and his fiddlers three) on the second day, a sure sign of returning health, was slow to leave his bed, preferring to smoke and write his journal, and have meals and hot drinks brought to him on a tray.

'Crozier, old man, how many "r"s in "heroic" – one or two?'

'One.'

'And "valiant"?'

'No "r"s in "valiant".'

'You know what I mean.'

'One "l".'

'What about "spunky" – "y" or "ie"?'

Crozier was standing at the porthole, which he had opened, ignoring bleats of protest, to alleviate the tobacco fumes (a fresh tin of Balkan Rumpus). An oxygenated breeze wafted off a rifle-green sea. The ship was creaking along at a tentative four knots. He could hear the sound of sawing and the tap of a mallet coming from the wheelhouse; from elsewhere, voices on the breeze. Rafferty? No. He was probably below deck somewhere with Phoebe. Spending more and more time together, it seemed. Hatching plans to save the world.

'That would be a "y".'

'Thanks. Tricky business, this writing lark.'

Crozier glanced over. Fitzmaurice was sitting up in bed, the portion of him not hidden under many blankets encased in a Savage Newell 'Alaskan Dandy' with the fur-lined hood pulled up. He hadn't shaved for several days and his frizzy beard happened to be the same colour as the fleece in the coat, giving him the look of some peculiar species of bear. He was puffing on his Meerschaum, his pen poised in the other hand, his journal propped up

157

against his knees. Restless light congregated on the wood panelling behind him.

'So I believe.'

'Yes, very hard work. Think I'll stop now. Excellent tea, by the way.'

'You're welcome. Feeling any better?'

'Slightly. Haven't had a shivering attack for a while but still a bit queer. My toes haven't thawed out completely yet and as for my head...'

'That's good. I'm sure you'll be up and about in no time.'

'I dare say. Mustn't rush these things though. I was in a tight spot back there, you know.'

'You certainly were.' Crozier turned back to his breathing hole. 'Mind you, we all were.'

'Yes, but...' Fitzmaurice broke off for a coughing fit that sounded at times not unlike the yelping of a small dog. 'Yes, but *I* nearly died.'

'You'll be dead soon enough if you don't stop sucking on that infernal pipe.'

'What? Nonsense. It's good for the tubes, keeps the airways clear. Not as healthy as cigarettes, mind you, but damned nearly. Ask Rafferty, he's a medical man.'

Crozier snorted. The bird that was dipping on the wind in the middle distance appeared to be a glaucous gull *(Larus hyperboreus)*. Or possibly a glaucous-*winged* gull *(Larus glaucescens)*. He considered fetching his field glasses.

'Crozier, old man...'

'Yes?'

'You know when people die?'

'Yes.'

'Is that the end of it, do you think?'

'Are you asking whether I believe in an afterlife?'

'Yes.'

'No, I'm afraid I don't.'

'Really? Nothing at all?'

'I can't see it.'

'Cripes, that's a bit bleak. So, have you given up on God now altogether?'

'More or less. I think, as Comte says, that humanity should be our only god.'

Fitzmaurice attempted to blow a smoke ring and choked. Out at sea the constant agitation of light on the undulating waves was mesmerising. Crozier felt for a moment outside time.

'Remind me,' Fitzmaurice said. 'Your background. Methodist?'

'Presbyterian.'

'Ah yes. The chutney-makers, right?'

'No, that's the Methodists. Presbyterians make little cakes.'

'And Catholics?'

'Scones. What about you, did you tell me your people were Quakers?'

'There's Quakerism somewhere in the family, but my side would be mostly Anglican or Church of Ireland. Don't ask me what we believe in – I never paid much attention -- something to do with the Thirty-Nine Articles I think. Or is it the Forty-Two? Twenty-seven? Not sure. I'm fairly certain we get an afterlife though, if we sing an occasional hymn and don't abuse the poor. Anyway,' he set down his pipe, 'time for a nap, I think.'

159

Crozier remained at the window. The gull, he decided, was either an Iceland *(Larus glaucoides)* or a hybrid of some kind, a mongrel. He watched it glide towards the ship, then bank and gain height until it was out of eyeshot. What were they up to, birds? This was something he often asked himself. Most people, he was sure, dismissed them as random, spindrift creatures of little brain ('bird-brained', in fact) but the more closely he observed them, the more purposeful they seemed: always on the way to some secret rendezvous – a specific tree, a nook beneath the eaves of a barn, the thatched roof of an African hut – not blown willy-nilly by the wind, but in control, harnessing it as a ship does, negotiating currents and channels to important destinations. The homing instinct – now, *there* was a mystery. Magnetism? The stars? More than anything else in the animal kingdom (even the ants), birds were *up to something*.

He thought of the larks above the bog meadow near his father's house, treading the blue air (if you searched the sky long enough, it felt as though you were falling into it) and putting their joyous, high-voltage song inside your head until you could hear nothing else. He wondered what was happening back at home. He imagined the shockwaves news of their drowning would have sent through a dozen little worlds. He wondered if they would ever see home again.

He secured the porthole and turned to leave. Fitzmaurice was snoring, head tilted back on the pillow, mouth slack. His journal had slipped close to the edge of the bed. Crozier lifted it and took it to the desk where he set it down and, with a quick glance over his shoulder, flipped it open at the latest entry.

160

A Conversation

Wendesday, 26th of April, 1916
Third day in sickbay after my heroic actions during the
storm (actually more like some terrible kind of tyfoon
or hurrocane). It was an eventfull night. First I was
awakened by noises on deck and went to find Harris &
Doyle up to no good with my igwana. Poor thing was
terrorfied! I retreeved her and warmed her up with a hot
waterbottle. (She is still sneezing but much better and has
eaten a bisciut.)

While I was tending to her an extradinairy fight broke
out between C & R who have been quarelsome for some
time now – I suspect it has something to do with Phoebie.
Anyway, using my arthority I managed to sort it out.

Then it was all hands on deck and an almightey battle
with the elements. Due to my notting skills the captin
chose me to repare a sail while the others kept warm
in the engine room. It was a valiunt effort but soon
my braverey was required elsewhere as the ships' dog
appeared and I could see the captain feared for it's life.
Just as I was about to rescue the poor creeture a huge
wave crashed over. I was soaked, concussed and close to
death but I am nothing if not a spunkey—

He closed the book.

17

Mr Rafferty Faces a Challenge

That Sunday, running before a strong wind, they sighted land – according to McGregor's calculations, the tip of Cape Farewell — and by sunset the *Dolphin* was anchored in a small bay off a trading post marked on the chart as 'The Place of Polar Bears' (Lat. 60° 08′ 19″ N, 45° 14′26″ W). At first light, the ship's launch having been lost to the storm, the bosun signalled to the harbour, and after a time two men rowed out in a longboat and began ferrying them ashore.

'Do you think there *are* polar bears around here?' Fitzmaurice said.

They were standing on a rocky outcrop on the western side of the port, looking across at the town, a grim configuration of stone houses and rudimentary streets in the shadow of a vast mountain range. Danish flags flew from several of the larger buildings. To the rear, on open ground before the onset of dense pine forest, was a settlement of flat-roofed sod huts where figures clad in silvery seal skin – 'blubber-munching squawmucks' in McGregor's estimation – were up early and hard at work.

'More than likely,' Crozier replied. 'Though I'd say it depends on the time of year, where the ice floes are, and so on.'

'And what time of year would that be?'

'Probably around now.'

'Oh that's just... splendid.'

'I read somewhere,' Rafferty said, 'that their first instinct in attack is to claw the top of your head. Often this results in your scalp being ripped off.'

'Who?'

'Polar bears. Sometimes, apparently, your whole face comes off.'

They digested this information.

'That would definitely put you at a disadvantage.'

Behind them, a wooden church was under construction, nearly completed except for parts of the roof and the top of the bell tower. Piles of bricks, tiles, planks and loose timbers lay around. To one side was a small corrugated tin hut, and at that moment the door squeaked open and a bleary face squinted into the morning sun. They waved but the man just yawned, rubbed his eyes and withdrew.

Rafferty turned to Crozier. 'Nightwatchman?'

'I suppose so. Though I can't imagine there's much crime. The Danes are known for running a tight ship.'

'Bloody imperialists.'

'Speaking of tight ships, is that McGregor?'

At some distance below them a stocky figure was scrambling up the steps from the harbour.

'Crikey,' Fitzmaurice exclaimed. 'I've never seen him on dry land before. He looks much shorter than he does at sea.'

'And twice as ugly.'

'Don't be cruel,' Phoebe said.

The skipper arrived, moustache flapping, on the mount

and lit a Navy Cut. It was a minute or two before he was able to speak.

'I'll tell yis what,' he wheezed. 'That's goin' tae be one fit f—ing congregation.'

The others agreed. He surveyed the building site.

'I'm tae see a wee man about timber for the mast – is he in there?'

He started towards the hut, then swung round and pointed at Rafferty.

'By the way, the first mate needs an operation on his finger. The doctor's upcountry so you'll have tae do it.'

'*What?*'

'Aye, that dirty f—ing lizard has it swole up like a Stornoway black puddin'. I could be wrong but I reckon it'll have tae come off.'

'Now, wait a minute,' Rafferty began, his eyes bulging against his spectacles. 'I'm not... that's...'

But the skipper was already away and hammering on the tin door.

'Don't worry, Frank, we're all behind you,' Phoebe said.

'Piece of cake.'

'I'll see if I can get the Magiflex working,' Fitzmaurice called, setting off down the hill.

News of Harris's finger spread rapidly. The Place of Polar Bears was a sleepy outpost populated mainly by whaling company workers and their families, and a handful of clerks and smalltime merchants. Apart from the occasional mauling, drama was in short supply. It was decided that the amputation, and there was no way around it given the digit's galloping deterioration, would be performed in the town's social club where the patient would have access to anaesthetic in the form of schnapps (the ship's stock of ether having perished in the tempest), and the surgeon to a stable work surface (the sea that day being choppy). By seven o'clock that evening the venue, a draughty, jerry-built hall within gagging distance of the blubber plant, was at capacity, a dozen deep on all sides, and thrumming with the kind of suppressed excitement that precedes a high-stakes sporting event.

Once he had overcome the compulsion to hide until someone else did the job, Rafferty knuckled down to a couple of hours' study of Henry Gray's *Anatomy: Descriptive and Surgical*, sharpened the tools from the ship's medical bag, rustled up saline solution and an ice pack, and steadied his nerves with a ration or two of grog. This was to be his profession, after all. More importantly, what would Phoebe think of him if he refused? The way she'd looked at him: she had seen his fear. But she had also seen beyond it. She had faith in him. This gave him strength.

As he and his team entered the hall, pushing their way past the overspill of fifty or more women and children outside, the crowd fell silent. Harris, flanked by McGregor and Doyle, was installed at a long bench at the top of the room, the table littered with evidence of his pre-op preparation. His face in the lamplight had a septicaemic pallor and he eyed both the Magiflex – salvaged from the hot spring incident by the Reykjavik police force – and Rafferty's instrument bag with bleary suspicion.

'You're early,' McGregor said as they approached. 'Patient requires another half bottle. At least.'

'That's fine,' Rafferty replied. 'I'm really in no hurry.'

'Will yis join us?'

'Don't mind if we do,' Crozier and Phoebe said in unison.

They took their places at the table and drinks were poured. The hubbub resumed. Curious onlookers began to accumulate around the Magiflex, which Fitzmaurice was affixing, with the usual grunts of exertion, to its tripod.

'Well, cheers.' Crozier raised his glass. 'Here's to a successful operation. Although we should perhaps bear in mind that Rafferty is a *student* of medicine rather than a qualified doctor.'

They drank the harsh spirit. Harris, who was not his usual convivial self, motioned sullenly for a refill.

'How's the hand now?' Phoebe enquired, and received a baleful stare in reply. The body part in question, resting on a cloth, was twice its normal size and the colour of a pomegranate, the doomed, sausage-like pinkie sticking out at a blunt angle.

'Serves him f—ing right,' McGregor snorted. 'Shouldn'ae been messin' with a wild animal in the first place.'

Harris lifted his head as though about to speak, but didn't. Reflexively, Doyle's fingertips sought the bald strip where his eyebrow had once been.

'Right, big smiles everyone.' Fitzmaurice held the flash tray aloft. 'Harris, if you could just raise your hand a little...'

The magnesium powder ignited with a crackle, there was a modest explosion (Fitzmaurice had learned his lesson) and every detail of every object and face in the hall was briefly illuminated as though by lightning, eliciting

166

a slaves' chorus of swearing, and universal eye rubbing.

'Perfect,' Fitzmaurice said, when he himself was able to see again. 'And we'll take another one afterwards.'

They drank on, McGregor having grossly underestimated Harris's dosage. Later in the evening, whether out of generosity or a desire to accelerate the proceedings, a group of whale flensers at the back of the room sent over a bottle of the super-strength liquor they were allocated on account of the unpleasant nature of their job. This did the trick. Gradually, Harris's head drooped until his chin met his chest, jerking up once, twice, and then remaining there.

With the help of a couple of enthusiastic locals, the table-top was cleared and the comatose Harris laid full stretch. Extra lamps were brought, and Rafferty set out his tools. With a jigger of the flensers' firewater, he sterilised Harris's hand – the patient twitched and gave a faint moan – then wiped down the scalpel and the saw and donned his surgical gloves. Phoebe, wearing a bandage as a face mask, was to assist.

'*Digitus minimus manus,*' Rafferty muttered to himself, as though incanting a spell.

The crowd craned in.

'Please,' he said, 'I must have room to work.'

'Yis heard what the doctor said,' McGregor shouted. 'Now f—k off!'

The crowd shrank back. Due to numbers and alcoholic thermogenesis the hall had become oppressively hot. Rafferty probed the tense surface of Harris's mitt with the tip of his knife.

'It is my opinion that I should sever the finger just below the metacarpophalangeal joint,' he announced.

167

A knowledgeable murmur travelled around the room (despite the fact that few spoke any English) and the crowd craned in again.

'I then intend to disarticulate the distal phalanx…'

Head-nodding along the front row.

'… remove the flail segment of the *proximal* phalanx…'

Chin-cupping and frowning.

'… thus preserving breadth of palm…'

Renewed head-nodding.

'…smooth the residual bone using a rongeur and file and, finally, seal the wound with a volar skin flap.'

Some clapping broke out but was quickly glared down by McGregor. Rafferty checked the edge of his blade and leaned in. The crowd shuffled forward a couple of inches. The surgeon took a deep breath and made his first incision, releasing a high-pressure jet of fluid that blinded several onlookers. The crowd sprang back.

'Should have anticipated that. Nurse, I mean Phoebe, if you wouldn't mind wiping my forehead. And my hair.'

The discharge drained, Rafferty completed the cut around the circumference of Harris's finger and took up the metacarpal saw. The crowd edged closer again.

'Flexor digitorum profundus,' he said to himself, then to Phoebe: 'Could you open the book at page three hundred and sixty-seven please, I need to consult.'

Phoebe took Gray's *Anatomy* from the medical bag, located the page and held it up.

'Yes, that's what I thought. Now I need you to elevate Harris's hand and keep it very still. That's crucial.'

In the bated silence the motion of the saw made a rasping sound that had every last whale-hacker and seal-clubber in the hall sucking their teeth and dancing on the tips of their toes. It was harder work than Rafferty expected, requiring two perspiration breaks, but finally the saw encountered no further resistance and the finger came free, suddenly and strangely light in his grasp. Elated, he waggled the appendage above his head. A cheer went up. He passed the dripping object to Phoebe who dropped it into a glass. Then he took up the pliers and began to trim the untidy edges of the remaining bone before filing it to a smooth nub.

'Now,' he mused, threading a length of catgut, 'what kind of stitch?'

A speculative buzz started up.

'Blanket?' Phoebe suggested. 'Or a hemming stitch?'

'Chain?' McGregor ventured.

'Actually,' Rafferty said, 'I missed the stitching class. Phoebe, would you mind doing the honours?'

They switched positions. Phoebe pulled the residual skin flaps together like the mouth of a purse and secured them, her tongue protruding, with a crossed buttonhole stitch that drew many clicks and nods of appreciation.

'There,' she said. 'All done.'

Rafferty inspected the stump, gave it a final douse of schnapps, and declared the operation a success. Thunderous applause broke out.

'Right, everyone in the picture,' Fitzmaurice cried. 'And *please* ... try to keep your eyes open this time.'

18

The Icebergs

A shout came from high in the rigging. It was the cabin boy. Crozier set down the breakfast dish he had been drying and hurried up to see what was happening. Rafferty and Phoebe were already at the starboard rail. Phoebe pointed. A line of white peaks loomed in front of them like jagged clouds rising from the water. They had seen icebergs before but much smaller and only in ones and twos. These were of a different order, some of them soaring to two and three hundred feet. McGregor was nearby, binoculars in hand, calling out instructions while Doyle and the twins hauled on ropes, adjusting their trajectory. As they progressed, the titanic scale of the formations became clear, their frozen spires, cambered and chamfered by the wind, towering over the ship, their high, winnowed archways like cathedral vaults.

At closer range the things revealed themselves not to be wholly white: here and there, where interior flaws were most stressed or where huge sheets had fractured and sheared off, they were striped with green and glacial turquoise. Smaller bergs, some as big as trams, many of them eroded into strange, contorted shapes, drifted in the avenues.

The *Dolphin's* engine was shut down for fear of

damaging the propeller and the vessel slowed almost to a walking pace, running on the fore topsail alone. But for the low groaning and creaking of ice, and the occasional bird cry, all was quiet. McGregor, leaning out over the rail, signalled by hand back to the wheelhouse and, gradually, they picked their way among the dazzling giants.

'Just imagine,' Crozier said, breaking the silence, 'only a tenth is visible.'

No one else spoke. They were each gripped by a sense that this field of crystal mountains, thousands of years suspended at their core, was a signpost, a boundary, a signal that they were entering another realm.

*

It had been several weeks since they had left The Place of Polar Bears and, with a stout new mast and refreshed sails, ploughed north into the Davis Strait bound for Baffin Bay. A vicious fall in temperature as they rounded the tip of Greenland had triggered urgent rummagings among the Savage Newell supplies, with the result that all onboard were now bulkier and slower moving. Even Bunion had finally been forced to wear the tartan waistcoat packed for him by the skipper's wife.

Harris took some time to recover, first, from the grisly aftermath of the flenser schnapps, and thereafter from the residual infection in his hand, which brought him to a point of fever so high Rafferty feared it might engulf him. At last, after a week of more or less continuous sleep, the first mate emerged, pale and shaky but with a ravening hunger, and was pronounced cured.

So successful had the surgery been that Rafferty was viewed with new and wondering respect by the rest of the crew and it wasn't long before they began to make their way to his cabin for consultations on various personal matters. First to show, one morning after breakfast, was Victoor, revealing a third nipple under his armpit, where it had been rubbing and chafing his entire life. With the numbing aid of a bottle of oil of cloves from the galley, Rafferty excised the rogue teat and sealed the wound with a passable cross-stitch. A quick application of O'Hara's Pine Tar Salve, and Victoor winced off back to the galley.

That afternoon, the cabin boy appeared, and after fifteen minutes of swivel-eyed mumbling, finally lifted his sweater to display a bulbous mole that all but obscured his navel. This was not quite so straightforward a procedure. Despite copious clove oil and ice there was much screaming and blood until eventually, much to the surgeon's relief, the boy passed out. As he threaded his needle, a newly confident Rafferty became infused with a sense of Hippocratic beneficence and, casting around in his mind for worthy recipients resolved, with great magnanimity, to carry out an act of mercy on the ship's dog's chin.

'I'm not sure that's such a good idea,' Phoebe said at dinner.

'Why not? The thing's an absolute sight. I swear it's getting bigger.'

'I just don't think it's fair. What are you going to do, make a dog drink a bottle of rum? Anyway, it's part of Bunion's identity.'

'Really? Do dogs have identities? As such? Crozier?'

'An interesting question.' Crozier set down his spoon. 'He responds to his name, so in one sense he *is* Bunion, but I don't believe he has sufficient self-awareness to justify the term "identity" as we understand it – that is, he doesn't look in the mirror and think to himself "I am Bunion and, you know what, I think that goitre on my chin really suits me".'

'That's because he doesn't have the necessary language. It doesn't mean he wouldn't miss his ... *is* it a goitre? Or a canker?'

'I think it's a carbuncle,' said Fitzmaurice.

'It's not a carbuncle, it's just a huge wart,' Rafferty slapped the table. 'And it's coming off.'

His crusading zeal was soon curtailed however. The next day, as he was examining Victoor's nipple under the microscope in Fitzmaurice's cabin, there was a smart rap at the door and the room was suddenly full of huge beards and flashing Nordic teeth. 'Skål!' The twins removed their woollen caps and stood before him, nodding and grinning.

'Good morning gentlemen, and what can I do for you today?' Rafferty eased back in his chair, tapping a scalpel against his thigh.

The twins both began to speak at once, an unintelligible babble of which he could discern only repetition of the word *doktor* and something else that may have been *dingle*. Perceiving after a while his incomprehension, the pair began pounding on their chests, pointing at him, and making snipping motions with their first and second fingers.

'I see. There's something that needs to be removed, is that it? *Snip snip?*'

'Ja, ja. *Sneep sneep*. Ja.'

'I thought as much.'

The twins continued to smile and nod.

'Well?' Rafferty made a wafting gesture with his hand. 'Which one of you?'

Puzzlement. They both slapped their chests again.

'*Both* of you?'

'Ja, ja.'

Rafferty's eyes narrowed and the scalpel ceased its tapping. He sat up.

'Right-so. I suppose we'd better have a look.'

Exchanging glances, the twins turned to face the door, then, with a sudden synchronised swoosh of oilskin, dropped their trousers and bent over to within touching distance of their toes.

'Oh Holy Mother of God,' said Rafferty.

They crossed the Arctic Circle (Lat. 66° 33′ 44″ N), at mid-morning on the 24th of May, marking the occasion with beakers of rum on deck. Shortly after, the sea became noticeably soupy and they had their first sight of pack ice: a vast jigsaw of white scruff stretching for many leagues to the northwest. Changing course in order to skirt it, McGregor began to fret that they were too early in the year, that there had been insufficient meltage, and that the voyage was futile.

'We've only a couple of months tae get in and out,' he grumbled. 'Once the big freeze starts again we'll be caught like rats in a f—ing trap.'

His mood infected everyone on the ship. Except for Fitzmaurice.

'*Fortitudine vincimus*, gentlemen,' he chirped. 'As my Uncle Ernest always says: by endurance, we conquer.'

Their next port of call was a trading depot on one of the

Whalefish Islands at the edge of Disko Bay, where they replenished their stocks of coal, taking on an additional twenty tons which they stored on deck. This brought their total to ninety-five tons, enough for nearly fifty days of steaming, used wisely.

Uncertain of both voyage duration and the supply opportunities ahead, they also purchased the last of their bulk provisions. These included ninety pounds each of salt-cod, caribou, ox, and whale suet, and forty pounds each of smoked ham, smoked herring, lump sugar, salt, flour and oatmeal. As well as extra coffee, tea, tobacco and jam, they stowed crystallised fruit, thirty gallons of rum, fifteen gallons of Rose's lime juice and ten gallons of vinegar, along with a flitch of dried narwhal for Bunion. Much to his surprise, Rafferty found medical supplies that had been out of stock at The Place of Polar Bears, including small quantities of sulphate zinc and cocaine, opium tablets, ether and chloroform, linseed poultices and various ointments and compounds, among them quinine, bromide and a vegetal laxative with 'caution' stamped in red letters across its label.

From the cheerful Dane in charge of the stores they learned that a whaler tracking bowheads along the coast had returned the previous week and reported that the ice was loose as far as the 75th parallel – news that came as a relief to McGregor as it greatly increased their prospects of reaching the Northwest Passage, some four hundred miles above them, by the end of the month.

Further good fortune materialised just as they were preparing to weigh anchor. A group of Inuit rowed out to them in kayaks with fresh goods to trade, and in exchange for knives, fish-hooks and brightly-coloured handkerchiefs brought for the purpose, handed over a dozen eider ducks and their eggs, four sacks of seal-meat and a haunch of something that, judging from the fearsome face-pulling and air-clawing, was probably polar bear.

'Are they Eskimos or Inuits?' Rafferty wanted to know as Victoor brought the dumb-show of commerce to a close.

'As far as I understand it,' Phoebe said, 'we say "Eskimos" but they call themselves "Inuit", with a single "Inuit" being an "Inuk". The word "Eskimo" just means "raw meat-eater".'

'Squawmucks,' McGregor muttered. 'Blubber-munchers.'

'You should have some respect. I'd like to see *you* survive here all year round.'

McGregor initiated one of his terrifying throat clearances, the resultant projectile landing with a loud splash. Three weather-burned faces jerked up in alarm.

'I'd like to see yon boys survive one f—ing week in the Gorbals,' he growled.

In the days that followed, the *Dolphin* made smart progress under sail through long swathes of open water, keeping to the eastern side of the bay, even though it was a longer route, in order to avoid the immense central ice field. Wildlife was in abundance, with many sightings of narwhals, walruses, seals, and beluga whales, the latter in particular showing great curiosity about the ship, their blunt white heads appearing to sniff the air as they surfaced. Announcing their arrival with jets of water blasted high in the air, the huge creatures would bob around in groups of up to a dozen calling to each other with incongruous, strangely bird-like whistling sounds. ('I could have sworn I was listening to a cloud of blackbirds,' Crozier exclaimed on first hearing them.)

The narwhals too were a source of wonder, the males clustering along the edges of floes clashing their long, spindly tusks together like bands of musketeers. Herds of seals, numbering into the high hundreds, passed them on several days heading north, and both the skipper and the cook were encouraged by their profusion. 'We could be needing a few of those wee buggers soon enough,' McGregor said, though he had struggled more than most with the cook's seal experiments to date, the meat being viciously fishy.

Of birdlife, Crozier listed in his notebook: skuas, Arctic terns, black guillemots *(Cepphus grylle)*, Brunnich's guillemots *(Uria lomvia)*, fulmars *(Fulmarus glacialis)*, little auks *(Alle alle)* and the usual gull suspects. One evening, loitering on deck before dinner, he witnessed a snowy owl *(Bubo scandiacus)* skim the ice to port and snatch a guillemot from a strip of open water before wheeling east with its victim flapping and protesting beneath it. *'Most surprising,'* he wrote. *'One would have thought, given their nature, that these predators would not venture beyond the tundra at these latitudes. (NB: report sighting to School of Zoology on return.)'*

The pack, after they passed through the field of giant icebergs, became thicker and more extensive and they had to take more care, having travelled for the best part of one day into a dead-end, in picking their leads. As they worked their way along the edge of Melville Bay, they settled on conning the ship from the crow's nest, with the fore-sail reefed for a clear view. This afforded them some warning of impenetrable stretches and enabled them at times to plot the course in advance. Watch was taken in turn by Harris, Doyle, and the cabin boy, with orders being called down to the wheelhouse and a wire running down to a bell in the engine room where one or other of the twins was on stoking duty. Where the ship became stuck fast they used steam power to reverse, then, under full sail and with engines at high pressure, rammed the ice repeatedly. The *Dolphin's* bows would rise and chunks of ice would buckle and tumble to either side, and eventually a lead would open up. It was laborious work and sometimes they spent whole days thrashing around, going nowhere.

Where the pack had broken up and was freezing over again 'frost-smoke' gushed from the surface and formed cumulus clouds, giving the impression at times that the *Dolphin* was sailing through the sky. The quality of light as they moved north also changed, the ice-haze in the atmosphere causing many distortions and mirages: double suns, land where there was none, icebergs and islands hovering in mid-air. At one stage Doyle was convinced he could see, far in the distance, the flat top of Ben Bulben, his native county's most distinctive mountain. Another day, McGregor was spooked by a ship following in their wake, a black-sailed schooner, that had evaporated by the time the field glasses were located. As it wasn't long until the summer solstice there was, after a while, barring heavy cloud cover, almost continuous sunlight, a phenomenon that soon began to blur the boundary between wakefulness and dreaming aboard the *Dolphin*.

19

A Wild Encounter

They entered Lancaster Sound (Lat. 74° 13' 0" N, 84°), the eastern entrance to the Northwest Passage, on the 27th of June, having found a channel of open water that led them the last hundred miles across the top of the central ice pack. Almost immediately, the weather took a turn for the worse, a northeasterly gale driving sleet and snow against them with such force that McGregor gave the order to reef the top sails. Within an hour the bow was encased in ice and they had no choice but to heave to for the rest of the day. Huddled around the mess hearth drinking cocoa made with condensed milk and rum, all agreed it was the coldest any of them had ever known.

'When I was up on deck earlier the moisture in my eyes actually started to freeze,' Rafferty said. 'It was agony.'

'I know,' Fitzmaurice moaned. 'I think I might be coming down with ice blink.'

Crozier thought about correcting him but left it. He wondered how far the temperature had fallen. He'd had his first encounter with real cold when he was seven, the severe winter of nineteen hundred and four. His father had taken him sledging in the hills and over the course of the afternoon his boots had filled with snow. He had ignored the discomfort because he was having fun, but by dusk the magnitude of pain was astonishing and by the time they arrived home he fully understood the meaning of the phrase 'frozen to the bone'. It was a week before he had felt properly warm again.

'How many layers are you wearing?' Phoebe asked.

'Five,' Rafferty said. 'And this coat.'

'Six,' Crozier said.

'Seven including my pyjamas.' Fitzmaurice held up his tin mug. 'Would there be a drop more?'

McGregor entered, his eyelashes white, his moustache a fringe of tinkling icicles. He glared around.

'Just wondering what the temperature is?' Crozier enquired.

McGregor removed a glove and lifted the jug Fitzmaurice had just emptied. He grimaced and set it down again. He headed for the door.

'No f—ing idea. Thermometer's f—ing frozen.'

In the early hours the wind began to moderate and by mid-morning the day was bright, with brilliant white clouds huge against the purest cobalt. The ice was drifting against them, in the direction of Baffin Bay, and they progressed with caution through loose pack and scattered fields of small bergs. On the chart, the Sound, which was free of islands and offshore shoals, averaged around forty miles in width but at times land seemed barely a league away and at others a hundred. A range of mountains, some of them a couple of thousand feet high, sparkled along the length of the southern side.

Crozier, taking a turn in the crow's nest that night while Harris slept, marvelled at the fiery gold of the peaks in the rays of a sun that did not set. The icebergs too glittered with many hues as the light changed: lime, indigo, crimson; whilst the vast mosaic of ice and water reflected the shimmer of the sky all the way to the far mirage of the horizon. There was an unearthly stillness at this hour that defied explanation. Why, he asked himself, should there be a difference when there was perpetual daylight? But there *was*: like a withdrawal, an intake of breath. Gazing out across the silent, gleaming tracts of ice, listening to the groans of the paralysed ocean – the scale of it, the majestic indifference – Crozier wondered if he'd ever felt more alive.

The next day they followed a lead that took them close to the northern shore. Here, the floes were thick with seals and the pools on top of the pack full of little auks. From the cliffs, colonies of eider duck fished for urchins and scallops. There were several bowhead sightings, and McGregor speculated that there might be whaling ships in the vicinity.

Around noon, as they were pushing back towards the centre of the Sound, conditions deteriorated, with strong winds churning up a heavy cross-sea and obliging them to hook on to a stable floe. Snow squalls arrived then, intensifying through the night, and by morning they were stuck fast, with the lead behind them closed over and no leeway even to attempt splitting the ice under steam power. There was nothing for it, the skipper said, but to sit it out.

In the afternoon, keen to observe the wildlife at closer quarters, Crozier proposed an expedition onto the pack ice, an idea the other three took up enthusiastically after the long spell of confinement. After an extended rummage in the Savage Newell hampers they descended the

181

ship's ladder and stood stamping the crusty ground in their walking boots. Doyle, armed with a rifle, joined them, followed by the cabin boy. A few minutes later a sledge, to transport the Magiflex and any game Doyle might bag, landed with a thump beside them in the snow. At the last minute it was decided that Bunion would benefit from some Husky-style exercise and he was lowered down in a rope cradle, his stumpy legs waving beetle-like in the air. On his release he immediately hopped onto the sledge and refused to get off. With a sigh, the cabin boy took up the reins.

The sky had cleared and the expanse before them sparkled under a halo-wreathed sun: 'God, it's bright.' Crozier shielded his eyes. 'I hope we don't go snow-blind.'

'This is definitely not going to help my ice blink,' Fitzmaurice said, wriggling onto his newly-acquired shooting stick.

'Ah, I nearly forgot.' Rafferty pulled from his pocket a tangle of metal-framed goggles fitted with glass of various colours. 'I found these in one of the trunks. Apparently they're experimental models. Our sponsors would like a report on them.'

He handed them round, retaining the red lenses for himself. After a brief tussle with Phoebe over the blue ones, Fitzmaurice settled for yellow, while Crozier took green. There was a brown pair left over but neither Doyle nor the cabin boy was interested so Phoebe attached them to the ship's dog, who seemed pleased enough.

To the east and west, immense floes had collided and ridden up over each other forming uninviting ridges, but to the north the pack was smooth and flat for several miles, culminating in a belt of hills or icebergs in front of which appeared to be a dark stretch of open water. It was towards this that the party headed. After a few hundred yards they came to a crack in the ice that extended a long way in either direction. It was no more than a couple of feet in width but it required them to manhandle the sledge over the gap, Bunion sitting high and sniffing the breeze like some bug-eyed sultan on an imperial litter.

As seemed to be the case of late, distance was deceptive, the walk being much further than they had anticipated. After a couple of hours they stopped to eat some biscuit and smoked ham, and to rest the cabin boy. Crozier scanned the horizon for birds. He was itching to see something rare — a grey phalarope (*Phalaropus fulicarius*) say, or a willow ptarmigan *(Lagopus lagopus)*. So far it was just the usual guillemots and terns, though sometimes it was hard to tell with the goggles on, the world, in Crozier's case, appearing as though viewed from inside a wine bottle. For Fitzmaurice the vista was one of sepia eternity, and for Phoebe of moving through a multi-dimensional sky. Rafferty's pink wonderland, meanwhile, was making him feel oddly optimistic.

They pressed on and at last arrived at the edge of the plain. Before them, across a quarter of a mile of open water, a number of large icebergs had fused together to form a continuous range, seabirds nesting in profusion along their ridges and crags. Below, on a network of ice pans connected to the main pack by a narrow causeway, hundreds of seals sprawled and lolled amid a holiday-camp cacophony of splashing and honking. As the party stood there, all of them at a loss for words, a bowhead surfaced, suddenly and massively nearby, its fountain of expelled froth reaching them as fine mist.

'Well,' Crozier turned and smiled. 'Aren't you glad you came?'

They were. It was agreed they would spend an hour before returning to the ship, so while Rafferty and Phoebe had a stroll along the water's edge, Fitzmaurice tinkered with the Magiflex, and Doyle and the cabin boy set up their fishing gear over an ice hole, watched sleepily from the sledge by Bunion. Crozier took the field glasses and ventured along the causeway as far as it was safe. The seals, unused to humans and having no reason to fear them, regarded him benignly.

Fulmars, Brunnich's, little auks, skuas and terns as expected, he wrote in his notebook, *but also a few Arctic (or Hoary) redpolls (Carduelis hornemanni), a Sabine's gull (Xema sabini) and, much to my delight, a group of phalaropes – unusual in the bird kingdom (remember to tell Phoebe) as it's the female that sports the colours and the submissive male that's left to incubate her eggs. Eiders in huge numbers, the males still in their winter plumage of black, white and olive. No sign, unfortunately, of the spectacled eider (Somateria fischeri) with its distinctive white eye patches. Large groups of snow geese overhead, and several types of seal around, including harp, bearded, and hooded.*

Fitzmaurice loaded a plate into the Magiflex. He had more or less dispensed with the instructions — it was such hard work and besides, after the hot spring incident it was fifty-fifty, he reckoned, as to whether the device would actually yield any more pictures. He slid the film holder into place *(fig. 7)*, flinched, as usual, at the pistol-crack of the springback mechanism *(fig. 8)* and cocked the shutter *(fig. 193)*. Crozier was on his way back but the other two were still some distance away so Fitzmaurice swung the camera round and took a quick study of Doyle and the cabin boy peering into their fishing hole (they were wearing Savage Newell hats so it counted).

'Group portrait,' he announced as they convened. 'With the icebergs and everything in the background. There behind the sledge. Mr Doyle, if you wouldn't mind?'

He showed the bosun how to release the shutter *(fig. 364)*, ordered the cabin boy out of shot, and took his place in the middle of the line-up. There was some jostling and bickering but finally they were ready. Bunion was woken and prodded into a sitting position.

'Mr Doyle, if you please...'

The resulting image, should it ever reach the light of day, would show four young people standing in a landscape few of their years had ever seen and that they themselves were unlikely to witness again. Of the quartet only one, the female, was smiling; the males were serious or thoughtful or distracted by bird cries; the one in the centre had his arms folded in a self-important manner. The eyes would have told more of the story but none were visible, the glass in four pairs of goggles reflecting eight dazzling snowscapes in tinted miniature. As for the pale, squat dog on the sledge, its head was in sharp profile as it stared over its left shoulder at something outside the frame.

Crozier was first to notice the sound, thinking initially that it was the creak of the current beneath the pack, but then he saw the raised hackles.

'What the hell's wrong with Bunion?'

'Wait, wait,' Fitzmaurice hissed, '...seven, eight, nine,

and… *ten*. Thank you Mr Doyle. Now, what was that?'

Bunion's growl had increased to the volume of a small engine. They turned in the direction of his gaze and gasped, more or less in unison. Bounding towards them along the causeway, head lowered and ears flattened, was a polar bear, a mature male of impressive dimensions. For a few moments they stood in shock, then Doyle sprinted for the rifle.

'No need to panic folks,' Fitzmaurice told them. 'It's that seal he's after, not us.'

A bull harp seal was dozing on the edge of the pack in a direct line between them and the approaching bear.

Phoebe looked dubious. 'I hope you're right.'

'Don't worry Phoebe, I'll protect you.' Rafferty put his arm around her but she shrugged it off.

Doyle slid the bolt of the rifle back. Bunion started to twitch. The seal, alerted by vibrations in the ice, started out of its reverie and rolled into the water in one motion. The bear, its eyes like hard black stones in compacted snow, did not falter.

'Ah,' Fitzmaurice said. 'Perhaps…'

'Might I suggest running away?' Crozier said. The creature was now no more than twenty yards from them and its intent was clear.

'Mr Doyle,' Fitzmaurice took a step back, 'you may shoot at will.'

The bosun raised the rifle, took aim and squeezed the trigger. The shot went wide. He reloaded and fired again. A splash of blood appeared on the animal's shoulder, but apart from a brief flicker of surprise it was undeterred. Again the bolt was pulled back and released. This time there was no sound. Doyle gave a cry of desperation and

186

began clawing at the firing mechanism. But it was too late.

The bear lumbered to a halt in a shower of ice crystals and, rearing up on its hind legs (the consensus later was that it topped nine feet in height), it gave a roar of such ravenous fury that each one of them felt their heart stop. The sound echoed to the edges of the plain, clearing the ice pans of seals and filling the sky with birds. The bear dropped back on all-fours and began to sway to and fro.

'If we all run in different directions it might confuse it,' Crozier murmured. He had the distinct impression he had been singled out.

'Fitz, stab it with your shooting stick, for Godsake.'

'We're done for,' Phoebe said.

The beast lifted its massive head and let out another bellow. Its teeth were startlingly large and yellow in the black interior. It shifted its weight onto its haunches, gathering itself to launch forward, but just as it was about to spring, another pale-coloured, heavy-set entity hurtled through the air and landed with a thump, four-square on the ice. Bunion! With slavering lip and corrugated snout, the ship's dog let loose a flurry of barrel-chested barking that caused the bear to rear back in surprise. It unleashed a couple of warning swipes. Bunion's guttural outrage became a continuous howl. The bear shuffled backwards, still nonplussed, but then seemed to recover itself, leaning forward with an indignant snarl and sending its opponent tumbling across the pack in a welter of legs and ears. Bunion skidded to a stop, shivered, and was still. In a moment of suspension everyone, including the bear, stared at the immobile body.

Another dog might, at this juncture, have reflected on

the terrible power behind that casual blow and called it a day. Not Bunion. He licked the blood from his muzzle and climbed to his feet, shaking his head like a punch-drunk prizefighter. Through the filter of his goggles, which had stayed in place despite the force of the slap, his adversary was a muddy blur. He flung himself forward with renewed ferocity. Again the bear was taken aback, again enraged by the smaller animal's impudence. It charged and batted, reared and jabbed, but Bunion was wise, scuttling around to nip at the hind-quarters, darting beneath to tear at the underbelly.

Round and round they went, first one way, then the other, the bear's howls of pain becoming ever more anguished, its flailings, as dizziness took hold, wilder. Only once more did it appear that Bunion might be in trouble – an uppercut that caught him under the chest and flipped him high in the air. He landed badly and had to twist from under the paw that almost trapped him. All the while, the bear was being driven back towards the edge of the pack and at last, extensively japped with crimson, it gave a yodel of frustration and plunged into the water.

'Right everyone, let's go,' Fitzmaurice shouted.

'Wait,' Phoebe said, pointing. 'Bunion.'

The ship's dog was staggering towards them, attempting to follow a straight line but tottering sideways as if inebriated. As they watched, it came to a standstill and collapsed. Doyle and Crozier rushed forward and between them managed to heave the comatose beast onto the sledge and, with the cabin boy hauling, they set off at a jog in the direction of the *Dolphin*.

After half a mile they slowed. Running on ice in many

layers of animal skin was hard work and after months at sea none of them was in peak condition. Panting, Crozier lifted the field glasses and scanned the way they had come.

'No sign,' he reported. 'With any luck he's turned his attention to the seals.'

'Thank Christ. Did you see the size of those teeth?'

'And those paws?' Phoebe said.

'I know. Have your face off in a jiffy.'

Rafferty was examining Bunion, who was still unconscious. 'Some blood coming out of his ear. When we get back to the ship I can take a closer look.'

They resumed at a walking pace. The sky had become congested and a fresh breeze was frisking out of the south, bringing a few shavings of snow. Up ahead, still several miles away, the outline of the *Dolphin* hovered on the horizon, wavering as though behind a heat haze. Fatigue, largely the after-effect of a deluge of adrenaline, was telling on the group and there was little conversation. Noticing that the cabin boy was about to drop, Doyle took the reins of the sledge. The hiss of its rails and the crunch of their boots were the only sounds in the dead silence of the bright Arctic night.

20

Land Ahoy

They had been labouring through sporadic squalls of snow for what seemed like days -- in truth little over an hour -- when Crozier spotted the bear again. At first he wasn't sure he'd seen anything more than an eddy of flakes, a ripple of white within white, but as he swung the glasses back and focused, a discrete shape melted into view and out again. A few moments later he saw it again and this time there was no mistaking what it was, or the trajectory it was following. The news was poorly received.

'On the plus side, he's still a good way off and more than likely following us by scent alone. I don't think he's seen us.'

'That's a great comfort.'

'We're only a mile from the ship,' Fitzmaurice said. '*Nil desperandum.*'

'Last one back's a sissy,' Phoebe yelled.

They quickened their pace, Fitzmaurice lending a hand with the sledge, but despite their efforts the ship never seemed to be any nearer. After a while Crozier stopped again to check on their pursuer.

'Gaining ground,' he reported.

They pounded on, the snow, which had turned icy,

sticking to their goggles, narrowing their field of vision. Up ahead, the ship was a smudge, a faint watermark glimpsed through wreaths of vapour. Driving them on, through the exhaustion, was the invisible predator at their heels. Crozier was seized yet again by a sense of unreality. He remembered a dream he'd had in childhood, an encounter with an escaped lion that appeared, inexplicably, in the back garden and how shockingly *actual* the creature was in proximity and how the fear – it was a nightmare really – had paralysed him even though he'd wanted, with all his being, to run away. All these years later he still recalled the horror in that feeling of powerlessness. He was tempted to stop and take another look – there was a chance the beast may have given up – but he didn't. He knew in his heart it was still loping relentlessly in their wake.

At last they came within range of the *Dolphin*, its dark solidity eliciting a chorus of relief. Harris waved at them from the poop deck and turned away. Smoke drifted from the funnel. Victoor, they surmised, would be cooking up one of his fiendish stews. A second later their elation turned to dismay. The crack they had stepped across without a care on the outward trek had widened by some fifteen yards. They stopped dead.

'What the hell do we do now?' Rafferty said.

They stared across the shivering black water. Crozier did a sweep of the horizon.

'I see him. About a quarter of a mile away. He's heading straight for us.'

Doyle, who had been stamping his feet along the edge of the pack, suddenly dropped to his knees and began hacking at the ice with his boning knife.

'Doyle, have you lost your mind? This is no time for fishing.'

As they watched, the bosun winkled the barrel of his rifle into the hole he had made and heaved on it until there was a cracking sound. A crevice opened up. Fitzmaurice leapt forward with a cry. He plunged the point of his shooting stick into the gap and he too started tugging with all his strength. A grumbling noise came from beneath their feet.

'Quickly, get the sledge over here.'

'He's definitely spotted us now,' Crozier reported. 'Speeding up. Looks angry.'

Grunting with effort, Doyle and Fitzmaurice worked at the fissure they had made. The ice creaked and splintered. The bear was visible to the naked eye now, barrelling towards them through the swirl.

'One more heave,' Fitzmaurice shouted.

With a huge sigh of release the ice pan they were standing on – and not much more – came free of the pack and they were adrift. Everyone cheered. Doyle, using the rifle butt, and Fitzmaurice his shooting stick, began paddling the unlikely raft towards the far side. It was unwieldy and tended to rotate as it moved, but the current was with them and they were halfway across within a minute. Behind them, their pursuer reached the edge and stopped, rising up on its hind legs.

'Can those things swim?' Phoebe whispered.

'I'm afraid they're excellent swimmers,' Crozier said.

Bang on cue, the bear crashed into the water and disappeared. They reached the other side, the ice pan slamming into the bank and sticking fast. They leapt off and ran, not daring to look back. As they approached the

192

ship, closing the last fifty yards, Harris appeared, walking briskly towards them with a rifle. He passed them by. Three shots rang out.

*

The pack had loosened sufficiently the following morning for the *Dolphin* to break out under steam and they followed a long lead west, dodging through several fields of small bergs, for the best part of three days before bearing south towards the Gulf of Boothia. Crossing the Sound took them a week, but once they entered Prince Regent Inlet the going was easier. Hugging the east coast of Somerset Island, and helped by a southerly current, they crunched through two hundred miles of young ice, often under full sail.

At the start of August, as they passed Cape Nimrod on the Boothia Peninsula, conditions worsened again. Gales and heavy seas battered the ship as it navigated along narrow channels between encroaching pack ice on one side and treacherous offshore shoals on the other. Several times they were nipped between moving floes. On one occasion, so convinced was he that the *Dolphin* would be crushed, McGregor ordered boxes of provisions to be hoisted up on deck in readiness for a swift exit.

Matters were not helped by the collective insomnia afflicting everyone on board (except the cabin boy who seemed unable to wake up). Though duty rotas were adhered to, people could be found sleep-walking around the ship at all hours: haunting the mess and the galley, pacing the deck, staring luminous-eyed into the radiant night. Tempers often frayed and the antagonism between Crozier and Rafferty flared more than once.

At last they entered the latitudes where Sir Hamilton Coote's map indicated they would find the object of their voyage. Leafing through the diary itself, Crozier read, under the entry for 14th of July, 1865:

We have laid McNeill to rest on an island – unmarked on the chart – located in the open water of a bay on the western side of the Gulf, some hundred knots south of Cape Nimrod. He lies at peace under a simple cairn of stones on a mountain-top on the southern tip of the island, which we have named Prospect Island after the County Tyrone townland of his birth, a place he loved well. I shall miss him greatly, but most especially, having endured another night of Jackson's filthy hoosh, his cooking.

Farewell, gentle giant.

Having had no sight of the coast for some time it was concluded that they had entered the bay referred to by Coote, but despite laborious calculations and several days of meandering they came across nothing more substantial than smallish bergs, and the carcase of a beluga whale decomposing on an ice floe.

'It disn'ae make sense,' McGregor said. He and Harris were leaning over the chart table. 'It should be right f—ing here.' He stabbed at Coote's map. 'Islands cannae f—ing vanish.'

'Atlantis did,' Crozier said. 'And what about Hy-Brasil? That only appears every seven years.'

The skipper and the first mate stared at him for such

a long time that he backed out of the room. Later, as he shivered in the crow's nest, he began to contemplate the possibility that they would not find Prospect Island. What then? Turn and head for home? Was he ready for that? Ready to re-enter his old life? There were moments, standing at the bow, head full of the white noise of wind and ocean, when it seemed to him they had been at sea for years. Decades. Centuries even. As though time had slipped free of its ratchet. When he thought about Dublin – the view from chambers, the cascades of cherry blossom in Front Square, the yeasty gloom of the Bailey — it was like trying to recall another lifetime, everything, himself included, just glimpses and fragments, drifting ghosts. The *Dolphin* had become their world.

He peered down through the rime-crusted rigging at the frosted decks. Far below he could see the twins tinkering with ropes, Fitzmaurice on the capstan puffing his pipe, Bunion licking himself – all oblivious. At first he had avoided watch duty, finding the exaggerated motion of the sea high on the mast nauseating, but now he had come to relish the cold cross-draughts and the sense of freedom, and to imagine, when under full sail, what it must be like to be a bird on the wing, gliding into the purity of perpetual horizon...

He turned his attention back to the interminable mosaic of the frozen sea. Fog had been lying along the starboard skyline all morning but now it was thinning, glimmers of refracted sunlight breaking through. He raised the field glasses. There was a dark smear in the clouds to the west indicating open water and he called this down to the wheelhouse. They changed course, and after a couple of hours entered a wide expanse of calm, with only the occasional floe to negotiate. For most of the day they travelled southwest, then tacked in a wide arc back to the northeast. Towards midnight, sea smoke began to billow around them, and after a while it became so thick the order was given to drop anchor.

It was late morning before there was any visibility. Crozier, his turn come round again, made his way up to the masthead. He had become adept, despite his gangly physique, at hoisting himself through the rigging (sometimes imagining he was Jack ascending the fabled beanstalk). He emerged onto the platform and straightened up. From his pocket he took a sandwich of biscuit and smoked ham saved from breakfast, chewing on it as he gazed around. The mist was on the move, dissolving here and there to reveal tracts of flinty sea.

From below he could hear the clanking of the ice anchor as it was hauled aboard. He turned a hundred and eighty degrees but in this direction fog, water and sky were one. He munched his snack, then stopped to listen: seabirds, faint, but lots of them. A colony. He tried to gauge their proximity between the breezes. Not far. Odd. They had seen very little wildlife for days, save for a scattering of terns on a floe. A bird squawked overhead and he glanced up to see the ghost of a skua float over. He shivered. The mist was damp on his face, forming scabs of thin ice. He brushed them away. His eyelashes were heavy and he wiped at them. He hadn't slept more than a couple of hours and his eyes felt gritty. In recent days the visual distortions had become more pronounced and more frequent, and it was increasingly difficult to distinguish between hallucination and mirage. What, for instance, was this dark shape looming through the sea smoke?

He tossed away the remainder of his biscuit and grasped the binoculars. Barely a knot away, steaming as though fresh from creation, was an island. Its khaki cliffs, rising hundreds of feet straight from the water, glittered with ice; birds, almost indistinguishable from the motes in his exhausted eyes, wafted in the thermals above them. The suddenness of its mass after the empty horizons of recent weeks was exhilarating, but sight of the island – so long anticipated – also brought another feeling. It took him by surprise and it was a moment before he realised what it was. It was fear. He cupped his hands to his mouth.

'Land Ahoy!'

21

And Dogs Might Fly

Prospect Island, Sir Hamilton Coote had neglected to mention, did not fling its arms wide to visitors. It took them nearly two days to find a landing spot, on the south-eastern corner: a tiny shingle beach at the foot of a steep gully between the cliffs, reachable by a long thin floe that stretched out into the bay. They anchored for the night and the next morning two sledges were dropped onto the ice followed by sheaths of heavy canvas, tent poles, climbing equipment, and enough provisions to sustain four people for a week. Fitzmaurice also insisted on taking the Magiflex, and Harris provided a rifle. At the last minute McGregor threw Bunion into the mix. ('Wee bastard's happier on dry land, and yis might need a watchdog.') This required the addition of canine rations, and while these were being organised, Fitzmaurice remembered he needed tobacco and some O'Hara's lip balm, and Crozier went back on board to fetch a couple of books. At last, they were ready.

'Don't be buggerin' about,' McGregor warned. 'Yon sea won't be long freezing up again.'

They departed, hauling their twin burdens up the slope. The going was difficult, and more than once they had to stop to secure spilled equipment, but at last they found themselves on the edge of a treeless plain of scrubby tundra streaked with snow and ice crust. A few miles to the northwest was a cluster of foothills above which towered a range of mountains, their snow-clad peaks dull beneath a sunless sky.

'I'd say our man's up there,' Fitzmaurice pointed at the nearest and smallest of the mountains. 'Do you see the little dip at the top, like on the map? If the map's right, of course.'

'I still don't understand why they had to drag him up there,' Phoebe said. 'Why didn't they just leave him on the beach?'

'Well, for one thing there isn't really a beach, as such, and for another... Actually, I have no idea.'

'Maybe they just wanted him to have a view,' Rafferty said. 'He'd been used to one all his life after all.'

They contemplated this as they gazed at the flat distance before them. Nothing moved. The air was still and breezeless. A skein of geese straggled overhead. The birds were up high, but the sound of their wingbeats was intimate in the silence.

'Nice day to go in search of death,' Phoebe murmured.

They set off across the plain, following the tracts of crunchy snow, but occasionally having to tug the sledges across patches of bare ground. Bunion sat on the one pulled by Crozier, between bags of tent poles, staring straight ahead, serious in his brown goggles. His tartan waistcoat, ripped during the polar bear encounter, had been repaired by Phoebe, who was unable to resist adding a handsome fur collar that gave him an oddly prosperous look. At lunchtime they stopped and melted ice

199

in a primus stove to make tea, and ate salt-caribou and Jacob's Cream Crackers. They had reached the foothills and the change in gradient was beginning to tell. Rafferty, gauging the forthcoming climb, glanced back at Bunion, who was gnawing on a chunk of dried narwhal.

'You know, that dog is bloody heavy, I'm damned if I'm going to haul him up there.'

Bunion's ears twitched.

'Rafferty's right,' Crozier said. 'He'll have to walk.'

Bunion ceased his chewing.

'Seems fair enough to me,' Fitzmaurice said.

They all tried to ignore the stare from behind the impenetrable lenses. It was unnerving.

Phoebe finished her tea. 'Perhaps we shouldn't be too hasty. After all, he *is* a hero. And he *is* here for our protection. He needs to conserve his strength.'

The dog scrutinised them a moment longer, then turned back to its lunch.

Rafferty lit a cigarette. 'We'll see.'

A few hours later they were nearing the top of the hill and Bunion appeared to be enjoying the vista from the back of the sledge. Rafferty, who had run out of swear words, sparkled with sweat despite the cold. He stopped to mop his face, pushing his goggles up to wipe his eyes. The hill was not particularly steep but large rocks and outcrops, and the fact that they were towing sledges, forced them to follow a meandering route. Wildlife was scarce: the odd snow bunting and ptarmigan, and once, skittering away across the slope, a short-eared hare that Bunion growled at but was too lazy to chase.

'Count yourself lucky you've got Phoebe on your side,' Rafferty told the dog. Stepping out of the reins he moved off a short distance and, standing in front of a boulder, began the process of relieving himself – always a delicate procedure at sub-zero temperatures. The others were some way above him and he watched them dragging their burden, inching along, tiny against the white radiance of the hillside. Once again he was struck by an intense consciousness, like an echoing in his head, of their peculiar situation. They were in the middle of nowhere. At the end of the earth. Looking for bones. He stared up at the sky, which was so pale as to be almost transparent, and several moments passed before he came to, jolted by a sound behind him. He turned to see the sledge, dislodged from inertia by a shift of dog haunch, set jerkily off down the slope.

'Bunion!' he shouted. He made a lunge but slipped, landing on his back and skidding several yards. Below him, the runaway vehicle was picking up speed, Bunion, apparently unfazed, still in position despite the bumpiness of the ride. From higher up Rafferty could hear the panicked yells of the others. He scrambled to his feet and took a few more sidesteps down the hill, then stopped and stared in horror. The sledge, whose pace had been restrained by its diagonal trajectory, had swerved onto a more vertiginous path and was hurtling inexorably towards the largest of the overhangs they had bypassed on the way up. It hit the hummock at peak velocity and rocketed high into the air, its contents scattering in all directions. Bunion, his shape clearly delineated against the afternoon sky, executed a series of somersaults and a final pirouette before falling out of sight, his goggles flashing once in the sun.

201

22

Bones!

Phoebe wasn't hungry. Or at least she said she wasn't. It was a protest. In fact, she was ravenous. Who wouldn't be after a day like that. But she wanted the others to know that what they had done was wrong. They should have gone back for Bunion. He couldn't possibly have survived, they said – the drop beneath the outcrop was a sheer hundred feet onto boulders and shale. But what if he *had* escaped – landed in a snow drift or snagged on a branch? And anyway, even if he *was* dead, didn't they owe him a decent burial? He *had* saved them from the polar bear after all. She watched them from the entrance of her tent and took some satisfaction from their misery. Fitzmaurice was slumped on his shooting stick, staring moodily into the distance while the other two attempted to coax a meal from the emergency rations.

The day had not gone according to plan. Not only had they lost the ship's dog, one of the sledges, and all their edible food, but establishing base camp had proved far more difficult than anticipated, hammering pegs into the iron-hard ground resulting in damaged fingers and frazzled tempers. By the time they fired up the primus it was midnight and, with the setting sun still obscured by cloud, they were working in murky twilight. The only spark of good fortune was the discovery that what they had climbed had turned out to be not a foothill but a shoulder of the mountain itself, making the following day a little easier.

'What on earth *is* this stuff?' Rafferty was saying.

'It's called "pemmican".'

'I know, but what *is* it?'

Crozier picked up the empty package and squinted at the label.

'It's "a highly sustaining food made from albumen and fibrin of beef, animal fat, and extractives of meat", if you must know.'

'...Jaysus. Is there any chocolate?'

'No.'

Below them, the plain they had traversed was in dark shadow, the edge of the island out of sight; behind them loomed the mountain, the cold blue glimmers of its muscular flanks daunting in the half-light. The wind was picking up, rattling through the canvas.

'That is truly heinous.' Fitzmaurice tossed away the remains of his hoosh. 'Time to turn in, I think.'

'Goodnight Phoebe,' they called, but she did not reply.

The next morning there were drifts of snow against the rear of the tents. The sky hung low, obscuring the mountain peaks and casting a dull mauve tint over the rest of the landscape. After a breakfast of black tea and stale crackers, they stowed the excess equipment and packed their rucksacks with the remaining rations in order to leave the sledge unencumbered, and began their trek towards the second summit. The wind in the night had been northeasterly so the slopes had been spared the worst of the precipitation, and they took it in turns to haul.

As he climbed, Crozier began to feel the effects of a broken night's sleep. At one point he had been awoken by what he thought was the howling of a dog, and then lay, rigid, convinced there was someone walking around outside the tent. Through half-closed eyes he watched shadows moving on the canvas but could not tell whether they were real, or snow flurries, or an overflow of his dreams. And so it went on until he emerged, exhausted, into the dawn.

When he arrived at the top, some hours later and after several much-needed rests, the others were sitting on a hump of rock surveying a sweep of hillocks and ridges made treacherous by layers of crusted ice. The pinnacle of the mountain was still some distance off and obscured by mist. He could see at once that there was nothing in the immediate vicinity even remotely resembling a cairn. He joined them. No one spoke. They drank meltwater and crunched biscuits. A large whitish bird soared overhead, which Crozier thought might have been a gyrfalcon *(Falco rusticolus)* but he was too tired to rummage for the field glasses.

'We'd better get cracking,' Fitzmaurice said at length. 'I don't like the look of that sky.'

Above them the clouds glowed with an opaque yellowish light. The four of them straggled off in different directions. Beyond the far edge of the summit the higher mountains ranged out of sight into the north. Crozier trudged about, kicking at likely-looking bumps and knolls, but after an hour fatigue got the better of him and he perched on a boulder, giving in to the conviction that they must have the wrong mountain. Perhaps even the wrong island. He was cold. It struck him that at home it was high summer and he tried to imagine what he might otherwise be doing: strolling on a beach in Donegal or Antrim, sunning himself on Stephen's Green, eating ice cream in Portrush; and he thought of all the other young men, many of them younger than him, fighting for their lives at the Front. He would have to go, he realised, if the war wasn't over...

He looked up. Rafferty was calling and waving from the top of a far ridge. He could see Fitzmaurice jogging back. He turned. Phoebe was a little distance away, already hurrying towards him. He waited, his heart thumping, until she caught up and they approached together. When they arrived, the other two were at the foot of the ridge beside an elongated mound that was thickly encrusted with ice. A pole had been driven into one end of it from which hung the tattered remnants of an unidentifiable flag. They stood for a while, gazing at the object of their quest. Then Phoebe broke the silence.

'Is that it?'

Fitzmaurice let out a bark of laughter.

'Of course it is,' he said. 'What in God's name else would it be?'

'No, I mean... well, isn't it a bit small?'

The mound, now that she mentioned it, was by no means, *giant*.

'Maybe he's in the foetal position,' Fitzmaurice said, deep uncertainty taking hold. 'Quick, give me a hand.'

They hacked at the ice, uncovering the bare boulders, and began to dismantle the cairn, which had been constructed in the interlocking manner of a dry-stone wall, the stones diminishing in size towards the top. For half an hour the only sound was the clack and thud of rocks hitting the ground. As they worked, the swollen sky began to give up its burden, gently at first and then more steadily, until each of them was furred in white. Eventually the cairn began to crumble and a hole appeared at one end.

'Bones! I see bones,' Fitzmaurice cried.

They kept at it, their efforts hampered by the snow which made the rocks slippery and difficult to grip. They were also obliged to stop every few minutes to wipe slush from their goggles and shake drifts from their arms and shoulders. As the afternoon wore on, visibility beyond the circle in which they worked diminished, but they were too busy to notice.

At last the grave lay open and they gazed upon the skeleton within: snowflakes were falling between the rungs of its ribcage, melting on its skull, twinkling in its eye sockets.

'I don't believe it,' Fitzmaurice exclaimed.

'Crikey.'

'Frank,' said Crozier, 'perhaps you'd give us a scientific view?'

'You're the naturalist,' Rafferty replied. 'Over to you.'

'Very well. It's big, no doubt about that. A male if I'm not mistaken, of mature years. Some signs of wear and tear but, overall, a fine example of *canis lupus familiaris*, and if I had to guess the breed...' he leaned closer, 'I'd say Husky.'

'Poo and onions!' Fitzmaurice shouted, spinning round and booting a rock into the white yonder. 'Bloody ... *arse parsley!*'

He stomped off. The others stood in contemplation of

the evidence at their feet. The skull snarled up at them, unassailable in death.

'What the bloody hell do we do now?'

'I can't believe we came all this way for a...'

Fitzmaurice returned from his tribal rage-dance.

'This can't be it,' he cried. 'We've got to keep going.'

'Fitz, it's over. It's a wild goose chase.'

'No! There must be another cairn. There has to be!'

'Hugh, we have to get back to camp. Look at the weather.'

Fitzmaurice peered around, as if noticing the snow for the first time.

'Buggering bollocks!'

*

Crozier stopped in his tracks and scraped at his goggles but it made little difference: there was nothing to see but emerald-tinted blizzard. Where were the others? The shouts he had been moving towards had ceased hours ago. Were they safely back at the tents drinking tea? Or buried under the snow?

He continued in what he hoped was a straight line but after a while the terrain became rough and boulder-strewn and, after falling over several times, he was forced into so many twists and turns that his sense of direction left him completely. Panic was beginning to build inside him and it was an effort suppressing it. He realised he was also fighting the desire to sleep and that this was a dangerous sign. When he licked some snow off his sleeve to wet his mouth it only reawakened the intense emptiness in his stomach. What he wouldn't give for a mess-tin of pemmican hoosh and mug of cocoa.

He halted again, straining to hear, but his breathing was too loud. He started forward again, struggling to free his boots in the deepening drifts. His next step was into snow so deep his foot kept going and the rest of him followed, tumbling for endless seconds into an explosion of ice crystals. Then blackness.

When he came to, his head hurt, and there was blood on his cheek. He pushed himself half onto his side. He was at the bottom of a narrow crevasse, walls of frozen rock rising sheer on either side. He gazed up at the crack of light above. It had stopped snowing, apart from the odd fluttering flake, and he could see a gash of papery sky. He tried to move his legs, but they were numb and unresponsive, so he lay back again, letting the full hopelessness of the situation unfold around him. This was it. The others, if they were still alive, would never find him here; he was injured and the cold was tightening its grip, drawing him towards its core. Crozier knew the signs. He closed his eyes: the blood-plush behind the lids was pale, the corpuscles sparking; flashing and melting, like snowflakes.

Death was coming for him.

*

A man that is born falls into a dream like a man who falls into the sea. Wreckage; a piece of planking with letters painted on it, dips and bobs on the surface of the ocean. It crests upwards with one small wave, then downwards on

208

the next, and the next. He reaches out for it but it keeps darting away, tugged by the current, always just beyond his fingertips. He is exhausted. His body is heavy. He is sinking into the slow spiral. He half wakes, suffocating, struggling to clear his lungs of water.

But he finds he is not in the sea: he is breathing air — air that is thick with the cloying stink of wet soil — and he is at the bottom of a deep trench. As his eyes adjust to the gloom he sees in front of him, embedded in the dark brown clay, the gleaming white rungs of a ladder, and he begins to climb. The rungs are slippery, and it takes all his strength to heave himself up, but at last his hands encounter flat ground, and his head emerges above the surface.

And there they are, clattering towards him out of the fog, the lines rocking from side to side: a regiment of skeletons stretching for miles behind, their ivory hands held out in silent supplication; the wind whistling through their gapped, insistent grins.

*

When Crozier next opened his eyes, the fissure above was no longer clear to the sky. The light was blocked by the looming outline of a head and shoulders, and his heart convulsed. Salvation! He blinked, trying to focus, and may even have croaked a name. The shape withdrew and for a few moments huge shadows passed back and forth. Then a face filled the gap, peering down at him. He struggled with the features, which were blurred and strangely out of proportion, but was unable to make them conform, and this dissolved the hope he had felt. There was no one there. A figment, merely, of his dying brain. His thoughts began to gutter. The face disintegrated, rearranged itself, zoomed out and in again, drew close. It examined him with great interest. With a curious detachment he realised it was smiling.

23

Strange Meeting

The room was large, and the whitewashed walls, beneath the high, dark-beamed ceiling, were splashed with sunlight. At floor-level nearby, a fire ticked in an open hearth; beyond it, the door was ajar, admitting a gentle breeze and the murmur of voices. Crozier watched fugitive wisps of woodsmoke writhe in the air above him and sought to triage facts from the fevered jumble of his mind: he had been lost in a snowstorm; he had fallen into a ravine; he had been close to extinction – now he was tucked up in a warm bed in the corner of what appeared to be an Irish country cottage. This dislocation flummoxed him to the point where he began, half seriously, to wonder whether he had passed into some kind of afterlife.

A series of images kept coming to him, in particular a dream-like fragment that was surreal yet charged with a strange clarity: a procession of giant men, a dozen or more, marching along a mountain path above a valley of lush green fields. They wore animal skins and fur hats. His view was from atop the shoulders of one of these men, and further up the line he could see the backs of his friends, each travelling in similar style. Birds wheeled above them in a cloudless blue sky; white peaks glimmered. The only sound was the rhythmic thump of

211

heavy boots and the occasional click of a scuffed pebble.

He sniffed. Cooking smells. His mouth watered. Surely not? Could it be? It *was*. The unmistakable aroma of bacon frying. His stomach writhed. Gingerly, he hoisted himself into a sitting position. His hand went to his head, which was tightly bandaged. There was a beaker of water on the table beside him and he took a sip. It was cold and sweet. He drained it, then swung his legs over the edge of the bed and slid off onto the stone floor. He noticed he was dressed in soft buckskin in the fashion of the Inuit traders. He slipped his feet into a pair of thick woollen pampooties. As he stood upright, dizziness caught him and he had to grip the table. He took a few tentative steps. He had the impression he had shrunk. There were tapestries on the walls, and here and there, large ornaments carved from wood and bone. He stopped by a shelf of leather-bound books, their spines worn smooth, and ran his finger along them: *The Arabian Nights, The Odyssey, Gulliver's Travels, The Pilgrim's Progress, A Tale of a Tub, The Tempest...* At the threshold he hesitated. Sounds of talking, laughter. Children playing? He pulled the door open, and blinked as his eyes adjusted to full daylight, then he stared in amazement.

Across a stretch of bare earth, on which chickens strutted and pecked, was a row of out-sized chalk-white cottages, the thatch on their roofs shining gold in the morning sun, smoke trickling from their chimneys. In the foreground, a group of men were talking, as men do anywhere, observing the weather, passing the time of day. Again Crozier struggled for a sense of scale, tried to gauge his own stature within the yawning dimensions of the doorframe. But there was no way around it. It was true. Each of the men stood well over eight feet tall.

To their left, was a long table at which a number of people – some of them infant-sized in comparison — were sitting down to breakfast. He slowly realised that this group included three familiar faces.

'Come on,' Fitzmaurice called. 'We've saved you some bacon.'

As if in a dream, Crozier started towards them, hens scattering before him. Some children of about his height raced past, shouting, pursued by another with a stick. An Inuit woman, of normal dimensions, crinkled her eyes at him from a doorway. The air, he noted, was warm, like a morning in late spring. As he arrived at the table he staggered a little and a young giant stood up and, taking him under the arms, lifted him onto the bench between Rafferty and a giantess with plaited hair to her waist.

'Feeling better?' Rafferty asked. 'After your eighteen-hour nap?'

Unable to form words, Crozier grunted.

'You must be hungry,' another giant said. 'Here.' He began spooning creamy scrambled eggs onto a large plate.

'Try the bacon,' Fitzmaurice produced his pipe, 'smoked reindeer. First-rate. And the soda bread. Better than your granny's.'

Crozier regarded the food piling up in front of him.

'I like your hat,' Phoebe said. He gazed at her vacantly. She leant across and stroked his hand. Her face was pale. The giantess nudged him and beamed, displaying huge, perfect teeth. He looked around the table. Everyone was smiling at him as though he were an ancient relative on the cusp of senility.

213

'Tea?' An enormous teapot loomed, blocking out the sun, and pale rose-coloured liquid gurgled into a cup. Crozier noticed that the vessels and utensils on the table came in varying sizes. 'Milk?'

He began to eat. Questions were still being addressed to him but he wasn't listening. It was the most delicious food he had ever tasted and he went at it with a ravenous, trembling hunger. Bacon, sausages, potato farls, pats of yellow butter... All were passed his way and all went swiftly into his famished interior. After a while conversation resumed, but for Crozier, it was just a faint rumble above the tumult in his mouth. Lastly, he chugged his quarter-gallon of tea, which was fragrant with unfamiliar herbs, and set the cup down. The company turned its attention back to him.

'Congratulations, Crozier old man, a heroic performance,' Fitzmaurice said. 'Now, let me introduce you. Sitting on your left, that's Aisling. This is Patrick, that's Niall, further up is Grainne and then Niamh, and beside her is Gobnait – did I get that right? My mistake. *Tara*. This fine fellow is Sean, that's his son Fergal, that lovely lady is Amaruq, and at the end there, is Eamon. Who? I beg your pardon, I mean Finn. Brian was here a minute ago but he went to fetch more milk.'

Crozier managed a weak, all-inclusive benediction. His belly placated, equilibrium was beginning to return. Around him, giants and Inuit were milling in all directions, occasionally stopping to speak to someone or other at the table. Some carried tools – scythes and hoes – others baskets of bread, fruit and vegetables. There was, in the space between the two rows of cottages, a kind of wide, truncated street, the bustling atmosphere of a marketplace.

'Finn is the eldest son, is that right? And Ossian is the youngest grandson. The children that just ran by are yours Patrick? I thought so, they have your brow. Amaruq is expecting a baby, that's why she's not eating – feeling a bit queasy. Over there on the step, that's Pinga, the lady of the house, the mighty matriarch, maker of the best scrambled eggs in the world.'

Seated in the doorway of the nearest cottage was an elderly woman puffing on a long-stemmed pipe. Beside her a great mound of turf was stacked almost to the eaves, and perched on top – Crozier started when he saw it – was a large snowy owl, white against white, its eyes glinting in the shadow of the thatch. A pet? The thought triggered a flash of memory, and he saw again, in slow-motion, Bunion's aerial farewell. McGregor was going to give them hell for that. For a moment he was back on the *Dolphin*, hearing the thwack of the sails, the scudding ocean. Fitzmaurice was still talking.

'Ah, now here's someone you *have* to meet...' Crozier turned at the sound of footsteps 'This, Walter, *this* is the man who saved you from certain death.'

Crozier blinked up at a pair of whiskey-coloured eyes set deep in a finely-lined face framed by a bushy grey beard and a shock of white hair.

'... the man whose grave you came to rob.'

24

Worlds Collide

Crozier's hand was enveloped in a firm dry palm. The giant gazed at him solicitously.

'Bernard McNeill is my name. A pleasure to meet you. How are you feeling? Did you get your breakfast?'

Crozier nodded. Speech was as yet beyond him.

'I think breakfast is my favourite meal,' the giant said. He'd retained a soft Tyrone accent. '*Bread, milk and butter are of venerable antiquity — they taste of the morning of the world*. Leigh Hunt. Do you know his work?'

Crozier shook his head.

'Listen, if you'll excuse me, we just need to sort out the duty rota,' McNeill said, 'but when I'm free, why don't I show you around?'

The others, save for the new arrivals, rose from the table. When they had departed, Crozier turned to his companions.

'These giants. Are they real or am I hallucinating? Is this a dream?'

'No, you're not dreaming, Walter,' Phoebe replied. 'They're as real as you or me.'

'But how did we get here? Where is this place?'

Rafferty related how they became separated in the blizzard, unable to find their way back to the tents, eventually giving up and lying down in the snow, and

216

how the giants appeared out of nowhere just as they were succumbing to final sleep. Having hauled Crozier out of the crevasse, they carried them all, half-dead, over the mountain to safety.

'This is where they all live. With a colony of Eskimos. Don't ask me why it isn't cold, though. That's just one of many things we don't know yet. It's all very odd.'

Crozier fingered his bandaged head.

'I don't understand. Why is McNeill..?'

'Still alive? That we don't know either. But he's promised to explain everything soon. Ah, speak of the devil.'

McNeill had reappeared.

'Come along, Walter, a stroll and a breath of fresh air will do you good. Your friends have already had a look around so it's just the two of us.'

He helped Crozier to his feet and, putting his hand on his shoulder, led him towards the opening at the end of the yard. As they approached there were sounds of commotion – a panic of beating wings and hysterical clucking — and, as if fired from a cannon, several chickens shot through the gap between the gables, leaving a squall of drifting feathers. A familiar figure shambled into view: pale, wedge head, stubby bowlegs.

'I believe you know this little fellow? Wandered in a couple of days ago in a very nasty mood.'

'Bunion?'

'An unlikely creature to be named after a famous Puritan, if you don't mind me saying.'

'Bunyan?'

The hound stopped in his tracks and stared, then diverted into the yard and sat down, baring his gnarly little teeth in a panting grin of pleasure.

217

'He seems happy to see you. You must have a way with animals. That's a good sign.'

Crozier allowed Bunion (or Bunyan – he was unsure now which) to slobber briefly on his hand as they passed. McNeill was saying something about an incident with the Husky bitches '… result in several litters. Lord only knows what the offspring will look like, but it can't be helped.'

A short distance beyond the cottages the plateau they were on fell away into the deep scoop of valley Crozier had glimpsed during his moment of consciousness some days earlier. It was even more beautiful than he remembered, its slopes a patchwork of crops and orchards divided by dry-stone walls into oblongs of varying shades of green. Far below, a glittering blue river meandered west through the centre of the basin, met on either side by fields of wheat and barley. To the east, above a forest of pine trees, a waterfall cascaded, uninterrupted, for thousands of feet down the face of one of the mountains that encircled them. Here and there, people were at work with oxen and ploughs, carts rolling along the narrow tracks between the vegetation. A light haze moistened the air, which was bird-loud, and rich with earth scents. Crozier gulped it down.

'You probably didn't expect to see a view like that at these latitudes,' the giant said. 'When I first saw this valley, Walter, I thought I'd died and gone to heaven. Of course, it was much wilder then, overgrown with brush and brambles, and in terms of food mainly just roots and berries. I brought the cereals, potatoes, appleseed, taught the locals how to cultivate them, irrigate the soil, that kind of thing. That was, it's hard to believe,' he stamped

218

his foot on the ground, 'fifty-one years ago.'

Crozier found his voice.

'But aren't you supposed to be, I mean, we thought you were...'

'Dead?' He smiled. 'By rights I should be – I'm told my kind don't generally pass the age of thirty – but as you can see I'm in robust health. People tend to live a long time here. Makoktok, for example,' he turned and pointed at a nearby cottage, 'who lives there, she'll be be one hundred and eighty-five at her next birthday. My wife Pinga, her mother lived well into her second century.'

'Extraordinary. But...' Crozier trailed off again.

'All in good time, Walter, I'm sure you have plenty of questions. By the way, here's one for you, I forgot to ask the others, how did you find this place at all?'

Crozier struggled to focus.

'Your friend, Sir Hamilton,' he said. 'In his journal he made a sketch of the island and gave approximate coordinates.'

'Did he indeed?' The giant chuckled. 'Silly old Coote. Still, you're the first outsiders to make it this far. Apart from me, of course.'

They moved on. To the right, at the top of an incline, set apart, were two larger constructions, one of them a schoolhouse, the other a circular building of varicoloured stone with a flat roof and an elaborate entranceway above a set of steps.

'Is that the church?'

'No, it's not a church. There's no religion here. That's where we tell stories and read books to each other. Most evenings, in fact.'

'No religion?'

219

The giant made a face.

'Not as such. Some customs and rituals, mainly to placate the souls of the animals we eat, but it just doesn't seem... relevant. Not when you have imagination.'

'Some might say you need to put limits on imagination.'

'I know. And isn't that a terrible thing?'

Crozier fell silent, then, 'Do you have *many* books?'

'Only the dozen or so I brought from Coote's ship,' McNeill stroked his beard, 'but luckily they're good ones and have borne re-reading. We're half way through *Gulliver's Travels* again at the moment. You know, it must be about the fiftieth time, but it still gets a laugh... Come on, let me show you my new wine press, I'm very pleased with it.'

They made their way through a throng of children (of vastly differing statures – 'but they're all treated equally') across a manicured patch of green and down a slope into a large vineyard laid out in rows from south to north, the bushes heavy with fruit.

'How on earth did grapes come to be here?' Crozier said. McNeill made a theatrical gesture, raising his hands to the sky.

'A gift from above.'

'You mean...?'

'Yes. The birds have bestowed many little blessings on us. But this is the one for which I thank them most.'

They arrived at a long wooden barn and the giant swung open the door, releasing a waft of fermented sweetness. Inside, moving between broad stripes of sunshine, people were at work, stirring and tamping, rolling barrels around. In the centre of the floor was a huge

220

basket-shaped receptacle made of thick planks. Hanging over it, suspended by ropes and pulleys, was a heavy stone disk.

'Well, what do you think? Isn't she a beauty?'

'Certainly is.'

The giant became animated over the technical details.

'Should speed up production no end. Ah, thank you, Tonraq.' A beaming Inuk had arrived bearing two beakers of golden wine, one of them bowl-sized.

'Isn't a bit early in the day? Thank you.'

'Someone has to try the latest vintage. To your health – *this is life eternal*, as the man said.'

The wine was like no other Crozier had ever tasted. It sang in his mouth. It delighted his throat. It warmed him from head to toe. It seemed, instantaneously, to enhance the quality of his vision, making the sunlight and everything touched by it, more vivid.

'Well, what do you think?'

'Delicious.'

'The spirit is strong in those particular vines, but I think perhaps another month. Now, wait till you try this one. Good man, Tonraq...'

*

'... *But this I conceived was to be the least of my misfortunes; for, as human creatures are observed to be more savage and cruel in proportion to their bulk, what could I expect but to be a morsel in the mouth of the first among these enormous barbarians that should happen to seize me?*'

221

Grainne, whose eyes were unmistakably of the same cut as her father's, paused while the laughter died away. She continued: '*Undoubtedly philosophers are in the right when they tell us that nothing is great or little otherwise than by comparison.*'

Applause broke out.

'And I think we'll leave Mr Gulliver there for this evening,' she said with a smile, closing the book and stepping away from the lectern. The audience rose, still clapping, and began to disperse, some lingering in knots to chat. McNeill, seated at the front with his guests, stifled a yawn and stood up.

'I've had a long day,' he announced. 'So, if you'll excuse me, I'm going to retire.'

There was some protest.

'We were rather hoping,' Fitzmaurice said, 'that you might relate how you came to be here, and answer some of our questions. You said you would.'

'Did I?' The giant ran an enormous hand over his huge face.

'You promised,' Phoebe said. 'After all, we've told *you* a great deal.'

'Oh well, in that case, let's make ourselves more comfortable.'

He led them to the back of the hall and into a room where an old Inuk sat at a desk reading by lamplight. The man glanced up as they entered but did not speak.

'That's Injuquaq,' McNeill explained. 'One of our memorisers. He spends his time learning the books off by heart. Just in case.'

At the far end of the room were a number of chairs of various sizes and designs, and McNeill settled himself

222

in the largest of them. A low fire crackled in the nearby hearth providing the only other source of light, for there were no windows. The walls, below the level at which they disappeared into the darkness of the rafters, were rich with tapestries, the floor thick with rugs. The giant sat in silence for a while.

'I suppose I may as well begin at the beginning,' he said at last. 'Most stories do, after all.'

'Quite so,' Phoebe said.

'Very well then.'

He leaned back, spreading his knees wide as he gazed into the flames.

25

A Tale Within a Tale

'I was born, the last of six children, on a small farm in the northwestern corner of the county of Tyrone, in the early hours of the tenth of March, in the year eighteen hundred and thirty-eight. It was the tail-end of the worst winter for decades, snow as high as a man for a month, then a false spring, then the blizzards back with a vengeance. The night my mother laboured with me, my father was out in the fields pulling perished lambs out of the drifts; Easter was a lean affair that year. Our neighbour's son, who was helping him, lost three fingers to frostbite and my father was lucky, they said, not to lose his nose.

'It was a long and difficult birth, and my mother was a whisker from death by the end of it, but, to all appearances, I was a normal, healthy baby. There was nothing about me to hint at the extraordinary life that lay ahead. And nothing, indeed, for the best part of my childhood – an idyllic time, I can't deny it, lived between hedgerow and river, without a care in the world.

'But then, when I turned nine, it all changed. I began to suffer terrible headaches, sometimes for weeks on end. My limbs ached constantly. And I began to grow. Very rapidly. Within a year I was bigger than everyone in the family. At the age of twelve I was six feet six inches tall and had to have my shoes made specially for me. By my fourteenth birthday I stood well over seven feet and was too big for school. Luckily I had already learned to read and write. My father built an extra-long bed for me in the barn and from then on I spent my days helping out on the farm. I was strong, ' he held a fist in the air, 'like Goliath. I could do the work of three men. And I did, and I enjoyed the outdoor life, but I found myself drawn also to the kitchen, or, perhaps more accurately, to where my mother happened to be, for it was my impression, rightly or wrongly, that growing so large, so fast, I had missed out on the physical affection shown to other children. It was *her* attention that I craved, my father being a some-what austere man. Of course, to be with her, I had to make myself useful – a farm is a busy place – so, I learned to work with food.

'My mother was a marvellous teacher, and one of the most instinctive cooks I ever met. She had only basic ingredients but she understood how to use them, how to – it sounds almost foolishly elementary to say it — *make them taste good*. My love of food, and the excitement I still feel about the art of seasoning, the science of baking, the...' he screwed his eyes shut, 'the *alchemy* of flavour, comes from those mornings, the pair of us working side by side, the smell of scones on the griddle pan, little clouds of flour settling through the sunlight.' He lapsed into silence, a faint smile on his lips, for such a long pause that they began to suspect he may have fallen asleep. Then he continued.

'I was over eight feet by this time, and people were coming from all over the county to "see the giant". On Sunday mornings, after church, a crowd would gather at the gate, shouting and laughing. Pointing. They'd bring picnics, make an outing of it. Most of the time, I would hide in the barn, but one morning I could hold back no longer. I took up a pitchfork, burst out of the doors and ran down the lane at them, roaring like a mad man.' He threw his head back and let out a shout of laughter. 'By God, they scattered like mice! You should have seen their faces. As though they'd encountered the Devil himself.' He sighed. 'Unfortunately, that little temper tantrum was my undoing. My fame, or rather, my infamy, spread like blight. Soon people were coming from as far afield as Dublin to catch a glimpse. And not just on Sundays, it was *every* day: morning, noon and night. As time went on they grew bolder, marching up to the door, staring in through the windows, demanding that I appear. It became unbearable.

'Eventually, my parents were at their wits' end. My father sat me down – we'd been stacking bales together — and took out his pipe, very quiet, very serious. He told me it grieved them greatly, but that it was no longer possible for me to remain at home. I would have to leave. Fend for myself. I was a big boy now, he said. Hah! I was devastated, as you can imagine. I may have been large in stature but temperamentally I was little more than a child.

'Anyway, I learned that it had been arranged, through a relative, for me to join a variety troupe in Belfast, where, in return for five public appearances a week I would receive lodgings and a small wage. At first I was heartbroken at the thought of leaving the farm, but after a while the prospect of being in a big town for the first time, earning my own living, was...'

He pushed his fingers upwards through his silky hair, which glimmered white in the firelight. He cleared his throat. The whisper of a page turning came from further up the room.

'In all, including myself,' he said, 'there were ten "acts" that paraded daily across the stage of that dingy little music hall in York Street. Let's see if I can remember them – there was,' he began counting off on his fingers, 'the Bearded Lady, Baron Blue-Face, Ratboy, the Double Duchess, the Human Owl, Luigi the Legless Acrobat (how could I forget him?), Crocodile Girl, the Balloon-Headed Baby and,' he was snapping his fingers, 'oh yes, and a dwarf called Eric. Extraordinary people, and all very nice – well, apart from Eric, he had a bit of a temper – but they'd all seen better days, and admitted as much. We all rubbed along together well and helped each other out. I was particularly fond of the Crocodile Girl – Freda, her name was -- who was extremely cheerful despite her painful skin condition, and an excellent singer of ballads.

'As for the excitement of the town, I experienced very little of it. The owner of the show didn't like his *artistes* out in public, you see, he said it diminished the element of surprise for the paying customer. So we were confined to our quarters most of the time, icy rooms in a disused sanitorium near the docks. Every night, after work, we'd all gather around the furnace in the basement for warmth, and swap stories about our lives. I was the youngest so I didn't have much to tell, but the others had travelled the world and seen many strange and wonderful things.

'Sometimes, in the early hours,' he went on. 'Me and the Human Owl, a Hungarian by the name of Konrad who could turn his head through a hundred and eighty

227

degrees, would slip out and wander around the back-streets of Sailortown. Most people were drunk by that time, so they just thought they were seeing things anyway. We'd watch the ships coming in, from Liverpool and Rotterdam, the Americas, the Indies, cargoes of linen and tobacco on the quayside, convicts on their way to Van Diemen's Land and Botany Bay, the sailors staggering in and out of the bordellos. It was a far cry from where I was reared, I can tell you.

'In the centre of town, there was a hotel, the Grand Hibernian, and one morning as we made our way back there was a notice in the window: KITCHEN PORTERS REQUIRED. ACCOMMODATION PROVIDED. It had been six months since I joined the troupe and, while the others seemed to consider the way of life reasonably agreeable, or at least not as hard as it would be otherwise, I found it humiliating in the extreme. As far as I was concerned we were not performers, we were exhibits, curiosities, figures of fun for novelty-seekers. It was *infra dignitatem*. (Though I never said as much to the others, it was their bread and butter, after all.) A few days later I presented myself at the head porter's office and offered my services. He was surprised, to put it mildly, but all credit to the man, he set that aside and asked me all the questions he would have put to anyone. "Well, I can see you're strong," says he at last, "but I'm afraid we wouldn't have a bed to fit you." I replied: "Just give me a bit of floor," and that was that.'

(He paused to direct a quizzical stare at Fitzmaurice, who, seated closest to the fire, was having difficulty suppressing his yawns.)

'The Grand Hibernian was founded by linen traders

228

confident of a prosperous future for their rapidly-growing town, and was built on a lavish scale – mosaics, marble pillars, chandeliers, the lot. Most importantly, from my point of view, the ceilings were high, even in the kitchens, which were in the basement. It was a busy world below stairs, and the labour was hard: unloading fruit and vegetables at all hours, ferrying sides of meat, hauling barrels. The hotel had a reputation for food, and the dining room, which was vast, was always full, thanks to the talents of the head chef, a Frenchman by the name of Jean-Claude. His parents, fleeing the cold kiss of the guillotine in seventeen ninety-four, had taken him to London, where he was expensively schooled. Thereafter, shunning a career in banking, he had dedicated himself to cooking, working his way through the kitchens of lowly inns and taverns to become second-in-charge at Brown's of Mayfair, from where he was lured to Belfast by the Hibernian's owners. He was a Catholic, but a French one so that didn't matter. He was also a genius. Pure and simple. And so far ahead of his time that...'

The giant succumbed to another short, beard-stroking reverie.

'Sorry, I was just remembering the fragrant little shell-shaped cakes he used to make... so delicate. Where was I? Ah yes. That winter there was an outbreak of influenza and half the hotel's staff were out. One morning, I was hanging beef in the cold room and Jean-Claude called for me. He had noticed I had an interest in the goings-on of the kitchen. Did I know anything about baking? Could I make a loaf of bread? Well, I rolled up my sleeves and started kneading, and in an hour six perfect loaves, if I say so myself, were cooling on the rack. He was impressed.

"Le grand homme a les mains d'un ange," he said, slapping me on the back. I spent the rest of the week at his side and when one of the under-cooks failed to rise from his sick-bed, I took his place.

'I don't need to tell you that my life after that was transformed, but for the first time in a good way.' McNeill held his hands in the air. 'I was apprenticed to a great craftsman, to someone with sublime vision and uncommon talent, and I dedicated myself to learning everything I could from him. He had studied and absorbed the writings of his countrymen: La Varenne, Massialot, and the other one, Carême; and he used this knowledge to develop his own cuisine. Under his tutelage I mastered what he referred to as "the mother sauces": the *béchamel*, the *velouté*, the *espagnole*, the *allemande* – the four fundamental emulsions from which all others come and which, in themselves and by their variants, can elevate any vegetable or victual. This was just one of many revelations. I also learned about the applications of heat and cold, how to extract rich stocks and glazes, how to bake and fill sweet pastries, how to balance opposing flavours, and how to make food look elegant on the plate. The Frenchman was a hard taskmaster, a perfectionist – he wasn't above saying hurtful things — and it was a slow process: I worked night and day for three years, rarely leaving the hotel, but eventually, through practice and close attention, I was sufficiently skilled that he would leave me in charge when he went off on his travels, to London, Paris, Milan, all over Europe, in search of inspiration.

'Shortly after he returned from a trip to Bilbao, where he had been very excited by the local fondness for elvers,

230

he was adjusting the mother sauces for the first service when, with the words, "Une autre plaquette de beurre dans ça", he dropped dead, right there on the kitchen floor. He was not a young man, of course, and had become very portly and afflicted with gout, but nevertheless, it was a terrible shock to everyone. His funeral brought the town to a halt, the streets lined with distraught traders weeping and waving linen napkins. Or so I'm told. I stayed away. I was afraid my attendance might cause a fracas. But the rest of the kitchen staff, all wearing black aprons, marched at the head of the cortège. I believe it was quite a spectacle.' The giant sighed. He sat forward. 'Do you know, I think if I'm to finish my story I'll need refreshment. Walter, would you mind having a look in that dresser?'

26

An Unexpected Turn

Crozier located a terracotta flask, poured its contents into five cups and handed them round, (having first to nudge Fitzmaurice, who had nodded off). He gave the largest to McNeill who, even when seated, was taller than him.

'Ah, that's better. *O, for a beaker full of the warm South*, eh? To your health.' The giant drank deeply and gestured for a refill.

'So, there I was, barely twenty, and in charge of the finest kitchen in Belfast. Business was good. The town was thriving, despite the occasional donnybrook between Protestants and Catholics. It had a theatre, a railway, botanical gardens, its own newspaper. People were flocking from all over to work in its mills and factories. The merchants had money to spend, and where better than in the dining room of the Hibernian? We had the best meat and fish and an unrivalled wine cellar, and there was always something new to delight the palate.

'One evening past closing time, I was preparing dough for the following day when one of the boys appeared, sent to request my presence in the dining room. This was a rare occurrence and one that I would otherwise fend off with pleas of exhaustion or modesty, but this time, knowing there could be few remaining there, I went up.

In fact, only one table was still occupied, and by a solitary drinker, his party having said goodnight. He was a large man in a white shirt and dark waistcoat, high of forehead and florid of complexion, and with a brightness to his eye that hinted of the outdoor life. He looked me up and down, then addressed me.

"Are you the man responsible for the food?'

There was a sharpness to his tone and my mind began racing back through the evening's service. Had something slipped through? Had I missed something?

"I am, sir," I replied. "I trust all was satisfactory?"

He regarded me a while longer, and I must admit I had no clue as to what he was thinking, though I noted that he seemed to sway a little in his chair.

"Forgive me," he said. "I am a little taken aback by your…"

"Height?" says I.

"Youth," says he. "I had expected someone more experienced in charge of a kitchen of this quality. It has quite a reputation."

"I hope you weren't disappointed," I said, still braced for criticism.

"On the contrary," he replied, smiling at my nervousness. "I have to tell you, I am a well-travelled man and have dined with princes, potentates and panjandrums of all description, but what I ate at this table tonight knocked every one of those dinners into a cocked hat. It was, beyond a doubt," his words were somewhat slurred, "the finest meal I have ever eaten." And with that, his head hit the table with a bang, and he passed out, dead drunk.

'That, my friends, was my introduction to Sir Hamilton

Coote: gourmand, explorer, naturalist, scholar, mercenary, veteran of wars in Zululand and Burma, and owner, twelfth generation, of one of the finest estates in County Tipperary. A restless man (a razor without a strop, one might say), he had led expeditions to the Amazon to gather specimens of birds and insects (he discovered an unknown species of waterproof butterfly), to Mexico, in search of the Lost City of Gold (its name, unfortunately, remained unchanged), and to China where, disguised as a coolie, he spent two years attempting to steal tea plants for the East India Company.

'He had come to Belfast to check on the progress of a ship he was having built to replace his previous vessel, which had caught fire off the coast of Malabar, and while in town he ate at the Hibernian every evening. On his last night he called for me again. "I have a proposal for you," he said. "I've made no secret of my admiration for your food, and I would pay handsomely to have ready access to it. At present my house is without a cook."

'I knew what he was about to say and my head swam. I had little need of money – most of what I earned I sent to my family to help with the farm – but I was intrigued by this impulsive man and the aura of adventure and possibility that surrounded him. I was yet young, and although my employment gave me good satisfaction, my activities beyond the Hibernian's underworld were severely constrained by public curiosity. I felt a pang of guilt at the thought of leaving my co-workers, but it was fleeting. I accepted his offer.'

McNeill sipped his wine, savouring the aftertaste. In his pod of light at the end of the room, the old Inuk stirred; murmured to himself. Fitzmaurice snored gently.

'Life at Ithaca Hall suited me well,' the giant said. 'The kitchen might have been better equipped, but it was workable. More importantly, there was a mature vegetable garden, a teeming lake, and copious amounts of game (I later secured my brother a position as a keeper there). The Cootes were extremely sociable and I was kept busy with dinners and shooting parties, but there was also plenty of time for me to fish and hunt. The children of the house, a boy and a girl, had a governess and she was kind enough to help me brush up my education. Over the years, the family had built up a magnificent library and I spent many spare hours there. To commune with other minds, with great writers, in that way, to escape from the prison of the self... it was the greatest revelation of my life: literature, history, poetry, the classics: Homer, Chaucer, Milton, Shakespeare; I devoured them all.

'Meanwhile, Sir Hamilton's new ship, the *Antaeus*, a three-masted schooner of some four hundred tons, was nearing completion, and he was planning her maiden voyage. Would I, he wondered, consider accompanying him as ship's cook? He understood that, given the cramped circumstances of life at sea, this would be no light undertaking, but if I agreed, he would order modifications – opening up the galley, for instance – to make me as comfortable as possible. He valued my culinary skills but he had also come to regard me as a friend. It was a chance to see the world. How could I refuse?

'Our first expedition, under the auspices of the Royal Society, was to the banks of the River Nile where, with the assistance of a well-known scholar, Coote was to carry out a survey of the Valley of the Kings. It was a difficult voyage. A couple of days in, the second mate fell

overboard and drowned, we had a skirmish with priva-
teers, and a whirlwind near the Pillars of Hercules nearly
sank us. Cooking for fourteen people in a galley no wider
than a broom cupboard, sieving the flour for maggots
and mouse droppings, was challenging, and more than
once I regretted my decision. But, as time went on, I
adjusted to the routine and became used to the moods
and rhythms of the sea.

'After ten months in an encampment in the Theban hills,
where we endured intense heat, sandstorms, and dysentery
– and I became an expert in goat charcuterie – we retraced
our steps and set sail for home. Our expedition had taken
two years. The survey had been a success. *Topography of
the Tombs* was published the following spring and hailed
as a milestone in the study of Egyptology.'

The giant set down his cup and, with effort, stretched
out his legs.

'Central Africa was our next destination. A grand palm
house was planned for the National Botanical Gardens
in Dublin and Sir Hamilton was engaged, via a relative
on the board, to travel to the rainforest and bring back
plants to put in it. After a slow voyage – the best part of
a year – we arrived at Bagamoyo on the east coast, near
Zanzibar, assembled our equipment, hired bearers, and
began the perilous journey into the interior. There were
many adventures along the way, far too many to detail
here,' he paused, 'but for one, which I'll sketch briefly.

'We were deep in the forest, searching for a carnivo-
rous plant to complete our collection, when we came
suddenly into a clearing at the centre of which was a
brackish pool. To our utter amazement, gathered around
the edge of it, filling their water-gourds and chattering

among themselves, was a group of tiny dark-skinned men, not one of them more than three feet high. It was an extraordinary sight. But only momentary. One of our party stumbled over a log and alerted them and quick as a flash they disappeared among the trees. Coote sent two bearers in pursuit and they returned with one of the little fellows wriggling and yelling between them. He was completely naked but for a girdle of leaves around his middle, and impressively muscled despite his diminutive stature – it was all they could do to hold on to him. The poor creature was beside himself with terror, especially when he saw me, but Coote was delighted and resolved to take him home and donate him to science, saying we had "plucked something marvellous out of the mists of legend". Our captive was trussed and slung from a pole and, despite my personal misgivings, in that manner accompanied us on our journey.

'Or part of it. His friends had other ideas, although it was several days before we realised, so stealthy and invisible were their ways. Traps and snares, indistinguishable from natural hazards, hampered our progress out of the forest; two members of the party became lame from stings and punctures in their flesh; strange noises in the night spread unease among the bearers. At last we ran into an ambush, though we could not see our attackers: a rain of tiny arrows, shower after shower, like swarms of hornets until, in fear of our lives, we scattered in disarray. When we regrouped, our captive and his rescuers had vanished like steam off the river. We had not sight nor sign of them again.'

The giant sat up and looked at each of his audience in turn.

'Which brings me to the story of how *I* came to disappear.'

He motioned to Crozier, who went around again with the flagon. Rafferty, who was nearest to the fuel, tossed another lump of turf onto the fire, which seethed and flamed with a bubbling sound. Fitzmaurice mumbled in his sleep.

'Coote was much intrigued,' McNeill continued, 'as were many others in those days, by the fate of the explorer Sir John Franklin, who went missing, along with his two ships and one hundred and thirty men, in the Arctic Archipelago in eighteen forty-five. Although there were a number of search expeditions (spurred largely by the prospect of a handsome reward) only a few clues materialised. Coote wasn't satisfied. He decided to join the hunt himself. At great expense he had the *Antaeus* reinforced, insulated, and fitted with steam boilers, and assembled a crew of a dozen hardy men. I was in two minds myself – our previous outings had put us squarely in the face of mortal danger, but this... this seemed particularly foolhardy. Eventually, however, I was persuaded.

'The voyage was arduous, I need hardly tell you, and we made slow headway following Franklin's route, passing several months at various junctures trapped in the ice. When we rounded Somerset Island we found Peel Sound locked solid. Utterly impassable. But rather than abandon the expedition, Coote proposed that we should instead navigate south through the Gulf of Boothia and cross the peninsula towards King William Island, Franklin's last known whereabouts, on foot. This plan did not go down well with the men, but Coote was adamant.

'The Gulf proved hazardous, and we couldn't even

get near the coast, so extensive was the ice. Finally, we were nipped again and it seemed all was lost. Food was running low and even the seals had become scarce. One day, while out hunting on the pack, the mist cleared and the men had sight of an island – *this island* – not marked on any of our charts. Coote organised a party, including myself, and we took the jollyboats and a team of dogs and, after some difficulty, found a landing place. The island was abundant in game and we returned with a bagful of ducks and hares that went some way to restoring morale.

'With the ship stuck fast we had plenty of time to divert ourselves and soon returned to the island. Venturing up into the hills one morning to get a better sense of the landscape, Coote and myself came across a caribou, a lone male, grazing among the rocks. He bolted and the dogs set off in wild pursuit with us trailing behind, trying to load our muskets as we ran.

'The chase took us across a series of little peaks and higher, into the mountains proper. I wanted to give up and let the dogs take their chances but Coote was very attached to one hound in particular, whom he had named Rex, and refused to turn back. We pressed on, following the sound of baying, further into the range for an hour or more until at last our way became blocked by a wide wall of rock. We could still hear the dogs but only faintly and could not tell the direction.

'What happened next, neither of us really knew. There was a cracking beneath our feet that we strained for a moment to make sense of, then the ground gave way and we found ourselves hurtling, as if on a chute, for some distance into the earth. When we came to, we were in complete darkness. As we began to despair, we saw a burning torch in the distance, and to our amazement a group of Eskimos appeared before us. I think it's fair to say they were even more amazed, but they helped us through the mountain and brought us,' he gestured with out-turned palms, 'to this place.' He picked up his cup and drank, then peered into it, swirling the lees.

'The first thing you notice is the air, the warm breeze, then the green, so vivid after the eternity of white. And the trees...' He looked up, his eyes shining in the half-light. 'They had never seen an outsider, but they took us in nonetheless and tended to our wounds and fed us, and we stayed for several days. We had no words, but communicated well enough through signs and by drawing in the earth with sticks.

'In the following months Coote and I made a number of visits, bringing goods from the ship – axes and pocket knives, sugar, tobacco, a spyglass – in return for fresh fruit and meat. It was strange, after a while I began to notice that when I was there I no longer suffered from the ailments — the headaches, the pains in my limbs — that had plagued me all my life. I couldn't explain it. I also became enamoured of a young lady named Pinga whose eyes bewitched me from the moment I saw her.

'When the ice that gripped our ship finally began to loosen, it became clear to me that I could go no further. What was there to go back for, anyway? To be followed through the streets by laughing idiots? To end my days as an object of curiosity? A freak of nature? I took Coote aside and we talked for a long time. He used all his arguments to dissuade me but they simply stiffened my resolve. He wept most piteously. At last he accepted my wishes. We agreed that I would stay and that the existence of the valley would be kept a secret, to prevent others coming in search of it. He would record my death in the ship's log and this would mark the beginning of my new life. My rebirth. He was a true friend.'

There was a catch in the giant's throat as he uttered these words, and he reached up to brush away a teardrop.

'Forgive me, I haven't spoken of this for many years,' he said.

'Don't worry. We understand.' Phoebe rose and touched his sleeve.

'What about the cairn?' Rafferty asked. 'Why was there a dog in there?'

'Oh,' McNeill said, 'that was poor old Rex. He died on his final trip out of the valley. Coote was heartbroken.'

'And what about Franklin? Did they find anything?' said Fitzmaurice, who had woken a minute earlier, apparently unaware that he had been asleep.

'You mean you haven't met him yet?'

'I beg your pardon?'

'He's been living here for years.'

'What?'

'I'm only teasing. I think you're more likely to have news of him than I am.'

'Sorry. Silly question.'

'So,' Crozier said, 'you stayed. And you're still alive and kicking.'

'That's another thing I can't explain. Life is long here. I've lived to see my great-grandchildren: not many men can say that.'

'Didn't you ever miss home?' Rafferty asked.

The giant laughed.

'Look around you. Sure, isn't it more like Ireland than Ireland itself?'

They all agreed it was.

'No, there's no doubt about it.' McNeill's tone became grave. 'What I have built here is very precious. It gives me great pride. It has made me very happy. My life before, though I concede I was luckier than most of my kind, was full of pain. I was made to suffer because I was different. I was forced to hide away. Here, no one judges: big or small, we're all equal. My children, I fathered ten of them, and their grandchildren, and their children after that, will live here in peace and freedom, beyond the reach of the world I left behind.' He edged forward in his chair. 'As long, that is, as the valley remains a secret. That is *imperative*. No one must know we are here. Which is why, my friends,' he climbed to his feet, '... *you can never leave this place.*'

With a sigh, what remained of the fire collapsed in on itself. From behind them came the soft thud of a book closing and the old Inuk's chair squeaking as he leant back. The giant towered before them, his face lost in shadow.

'I'm aware,' McNeill said, 'that probably sounds a little... dictatorial, but I really cannot allow our community here to be jeopardised. You know as well as I do that if people learned of this island it would only be a matter of time before they came in search of it.'

Phoebe was the first to recover her voice.

'But you can't keep us here against our will.'

'No, you're free to go.'

'I thought you said...'

242

'But you would never find your way out. The route is extremely treacherous. Unless you know how to get to the pass that leads through the mountain, and only a handful of us do, it is highly unlikely that you would survive the attempt.'

'What if we promise to keep quiet?' Rafferty said.

'Ah, now.' McNeill surveyed the rafters, 'If it was just myself I would accept your word, my young friend, but there are others to consider, and in my experience the only real guarantee of a secret is death. Unless, of course, you believe in ghosts.'

'This is outrageous,' Fitzmaurice spluttered. 'You can't be serious. Please tell us this is a joke.'

'I'm afraid I cannot. I *am* serious. But, honestly, is the prospect really so unpleasant?'

'Our ship is waiting for us. They'll send a search party.'

McNeill brushed the protest aside as though shooing away a fly.

'Sleep on it. I think you'll find the idea will grow on you. And, I tell you what,' he clapped his hands together, 'tomorrow night I'll cook for you. Something special. How about that?'

He left the room, his footsteps booming on the bare wood. The others sat in silence, too flummoxed to speak. Outside in the valley, an owl began to interrogate the night, the sound melancholy, urgent, almost human.

27

Time to Dance

In the days that followed, not knowing how else to pass the time, the four of them did their best to fall in with the rhythms of the valley, rising at dawn to help with the ploughing and scything, the harvesting, and all the myriad other tasks and labours of agricultural life. There was grain to be pounded, fruit to be picked, livestock to be fed. Fitzmaurice found he had a talent for milking musk-oxen. Sometimes, in the afternoons, they took a picnic lunch and slipped away to walk in the forest and swim in the rockpool beneath the waterfall. Occasionally, such was the beauty of the landscape, some among them forgot, briefly, that they were prisoners, and in Fitzmaurice's case, given that without the precious skeleton there was little glory awaiting him at home, even to embrace the prospect of a longterm future. Phoebe, however, was having none of it, and returned often to their predicament.

'There *must* be a way out.'

They were sitting on a ridge at the edge of the pines, with a view of the village on the opposite slope, the vast, whitewashed gables of the cottages brilliant in the afternoon sun.

'If I'm remembering correctly,' Fitzmaurice said, 'the trick is to stab the giant in the eye.'

'Come again.'

'Mythology. You know, Ulysseuss.'

'Ulysseuss?'

'Greek chap. Escaped from some giant by stabbing him in the eye. Dressed himself up as a sheep too, for some reason, s'far as I recall.'

'Oh, Hugh.'

'What?'

'I think you mean *Odysseus*, and I can't really see how that helps. For a start our host, though he would certainly appear to be a man of singular vision, is not a cyclops. Secondly...'

'Who do you think built those houses?' Rafferty interjected, his head on one side.

'What?'

'The cottages. Look at them: they're massive. They required a huge amount of labour.'

'The giants built them, of course.'

'Hold on. There was only one giant to begin with. He couldn't have done it on his own.'

'What are you saying?'

'I'm saying the Inuit built them. I think the Inuit do most of the work around here.'

Crozier groaned. 'Not the Oppressed People speech again, Rafferty.'

'Why not? It's...'

'What do you reckon,' Fitzmaurice said, changing the subject, 'old man McGregor is going to say when we don't show up?'

'Well, he definitely won't be pleased.'

245

'I imagine he'll say something like...' Phoebe shook her head, 'like: "where the —k are those b—ing —ing a—s? Where the..."'

Rafferty broke in. 'No, it'll be worse than that, more like, "what in the name of —k are those c—ing little —ers doing, the s—faced —ing ...'

'Anyone else hungry?' Fitzmaurice was on his feet. 'I wonder what's for dinner.'

They considered for a while.

'Don't get me wrong,' Crozier said, 'the food's incredibly good here, but it's so rich, so complicated. I'd kill for something plain... like hardtack, or... what's that stuff we had back at the camp?'

'Pemmican?'

'Yes. Some pemmican hoosh.'

In the wake of his decree, aside from hosting his promised 'special' meal (rare fillets of caribou with wild mushrooms and snow goose liver in a sauce of sweet wine and bone marrow), the giant kept his distance. They would see him from time to time strolling to or from his winery, and in the evenings, in the reading hall, he would wave or nod in their direction, but his demeanour was haughty.

Regarding the nightly entertainment, they had come to the end of *Gulliver's Travels* and embarked on *The Pilgrim's Progress*. Crozier was soon reminded of the soporific nature of his father's weekly sermons, and the effort required for concentration on the spoken word. During one particularly dry passage, read by an elderly Inuk in the manner of someone deciphering a handwritten prescription, he nodded off, dreaming that he was picking his way through a valley of scorched bones. When he awoke (with a loud, involuntary snort), he looked up to find one of the young giants, Ossian, who was sitting across the aisle, watching him with a curious expression.

Ossian was the youngest of McNeill's grandsons, and, at barely a sunbeam off nine feet, the tallest. He was also the least blessed in the areas both of aesthetic appeal and intellectual reasoning, deficiencies he made up for with an abundance of puppyish enthusiasm. Flirtatious, eager to please, and extremely clumsy (he was constantly bandaged and patched as a result of stumbles and collisions), he was something of a contrast to his brothers and uncles who, after the initial courtesies, had retreated to a state of reserve that bordered on *froideur*. Crozier winked at him and, the young giant, seeming to snap out of a reverie, flushed and averted his eyes.

The next day, taking a break from scything, the four voyagers were lying beside a wheat field, eating their lunch in the sunshine. Heaps of golden stalks lay around them; other workers sat in groups at intervals, talking and laughing. In the adjacent orchard, a woman was singing. Above them, impossibly high and far, the mountain peaks gleamed though ribbons of cloud.

'Well, I'm getting used to it.' Fitzmaurice popped a cherry into his mouth. 'And let's face it, what have I got to go back to? Without the bones I'll be frogmarched straight out of College. On the other hand it would be good to see home again. Give old Ninian a punch on the jaw.' He shielded his eyes. 'Hello there.'

The sun was blocked out and above them stood a smirking Ossian. It transpired that he was wondering, if it wasn't too much of an imposition, if they wouldn't mind talking some more about the country of their forebears.

He had only ever heard his grandfather's version, and it was from so long ago. (Crozier wasn't sure things had changed *that* much.)

'Is there anything in particular you want to know?'

The young giant squatted down.

'What's Ireland like now? What's it like to live there?'

They each pondered the question. Crozier pictured the rain-dark factories and churches of his native city in its cradle of hills, heard the clang of the shipyard and the clatter of drums, the wingbeats of gaudy flags, silver drizzle sweeping across Belfast Lough. Phoebe was back in Ennisfree, in the cold hush of an unheatable house, looking out at drenched greenery and recalling the sense she had often had in the Irish countryside, that secrets beyond telling lay beneath the drowned soil. Rafferty found himself on the Dublin quays, inhaling the scent of roasted barley from St James' Gate — bitter, savoury: the city's essence, like the smell of home-cooking; saw also the cliff-like terraces and pillars, the statuary of a foreign power, and felt the familiar flash of heat in his blood. It was Fitzmaurice, emerging from a daydream about riding to victory in the Kilkenny Donkey Derby, who finally spoke.

'Most of the time it's jolly good fun.'

'And is it really as green as my grandfather says?'

'Very much so. You see, it rains a lot.'

Ossian twisted and pulled at the plait of hay in his hands. Perspiration gleamed on his forehead. A pulse twitched in his neck.

'And the *colleens*, the sweet colleens!' he blurted. 'Are they really as beautiful and mysterious in their ways?'

They all laughed. The young giant, most of whose waking hours were spent in dogged but ineffectual pursuit of the young Inuit women, blushed.

'Oh they're *mysterious* all right,' Crozier told him.

There was a tinkling of harness bells and a rumble of wheels as an oxen cart passed behind them.

'But the girls here are lovely too,' Crozier added.

Ossian mumbled something, wrinkling his long, wide nose.

'And it's undeniably green.' Crozier glanced furtively at the others, recognising their shared thought in that instant. They had to chance it.

'Listen, Ossian,' he said. 'Charming as it is here, we were just talking about how much we miss Ireland – the sweet colleens and the green fields and what have you — and how we'd love to go home. I don't suppose... What would you think about showing us the way through the mountain?'

The giant shook his head as though trying to clear water from his ears.

'My grandfather would kill me.'

'Well he wouldn't find out until afterwards. Perhaps he wouldn't mind so much?'

'He'd kill me. That's for sure.'

There was a pause, and Crozier gazed across the fields, flicking through possibilities. Then he looked up at the young giant again.

'You could see our ship.'

A gleam came into the big cow-like eyes. Snow geese, in a loose, wishbone formation, flapped overhead.

'Could I come with you?'

Crozier pictured this colossal man-child lumbering

249

through the streets of Dublin pursued by clamorous mobs of gawkers. He put the thought from his mind.

'Would you *like* to come with us?'

*

It was the only full moon they had seen since crossing the Arctic Circle. (In its other phases it had bobbed around the horizon throughout the voyage, often accompanied by a phantom twin and, once, in Lancaster Sound, by a pair of mirage siblings so sharp it was difficult to tell which was the real one.) Ghostly at first, it had grown more vivid as the sun dipped behind the mountains, until at last the valley was flooded with silver light. In the middle of the green a huge bonfire sent orange flakes zig-zagging into the sky. Long tables had been laid out with food and jugs of wine; joints of meat sizzled on spits. Dancers, in buckskin parkas of intricate design, were parading back and forth to the rhythm of drums, while young Inuit women, silhouetted against the flames, sang whooping, breathy songs.

It was the night of the *ceilidhe,* a monthly tradition in the valley, and all the residents, men, women and children, were gathered. At the table of honour, in the shadow of the schoolhouse, the four adventurers sat with McNeill and Pinga, and various senior giants. It was the first time they had broken bread together since the old man had told them of their fate, and though the wine was flowing, conversation was an effort. Ossian continued to dither over his decision. The young giant, patently subdued, was sprawled on the grass some distance away, glancing over from time to time with a haunted expression. Catching one of these, McNeill turned to Phoebe.

'Poor Ossian seems out of sorts, don't you think?'

She started, then recovered herself.

'Does he? I hadn't really noticed.'

'Hasn't been himself for a while now. Very… restless.'

Phoebe sensed the giant was watching her.

'Maybe he's in love.'

McNeill laughed.

'Well, it certainly wouldn't be the first time. And if that's the case it won't last long, but I don't think that's it. I just hope he's not tiring of our life here.'

'Oh, I doubt it. Where could be better than this?'

'Where indeed? You're settling in, then?'

'It's lovely.'

'And the others?'

There was a sudden hush and a bustling rearrangement took place around the fire. Several giants appeared carrying huge stringed instruments, and from out of the dusk came a tentative skirl of pipes. The musicians settled themselves, the eldest son, Finn, tucking a fiddle the size of a cello under his chin, and began to tune up.

'I think they could be very happy here,' Phoebe replied.

The giant nodded.

'*Fertilior seges est alieno semper in arvo*,' he murmured.

'Pardon?'

'I said…' But his words were drowned out by the sudden onset of music: the clattering, rashers-and-sausages rhythm of a double jig, at deafening volume. Immediately the giants rose, whooping, from the table and, seizing various partners, rushed onto the grass. From all sides others came running, and within seconds the green was a whirl of flailing limbs.

251

'Time to dance,' McNeill yelled in Phoebe's ear, and plucking his wife up like a rag doll, he entered the fray. Phoebe cast around for the others. Both Rafferty and Crozier, fear in their eyes, were sprinting towards her, pursued by a pair of giantesses. Rafferty arrived first and fumbled for her hand. Crozier was collared and, with a cry, hoisted into the air by his triumphant captor and whisked into the midst.

It was hot in there — the bonfire, the numbers, the exertion — and barely had they caught their breath than the next tune began. Fitzmaurice, a veteran from childhood of many a peculiar social event, was the only one of them relatively at ease, prancing around and waggling his head like an Indian street vendor. A variety of dance styles was in evidence, from text-book Irish to the tribal foot-stamping and arm-waving of the Inuit, but mostly it was a strange, jerky hybrid of both. On the edge of the crowd, Ossian was swinging his legs morosely to and fro. Crozier, his feet dangling, did his best, between violent gyrations, to watch for a sign that the young giant had resolved his inner conflict.

Round and round they went: jigging and reeling, horn-piping and stomping as though the world was about to end. Trapped in the giantess's sweltering embrace, Crozier began to feel faint. At last she paused to mop her brow and, peering over her shoulder, he saw that Ossian was also standing still. Their eyes met and the giant slowly nodded his head. And then they were off again, caught in a wheeling blur of shadows and flames, in a din of pipes and drums, under a bouncing moon.

28

Wolves in the Moonlight

By Crozier's reckoning it was around three in the morning, and they had been climbing on a diagonal path east for more than an hour. He had stopped to catch his breath; his three friends were up ahead, beyond them, the hulking figure of their guide. As he turned, something moved among the trees on the lower slope and he strained to see in the gloom. All was still. Just a hare, or a deer perhaps. But he began to run nonetheless.

A little further on he looked up and realised that the others were out of sight. He came to another halt. The path had degenerated into brush and scree where it met a sharp bulge in the mountainside, and it was unclear whether the way was around or over. He gazed at the moon, which was warped, almost ovoid, its cratered face sharply delineated: Mare Imbrium, the Sea of Rains, that was one of the eyes; the open mouth, he was nearly sure, was Mare Nubium, the Sea of Clouds. But he couldn't recall the others. At that moment, from somewhere high above, back behind the crags, came a drawn-out, plaintive howl, pure in the silence, that made his scalp tighten. Barely had it subsided than another began, hungrier, lonelier than the first, and then another, and from the darkness of the mountains more cries emerged until they had swelled to an inconsolable chorus. Down in the village, several Huskies were roused to answer, and then, just as suddenly, the sounds ceased. He made his choice and set off.

As he ran, Crozier pondered again what it was he was escaping from. Life in the valley was no hardship. On the contrary, it was extremely pleasant. Idyllic even. The people wanted for nothing. They worked, they played games, or made music and told stories, or had books read to them. They lived off the fat of the land. Every one of them seemed to be a first-class cook. Man and woman, big and small: all were equal. And the wine!

He thought of the world he was running towards, with its heaving cities and turmoil, its cruelty and bloodshed, its traps and snares, its heartache. But, as Phoebe said: however lovely it might be, they were *prisoners*, and without free will it couldn't be paradise. McNeill, she grumbled, was a tyrant. 'He's forcing us to be his children. He's emasculating us, don't you see?'

Just as he was beginning to fear he had taken the wrong path, Crozier rounded a bend and almost collided with the others.

'Where the hell were you?' Rafferty demanded. 'We need to hurry. Ossian says they may already be after us.'

The air, as they climbed higher, grew colder, and beneath their feet the pebbles became slippery. The trail itself narrowed to the width of a man's shoulders, falling away steeply to one side so they were forced to lean into the mountain as they ran. At one point the ledge gave way and Rafferty, momentarily off balance due to the weight of his pack, teetered and would have fallen if not for a timely shove from behind. Skeins of cloud dimmed the moon and they pounded along blindly until, at last, the ground began to level out and the path curved in towards a plateau that led to the base of the sheer wall of the summit.

They stopped to set their backpacks down and drink some water.

'Not too far now,' Ossian said. 'Another hour or so.'

'Do you think anyone saw us leave?' Rafferty peered back down the trail.

'We were careful, but you never know.'

'What will your grandfather say when he finds us gone?'

Ossian surveyed the distant valley. The glow from the dying bonfire was still visible.

'I don't want to think about that.'

Crickets were fidgeting in the undergrowth nearby. Phoebe took a meditative slug of water.

'Fitz, I can't believe you didn't bring Bunion. We're going to be in big trouble.'

'I tried, I really did,' Fitzmaurice said. 'Little bugger did Stiff Dog like you wouldn't believe. And bear in mind, he's deceptively heavy.'

Another howl descended through the night. Ossian picked up the rifle Harris had provided when they left the *Dolphin*. It looked like a child's toy in his hands. They reattached their packs and set off across the plateau towards the cliffs. After a while the ground became increasingly uneven, undulating into a series of steep ridges they had to clamber up on all-fours before edging – or in some instances sliding and swearing – down the other side. Fitzmaurice, encumbered as he was by the Magiflex and its accoutrements, found this particularly taxing. The dense dusk through which they were travelling did not help. Eventually they came to the last rise, and Ossian, reaching the top first, held up a hand to halt the others as they arrived.

'Oh my God.'

'Jaysus.'

'My word.'

'Cripes.'

They were gazing down into a chasm, a long split in the shelf of the mountain some thirty feet across and so deep that the darkness far below was absolute. The cold breath of eternity wafted up at them.

'Bit of a challenge this one,' Ossian said. 'But don't be afraid.'

He led them further along the lip, stopped, and peeped over.

'When you're ready, I want you to follow me.'

'Wait a min—' Fitzmaurice began, but the giant had stepped into the abyss.

Phoebe clamped a hand over her mouth to suppress a scream, and they stood in shocked silence. A moment later, Ossian's head reappeared at their feet.

'Right. Who's first?'

The ledge on which he was standing was connected to the opposite side of the chasm by a bridge made of rawhide ropes interlaced with slats of wood and animal bone, and secured by iron pinions driven into the rock. It had evidently been around a long time and, it was noted, sagged significantly in the middle.

'Don't worry, it's quite safe. It held my family with you on their shoulders after all,' Ossian said.

'We don't remember that.'

256

'Not surprising, as you were unconscious.'

Crozier went first. The rawhide made for springy suspension and the bridge bounced up and down at the least provocation. Weight management, and rhythm, were the key. Though he was careful not to look down, he was aware of the dark suck of gravity beneath him. He was recalling crossing, as a child (what were his parents thinking?) another, much longer rope bridge slung by fishermen between the mainland and a small islet off the Antrim coast, how it swung wildly in the wind, the swarming, marble-flecked agitation of the Atlantic a hundred feet below, the exhilarated relief of completion. Already a lifetime ago. This was easy by comparison. He gripped the hand supports, focusing on the steps up ahead that led back to terra firma. The ropes were creaking and he paused to let the bridge stabilise.

'Keep going,' Ossian called.

'Nearly there,' Phoebe said.

It was steeper after the mid-point and he had to haul himself towards the ledge, his boots sliding on the damp slats. At last he was at the other side, scrambling up onto the plateau.

Rafferty was next to cross, followed by Phoebe. Fitzmaurice, despite his mountaineering experience, required some coaxing.

'I don't like the look of it.'

'It's perfectly safe. We all did it.'

'I don't like the way it creaks.'

'That's normal. All rope creaks.'

'Not like that it doesn't.'

'Do you want Ossian to carry you?'

'No.'

He set off gingerly, keeping an ear to the groaning of the cords, and made good progress until the halfway stage where he froze, hunched forward, his legs wobbling.

'Fitz?'

'Fitzie?'

'Hugh?'

Through gritted teeth, 'It's the Magiflex.'

Lashed to his back, the camera, attached to its folded tripod, had slipped forty-five degrees to the horizontal, the weight of it pulling the bridge off kilter.

'Release the strap, let it go,' Ossian advised.

Fitzmaurice began grunting and wriggling, heaving on the opposite rope in an attempt to shrug the camera back into position.

'Let it go!'

The bridge teetered and listed, Fitzmaurice holding on with one hand as he struggled with the other to grasp the Magiflex.

'Let it fall!'

But Fitzmaurice was intent. He flailed behind him with his free hand and, after a panic of fumbling managed, for a brief instant, to grip the underside of the camera. With a sound like the twang of a vigorously plucked bass-string, the bridge overturned, leaving Fitzmaurice dangling over the abyss and the Magiflex whistling towards the centre of the Earth. Eyes wide with anguish, Fitzmaurice watched it fall and appeared, for a moment, to consider dropping down after it.

'Bloody hell,' he shouted.

'Don't let go,' Ossian told him. Crouching on all-fours, the young giant began to edge along the upturned bridge.

'Stop it. Keep still,' he yelled. The dangler's attempts

to secure purchase were causing severe turbulence. The bridge steadied, Ossian set off again, the griping of the ropes increasing in pitch as he neared the middle. Once there, he braced himself as best he could, reached around, seized Fitzmaurice by the wrist and, with huge, quivering effort, hauled him half onto the slats, nearly causing the structure to overturn again. Amid the hysterical squeaking of over-stressed fibres, Fitzmaurice squirmed himself into a horizontal position.

'Nice and easy. No sudden moves. Let it settle... Now, slowly forwards.'

The pair of them inched along, urged on by the others. The bridge shuddered and lurched, and even Ossian, though outwardly confident, appeared once or twice to be questioning the reliability of Inuit technology. It held. Once up the steps, Fitzmaurice sat down and took out his pipe and did not speak for some time.

The entrance to the mountain was hidden to the casual eye by a projection of rock where the cliff fell away, and was further obscured, even when close up, by the positioning of several large boulders. The opening was narrow, and low enough that the giant had to bend almost double, but once inside, a seal-fat lamp revealed a high-vaulted passageway leading at an upward angle into the dark. The stone on either side was wet to the touch and the chill air had a metallic tang. They trudged in silence for half an hour and then the gradient eased and the tunnel opened up into a vast cavern. Ossian held up his lantern and the light flickered over gargoyles of twisted rock and limestone, growths and meltings; an aeon's worth of corrosions and metastases. Immense stalactites protruded from the ceiling far above; in the grottoes, mountain seepage dripped into glittering pools.

'If only I had the Magiflex,' Fitzmaurice moaned.

They passed through chamber after chamber, each more fantastically wrought than the last – one was electric-green with phosphorescence, another encrusted from top to bottom with enormous pink crystals – until the path descended steeply and they arrived at the edge of an expanse of dark water. Tethered nearby was a kayak. They climbed in, Phoebe crouching at the front with the lamp, and Fitzmaurice and Ossian taking up a paddle each. The surface gleamed like liquid obsidian. Crozier trailed his fingers over the side but it was as viscous as cold oil and he snatched them out again.

The boat slid through profound darkness. In the flare of the lantern the walls glistened; in places, the ceiling sloped so that it almost grazed the giant's hair, and the openings between one cavern and the next became so tight the paddles had to be brought into the boat. Elsewhere, they had to negotiate between reefs of stalagmites and divert around humps of stone, Fitzmaurice and Ossian calling out instructions to each other. Eventually the walls opened up again and they entered another cavern in which the water, untrammelled, expanded into a lake. Towards the far shore, beams of daylight split the darkness.

'Here we are.'

They tethered the kayak at the foot of a steep slope of shale and ice, at the top of which was a narrow oblong of sky. They climbed up and through the aperture, and found themselves looking out over the plateau where they had been lost in the blizzard, not far from the dog cairn. The moon, bleached by the dawn's rays, hung still in the sky. A single star sparkled. The air was chill and they rummaged extra clothing from their backpacks.

'Seems we have company,' Ossian murmured, pulling on his gloves.

Ranged along the crest of a nearby ridge, regarding them with vacant intensity, were the wolves, a dozen or more, some standing, some sitting, others lying with folded paws. They were barrel-chested but lean, dirty cream against the snow.

'Start walking, they won't bother us,' Ossian said. 'Be confident.'

The wolves watched them go. A few hundred yards later they were still on the ridge and before long they were out of sight.

The snow was patchy but ice axes were required on the steeper slopes, and there were a number of slips, Rafferty taking the prize with a high-speed slide of some sixty feet. After a while they came to the tents, half-buried, and while they had no further use for the equipment, Crozier went to the trouble of retrieving his books: a volume of Richter's *Birds of the Northern Hemisphere* and a copy of Lord Dufferin's *Letters From High Latitudes*.

They continued their descent, and after a few hours came to a plateau below the snowline where they stopped to eat the food they had brought. The edge of the island was now visible and beyond it the glint of sea. The wolves had reappeared, watching them from the rocks above. Ossian glanced at the rifle but went on eating.

'Have you never thought of leaving before?' Phoebe asked. 'You must have wondered what lay beyond.'

'Of course, but how? Without a ship, or a map?

Hamilton Coote is the only person to have left. Until now.'

'That is, of course, if the *Dolphin* is still waiting for us.'

Ossian seized the rifle and fired in the air. The sound of the shot echoed around the mountain and across the plain, and the wolves, which had been encroaching, scattered. Shortly after, refreshed, the party pressed on, the giant trotting eagerly ahead. The others descended in silence.

'You know we can't take him with us,' Crozier announced at last, hanging back a little.

'What? Why not?' Fitzmaurice stopped in his tracks. 'He'll make up for not having Bunion, he'll get on with the cabin boy – they're both mad for the ladies, he'll...'

'For the same reason that his grandfather couldn't stay. He'd be eaten alive.'

'But, we made a deal.'

'Walter's right,' Phoebe said, 'he can't come to Ireland with us. He'd die like a dog.'

'But surely – Frank, give me some help here.'

Rafferty gazed down at the oblivious back of the young giant, skidding and stumbling below them in his seven-league boots and bear-sized hat. He sighed.

'I'm afraid I have to agree with the others, Fitz. People can be cruel. It wouldn't be fair to him.'

At the foot of the slope, Ossian was sitting on a boulder waiting for them, an expectant grin on his face. As they drew closer and he began to perceive their grim expressions, this faded. They explained the situation.

'You tricked me,' he wailed, putting his head in his hands.

'Believe me,' Crozier said, squeezing his shoulder, 'we don't feel good about this.'

The giant began to bawl in earnest. Fitzmaurice took Phoebe to one side.

'We need something to distract him,' he told her. 'Give him something.'

'Like what?'

'I don't know. What does he like?'

'*Ladies*,' said Rafferty phlegmatically. 'He likes the colleens. The ladies.'

'That's right.' Fitzmaurice's eyes bulged. 'Phoebe, quick – give him something from you. Whatever it was you chucked at the Prime Minister. Give him one of your undergarments.'

Phoebe stared at him.

'... I beg your f—ing pardon?'

'Go on, it'll take his mind off things.'

'I certainly will not.' She was breathing heavily through her nose. 'Here's a better idea – why don't you give him that watch you stole from your uncle? With the mucky picture on it. He'll like *that*.'

Fitzmaurice glowered at her, then glanced at the bereft giant. He fumbled in his pack. He stepped forward.

'Ossian, old man, I have a present for you, something special, something to remember us by.'

The deviant pocket watch was received blindly into a massive hand. It was a moment or two before the giant, who was in the grip of long shuddering sobs, was able to focus. As the dial's fleshy scene began to take form, he faltered, peered more closely. The convulsions of his mighty chest slowed, and finally, ceased.

'That's a genuine heirloom,' Fitzmaurice continued. 'My uncle, who was squashed by a rock, wanted me to have it. Now I'm entrusting it to you. I hope you'll look

263

after it and, who knows, perhaps pass it down to the next generation. And the generation after that.'

The giant, transfixed, did not reply.

'So,' Crozier said after a moment. 'I suppose this is it. We'd better get on.'

'Yes, Ossian, thanks for everything. You've been lovely.'

'Say goodbye to your grandfather for us.'

'Chin up, big fellah.'

They turned and headed for the plain. When they looked back, the young giant, despite his enormous fingers, had prised the back off the watch and was holding it aloft and shaking it, as though the tiny couple inside might fall, still in their amorous embrace, down from its silver casing and into his open palm.

By the time they arrived at the coast, the sun was low in the sky behind them, and their shadows reached the cliff-edge a minute before they did. The *Dolphin* was still at anchor in the bay.

'There she is,' Rafferty said. 'Look, there's McGregor.'

A figure moving on the ship's deck stopped and stared up in their direction.

'What are we going to tell them, I mean about the giants?' Phoebe said.

'Absolutely nothing.' Crozier lowered the flaps of his Savage Newell snow helmet against the biting sea breeze. 'I don't think we should say a word to anyone. Agreed? We'll say we were lost in the mountains and lived on hares and snow geese.'

'Another thing,' said Fitzmaurice. 'Who's going to break it to him about a certain canine?'

'Not me.'

'Nor me. Crozier?'

'Don't worry, he'll just be glad to see us back safely, he won't be bothered about Bunion. Anyway, Bunion's a father now and has had more than enough of life on the ocean wave.'

They scrambled down the scree and made their way out along the floe towards the *Dolphin*. As they approached, the crew appeared on deck and the ladder was lowered onto the ice.

'Ahoy there!' Fitzmaurice called.

McGregor, gripping the gunwale with mittened hands, stared down at them.

'Permission to come aboard, sir!'

The Scot looked older, his moustache, which was rising and falling as if worked by bellows, bigger than they remembered. His eyes were the size of ball bearings.

'Reporting for duty...' Fitzmaurice faltered.

A wad of expectorate hit the ice.

'Where the f— is my f—ing dog?'

29

A Fresh Fall

A fresh fall during the night had given, to those emerging into the turquoise light of morning, the impression of one vast snowfield, of all boundaries blurred and obliterated. Hills and gullies had been levelled out, trees and hedges buried, rooftops caked; from Fair Head to Mizen Head, the whole island lay soundless and gleaming.

By lunchtime, the towns and cities had struggled to their feet, shrugging off enough of the snow to become workable, and citizens tip-toed along frozen thoroughfares. In Dublin the railways had been shut down but a few trams were running, and from one of these, half way along Sackville Street, the College cellarer alighted. Adjusting his woollen muffler, he stepped, with great care, on to the pavement and entered the confectioner's, which smelled of damp breath and aniseed. Sawdust had been scattered on the floor between the doorway and the counter and it was soggy underfoot. The cold of the meltwater penetrated his shoes.

'It's the farmers I feel sorry for,' a woman in a lambskin coat was saying. 'And the poor animals, God love them.'

'Certainly in my memory there hasn't been a winter like it,' the proprietor replied, peering up through the window at the putty-coloured sky. 'And looks like there's more to come. That'll be tuppence, when you're ready.'

Outside the shop, the cellarer tucked his newspaper under his arm and fumbled in his little bag of liquorice comfits. Up towards the river he could see cushions of snow on the parapets of O'Connell Bridge; opposite him the ragged edges of the once magnificent Hotel Metropole, its innards blackened by fire, were picked out in white. Nearly a year on, cascades of rubble still lay in heaps, and the hollowed shell of the General Post Office remained open to the weather, jangling in the city's consciousness like an exposed nerve. It was odd to see business going on as usual amid such ruination, he thought, but there they were, the bargain-hunters, the bicycles, the trams, the flower sellers; commerce crackling back to life like an electric current. Onward flow.

He stood for a moment, sucking his sweet, watching the passers-by walk as though they were wearing tight skirts. A motorcar laboured through the slush, its wheels spinning. He turned to regard the wrecked façade of Clery's department store. The place was a mess. He would have to go out of his way to purchase the linen cloths he used to polish his wine glasses.

He began to trudge in the direction of the river, pausing at the corner of Abbey Street to let a cart-load of bricks pass. The devastation here was almost total, only jagged foundations and part of a scorched balustrade remaining. He couldn't remember now what had been there originally. On the bridge an icy breeze gusted off the river and a seagull screeched overhead and, as he hurried in the direction of College, fragments of mayhem came back to him: the gunfire on the roof, the pounding of mortars, blood on the cobbles; the body of the dispatch rider, his face as smooth as a boy's, laid out for days in a room behind the porter's office. Even down below, deep in the cellars, dust had trickled from the rock and the precious liquids had shivered in their bottles.

The Senior Dean removed his spectacles and dropped them onto the newspaper that lay open on his desk. He rose and crossed to the window. Snow was falling again, flakes melting against the glass, the square below astir with soft movement. He stared up at the sky, at the drifting motes, and let himself be lost briefly, as children are, to a sense of slow and endless proliferation. Change was coming, he thought. Faster than ever. And there was no stopping it.

On the top of the campanile, two pairs of magpies were jockeying for dominance, knocking clumps of snow off the ledges. Some students were leaping about on the lawn, their shouts muffled, distant. The sight made him think of the three young men he had received before they had taken the Queenstown train south from Dublin almost a year ago. He tried to place them back in the square, large as life, but he couldn't quite remember what they looked like. So many had been and gone over the years, borne on the four winds...

He turned, ignoring, out of the corner of his eye, the portrait of himself which had recently returned from its third, expensive re-touch job. The hand that gripped the scroll was no longer puny. It was meaty. With muscular, sausage fingers. And the scroll itself – this, try as he might, he could not now unnotice – appeared, in certain lights, to have an oddly flesh-like tone and to be elevated at a suspicious angle. He tinkered for a few minutes with the fire and was just settling himself when there was a rap at the door and the Regius Professor of Zoology and Comparative Anatomy scurried past and threw himself into the armchair opposite.

'I know it's early, old man, but any chance of some grog?'

'Of course. Madeira?'

'Whatever you have.'

Hefting the decanter, the Senior Dean hesitated for a moment, listening to the snuffling sounds behind him, and poured himself a glass too.

'There you are, that should do the trick.'

'You're a gentleman.'

The Regius Professor, pink-cheeked and a little teary, contemplated his drink. His feet, which failed by some distance to reach the carpet, twitched inside their tight black shoes.

'It's all going to buggery, you know. Cheers.'

'Indeed... Sorry, what is?'

'Everything. We're all buggered.'

The Senior Dean waited.

'The Royal Irish Geographical Society met last night. It's buggered. Finished. The money's gone. No more dinners, no more trips, no more stipends. Twenty years I sat on that board. Some of the others much longer. Poor old Dobbin cried like a baby when the announcement was made. It was heart-breaking.' He took a ravenous slurp. 'And that's only the beginning. The rot is well and truly setting in. Ireland? Buggered. Beauchamp tells me that in Westminster there's talk of self-government within the year.'

'I know. It's all over the papers.'

'Apart from Ulster, of course, but who'd want to live there? I thought that after the uh... *unpleasantness* last Easter they might have thought better of it, but seems not. Home Rule. Within the year! Can you imagine? It's terrifying.'

'Might not be *that* bad.'

'Are you out of your mind?' the Regius Professor squealed. 'There'll be priests at Front Gate faster than you can say "who goes there?" and then where will we be? Buggered, that's where. Next thing you know, Commencements Day will be all wafers and bad wine. Speaking of which, have you heard about what's going on in the cellars?'

'Buggeration?'

'Bloody U-boats have kiboshed the Bordeaux route. Cellarer...' he swallowed the catch in his throat, 'Cellarer's threatening to ration the claret.' He sank back in his chair. 'I ask you.'

The Senior Dean stood up.

'Refill?'

'Go on then. For the nerves.'

Outside, the air was becoming thicker, and snow was beginning to accumulate around the edges of the windows, reducing the panes to ovals. Somewhere, far off, a bell was ringing, and the sound, faint but insistent, brought to the Senior Dean's mind, arbitrarily, his first day at boarding school. He was back in the sunlit dormitory amid the pillars of dust, the acres of buffed wood, lifting the lid of his suitcase on his hairy bed to find the Madeira cake, packed by his mother, wrapped in opaque paper and tied with string, the scent of home assailing his heart. He remembered how he'd eked it out, pinch by

270

pinch, over the weeks until it was just stale crumbs. The memory began to fade and as he snatched at its retreat, he experienced a kind of pain.

'And as for cricket, you can kiss *that* goodbye,' the Regius Professor said. 'It's buggered. There'll be camogie bats on the crease, slitters flying all over the place. That's if there isn't livestock trotting to and fro. I've gone a bit far there, but you know what I mean – ah, you're very good. Chin-chin.'

They sipped in silence and the Regius Professor, noticing for the first time his colleague's douleur, checked himself. Wriggling into a more upright position, he coughed, and in a firmer tone of voice said: 'Sorry for going on, but I'm finding all this rather distressing.' He wiped his lips with a thumb and forefinger. 'Is there any *good* news? Is there any word of our intrepid trio? Tell me, when's our giant coming home?'

'Funny you should ask.'

The Senior Dean fetched the *Irish Times* from his desk, folded it in half and handed it to the Regius Professor, who, blinking, skimmed through the latest from the western field of war, the voluminous casualty lists running down as far as the advertisements for cigarettes and Sanatogen, until, at the bottom right of the page, his eyes fastened on the following:

ARCTIC EXPEDITION SHIP FEARED LOST WITH ALL HANDS

(REUTERS AGENCY)

A report of wreckage from the lifeboat of a ship bound from Queenstown to the Arctic has raised fears for the wellbeing of her crew and passengers. Capt. Jacob van

Haarlem, of the whaling ship Nautilus, told maritime authorities in Copenhagen yesterday that he had seen parts of the hull from a small craft inscribed with "The Dolphin" in the sea off southeastern Greenland in June of last year.

The Dolphin, a three-masted schooner-barque of 320 tons, set sail last March to the Arctic Archipelago on an expedition funded by the Royal Irish Geographical Society. On board were three scientists from Trinity College Dublin, and a crew of six under the command of Capt. Ewan McGregor of Glasgow. The Dolphin's last contact was by telegram from Reykjavik a month after leaving Ireland--

'Oh bugger.'

*

Startled by a sound like the crack of a wet whip, Crozier turned to find Fitzmaurice sitting on a capstan with Bridie draped across his lap. The lizard was holding up a tiny hand and staring, with wall-eyed concentration, into space. It sneezed again.

'It's the fumes,' Fitzmaurice explained.

Crozier, who had just finished tarring the main-stays, dropped the turpentine-soaked rag with which he had been cleaning his hands into the slush-bucket and leaned against the port bow. He inhaled the breeze. The sea was mineral blue, and they were travelling at a stately five knots. Somewhere not far to the south were the Western Isles, and only a matter of days beyond, was Dublin. Behind them, more than a month of Atlantic was evaporating at the nearing prospect of home.

On the opposite bow, Rafferty and Phoebe were engaged in high-spirited conversation. Crozier couldn't hear what they were saying but as he watched, Rafferty stood on tiptoe, making himself big, and adopted a booming voice; Phoebe was laughing, her hair blowing back from her face, her eyes brimming with ocean light. At the sight of her Crozier felt his heart twang and heat rise in his chest.

'...a spot of fresh air,' Fitzmaurice was saying. 'After being cooped up for so long, poor thing.'

The others approached.

'Not far now,' chirped Rafferty. 'First stop, home cooking. Pork chops. Irish stew. Maybe even a bowl of coddle.'

Phoebe looked at him askance. 'What on earth is *coddle?*'

'That's a secret known only to the mothers of Dublin,' Crozier told her. 'Though I suspect it may have originated with one of Victoor's ancestors.'

'You do realise, Phoebe,' Fitzmaurice said, 'that you will be questioned very closely by a certain Mrs Rafferty regarding your intentions towards her son?'

'She's a formidable woman,' Crozier warned.

Phoebe laughed. 'I'm sure I can convince her that my intentions are honourable.'

Crozier smiled at her. The hull of the ship thumped against a random swell, then another.

'It's going to be strange being back,' Rafferty said. 'Feels like we've been away for a very, very long time.'

'Nothing will have changed,' Fitzmaurice caressed Bridie's dewlaps, 'and after a few days it will be as though we never left.'

'I wonder when the war ended,' Crozier mused. 'Presumably we won.'

Mention of the war stopped them in their tracks. They'd almost forgotten.

'What will you do now, Hugh,' Phoebe said after a while. 'Will you try and go back to your studies?'

'No.' Fitzmaurice hoisted the lizard further up his lap. 'No, I'd say that particular avenue is closed. Actually, I've been thinking I might work my journals up into a book. Exploration memoirs are very popular with the public these days, and I believe my writing has a certain style. Who knows, I might even do a lecture tour – England, the Continent, the United States. I'd have to take Bridie with me, of course.' He patted her flank. 'Might even have a little outfit made up for her. Something sparkly.'

The reptile, which had been resting its chin dreamily in its hand, jerked to attention, fixing the others with a fiery eye as though daring them to laugh.

'Or maybe not. We'll see.'

'The voyage of the *Dolphin*? I'd definitely read it. What about you, Walter, what's in store?'

'Oh, back to College. But I've decided to give up Divinity. I'm going to apply to read Zoological Studies instead. The natural world – its *outward form and inner workings* — is what really interests me.' He glanced at Phoebe. Then away. 'And you?'

She shrugged. 'The struggle goes on, of course. I intend to resume my role as a thorn in the side of His Majesty's government.'

'*And* to marry a handsome doctor,' Rafferty added.

'Perhaps. If you play your cards right.'

There was a squeak as the hatchway opened and the

bosun, reporting for his shift, ascended the steps to the bridge. After a few minutes, Harris, who had been in the wheelhouse since dawn, emerged yawning. He threw them a weary salute.

'I regret to have to inform you, ladies and gentlemen,' he called, pointing downwards, 'that lunch is now being served.'

The cabin boy, sporting several fresh pustular constellations, arrived with a thump from the crow's nest and sprinted towards the opening. The group at the bow began to break up.

'You coming, Walter?'

'Be there in a minute.'

Crozier gazed out at the ocean. He was thinking about Fitzmaurice's plan to write about their adventures, and their pact regarding the giants. Why should he worry? In the unlikely event of Fitzmaurice producing anything readable, no one would believe it anyway. Sometimes he had trouble believing it himself... His mind wandered back to the valley on that first morning, the mist lifting over the fields, the far-off rumble of the waterfall – and the memory was already fragile, almost beyond retrieval. The faces of the giants too, framed against the sun, were bleaching out, like photographs in reverse. He wondered if he and his friends had become ghosts to those they had left behind in Ireland all those months ago.

The wind was picking up and the sea turning choppy. Behind him the sails thrummed. He scanned the horizon. Landfall couldn't be far off: fragments of Europe that would mark the beginning of their final approach. Journey's end. Home.

A tingle of movement in the distance caught his eye, a

dark scintillation that dissolved as he tried to focus. He squinted but could make out nothing but restless ocean. Yet there it was again, a disturbance, a flurry of waves breaking the wrong way. His mind jumped back to the submarine on the outward voyage and, with a throb of foreboding, he moved further along the gunwale. Then he smiled.

There were nine, ten... no, *eleven* dolphins leaping and plunging along a furrow of sea. Their stone-smooth bodies glistened as they arced through the air. He found himself marvelling at how high they soared, and how fluidly they re-entered the water, as though formed from the same element. As he watched, they began to alter their course, until, after a few moments, they were coming square-on, two and three abreast, in a line, bursts of spray dispersing in their wake. They were closer now: he could see the sleek delineation of their domed heads, their ecstatic grins, and he could hear their cries, like birdsong, as they raced towards the ship.

Acknowledgements

My thanks to the following:

Patrick Murphy at Cobh Harbour Office for sharing his knowledge of sailing ships; John Fairleigh for his hospitality, and the peace and quiet of his Westmeath boathouse; Gerald Dawe and Dorothea Melvin for their advice and support; my son Milo for his candid and transformative criticism, and my wife Eve, as always, for her fortitude.

Selected bibliography

I May Be Some Time: Ice and the English Imagination by Francis Spufford (London: Faber & Faber, 2003)
Letters From High Latitudes by Lord Dufferin (London: John Murray, 1867)
South: The Story of Shackleton's Last Expedition 1914-1917 by Ernest
Shackleton (London: William Heinemann, 1919)
The Worst Journey in the World by Apsley Cherry-Garrard (London: Penguin Classics, 2006)

A Voyage to Baffin's Island and Lancaster Sound by Robert Anstruther Goodsir (London: John van Voorst, 1850)

Jeanie Johnston: Sailing the Irish Famine Tall Ship by Michael English (Cork: Collins Press, 2012)

Easter 1916: The Irish Rebellion by Charles Townshend (London: Penguin Books, 2006)

Dublin 1916: The Siege of the GPO by Clair Wills (London: Profile Books, 2009)

All Quiet on the Western Front by Erich Maria Remarque (Boston: Little, Brown, 1929)

Gulliver's Travels by Jonathan Swift (London: Penguin Classics, 2003)

The Voyage of the Dawn Treader by C.S. Lewis (London: HarperCollins, 1951)

Lord Jim by Joseph Conrad (New York: Norton Critical Editions, 1996)

The Valley of Adventure by Enid Blyton (London: Macmillan, 1947)